SOME OTHER ALAN MAITLAND ANTHOLOGIES TO ENJOY:

Favourite Winter Stories
from Fireside Al

Favourite Summer Stories
from Front Porch Al

Favourite Christmas Stories
from Fireside Al

Favourite Scary Stories
from Graveside Al

Favourite Seaside Stories
from Seaside Al

Fireside Al's
TREASURY OF CLASSIC STORIES

Selected and Introduced
by Alan Maitland

Penguin Books

PENGUIN BOOKS
Published by the Penguin Group
Penguin Books Canada Ltd, 10 Alcorn Avenue, Toronto, Ontario,
Canada M4V 3B2
Penguin Books Ltd, 27 Wrights Lane, London W8 5TZ, England
Penguin Putnam Inc., 375 Hudson Street, New York, New York 10014, U.S.A.
Penguin Books Australia Ltd, Ringwood, Victoria, Australia
Penguin Books (NZ) Ltd, cnr Rosedale and Airborne Roads, Albany,
Auckland 1310, New Zealand

Penguin Books Ltd, Registered Offices: Harmondsworth,
Middlesex, England

First published in Viking by Penguin Books Canada Limited, 1997
Published in Penguin Books, 1998

1 3 5 7 9 10 8 6 4 2
Introduction, Notes and Selection Copyright © Alan Maitland, 1997

Manufactured in Canada.

Canadian Cataloguing in Publication Data

Main entry under title:
Fireside Al's treasury of classic stories

ISBN 0-14-026618-6

1. Short stories. I. Maitland, Alan. II. Title: Treasury of classic stories.

PN6120.2.F57 1998   808.83'1   C97-930559-4

Copyright acknowledgments appear on page 325

Visit Penguin Canada's web site at **www.penguin.ca**

This story book is dedicated to Old Hark the hermit.
He wrestled with death for several days. When death finally
took the upper hand and was ready to deliver the coup de
grâce, the referee called the fight on a technicality. Here's to all
the refs—and to all us Old Harks.

*Never be completely idle, but either reading,
or writing, or praying, or meditating, or at some
useful work for the common good.*

De Imitatione Christi, Thomas à Kempis

THE LAND OF STORY-BOOKS

by Robert Louis Stevenson

At evening when the lamp is lit,
Around the fire my parents sit;
They sit at home and talk and sing,
And do not play at anything.

Now, with my little gun, I crawl
All in the dark along the wall,
And follow round the forest track
Away behind the sofa back.

There, in the night, where none can spy,
All in my hunter's camp I lie,
And play at books that I have read
Till it is time to go to bed.

These are the hills, these are the woods,
These are my starry solitudes;
And there the river by whose brink
The roaring lions come to drink.

I see the others far away
As if in firelit camp they lay,
And I, like to an Indian scout,
Around their party prowled about.

So, when my nurse comes in for me,
Home I return across the sea,
And go to bed with backward looks
At my dear land of Story-books.

TABLE OF CONTENTS

INTRODUCTION

As I sit writing these lines, Gretzky sleeping on the mat beside me, I am surrounded by friends—almost an embarrassment of friends, you might say, even though there's no one here but the faithful Gretzky and me. The friends I'm talking about are my books. Old brown leatherbound volumes that I recall my father reading to us on Sunday evenings. Well-thumbed paperbacks with dog-ears and turned-down corners, books I've carted around with me for years and wouldn't part with for anything. Black-spined classics, green-striped mysteries, and some beautifully designed modern paperbacks with oil-paintings on the covers. And an assortment of lovely old books from the Modern Library and Everyman's Library series—elegant and compact editions that promise a world of understanding and entertainment between two covers. I love to browse through these series titles at second-hand stores, and usually find I cannot resist carrying one or two home with me.

Among the more recent additions to my library is a proud new group: my very own collections of my favourite stories, so many of which I've been able to read on CBC Radio. There they sit, five of them now, and handsome, too. Hard to believe—and yet here I am introducing number six. I certainly do feel fortunate to have had the opportunity to bring the magical, meaningful world of stories to so many loyal listeners and readers over the years. Indeed, at moments like this, as I muse upon the power of the stories collected here, I find it hard to imagine a more rewarding occupation.

You may be wondering what it is that I consider makes a story a "classic." Age is certainly an important factor in my definition, since a story published last year can hardly be a classic. Before it can attain that exalted status, however meritorious it may be, it has to acquire a "critical mass" of admirers, a kind of currency among the reading public. In short, it must possess that timeless quality which all great stories enjoy, and the sort of universality that will enable it to endure. Whatever happens in this unpredictable world of ours, the classic story is like a talisman, a treasured possession that successive generations choose to carry with them as a testimony to the wisdom of the past, a source of strength for the present, and an inspiration for the future.

This particular anthology is by and large devoted to the writers I knew when I was young, before the era of such great Canadian short-story writers as Mavis Gallant and Alice Munro. Charles Dickens, Guy de Maupassant, Saki, Nathaniel Hawthorne, Anton Chekhov: all have acquired well-earned reputations, and we will cherish and preserve everything they left to us for as long as we value good writing. Personally, I feel as though these authors are old friends of mine, and when I happen upon an unfamiliar story of theirs, it is rather like reading a letter from a dear acquaintance. I hope you will have that same feeling when you encounter their stories in these pages—that warm glow of recognition and familiarity and comfortableness, the sense that these are worthwhile companions.

It's been a joy to bring together all these great writers, rather like organizing a grand dinner party. ("If I invite Guy de Maupassant, I should have another Frenchman for him to talk to. How about Alphonse Daudet?") And I tried to slip in one or two surprises, writers you may not have met before, or weren't expecting to meet at this particular get-together.

So, without more fanfare, welcome to the party. Now just come inside and make yourself comfortable; you know almost everyone here. Oh, and watch out for Gretzky—she gets a bit lively around company.

THE NECKLACE

Guy de Maupassant
(1850–1893)

When I was choosing the stories for this collection, there were a handful of authors whose inclusion was unquestioned: Guy de Maupassant was among them. And so it is with special delight that I open this volume with one of the best-loved stories of all time, by one of the masters.

"The Necklace" contains an entire world, complete unto itself, like a fine diamond buffed and polished to a perfect, shining lustre. Dripping with Maupassant's characteristic irony, it is chock-full of delicate observation, and the sorts of seemingly insignificant facts that together bring a fictional universe to life.

he was one of those pretty, charming young women who have had the ill fortune to be born into a wage-earning family. She had no dowry, no prospects, no opportunities of getting to know some rich and distinguished man who might have understood her, loved her, and made her his wife. Consequently, she let herself drift into marriage with a junior clerk in the Ministry of Public Instruction.

Though her tastes were simple, anything else having been out of the question, she felt as unhappy as though she had come down in the world. Among women, caste and birth are meaningless. Beauty, sweetness, and charm take the place for them of blue blood and family connections. Quick wits, instinctive elegance, and adaptability are the only degrees in their hierarchy, and can make of working girls the equals of the greatest of great ladies.

She was in a perpetual state of dissatisfaction, because she felt that luxuries and soft living were her natural birthright. The furnished flat in which she had to live, its squalid wallpapers, its shabby chairs, its hideous curtains and upholstery, were a constant source of torment to her. These things, which another woman with a background similar to her own might not even have noticed, she found unendurable and degrading. The sight of the Breton girl who did the humble domestic chores filled her with hopeless longings and idle dreams. She conjured up a vision of hushed entrance halls, hung with oriental fabrics and lit by bronze sconces, of tall footmen in knee-breeches dozing in deep armchairs in the drowsy warmth of a great stove. She dwelt in imagination on vast salons adorned with antique silks, on elegant tables littered with priceless knick-knacks, on perfumed boudoirs where she would sit in the late afternoons chatting with intimate friends—men well known and sought after, such as every woman wants to have dancing attendance on her.

When she sat down to dinner with her husband at the round table covered with a three-day-old cloth, and heard him say, with a delighted expression on his face, as he lifted the top from the soup-tureen, "Ah! vegetable soup; what could be better than that!" she let her mind run on delicious dishes served in exquisite porcelain, on whispered gallantries, and the sphinx-like smile with which she would listen to them while eating the pink flesh of a trout or the wing of a chicken.

She had no evening dresses, no jewels, nothing. And those were the only things she cared about. She felt made for the life they represented. She longed to be envied, popular, seductive, and courted.

She had one rich friend, a woman she had known in their convent days. But she no longer went to see her, only too well aware, from experience, that everything seemed so much worse at home when she got back from one of those expeditions. For days on end she would cry and cry, shedding tears of misery, regret, despair, and anguish.

One evening, her husband came home looking unusually pleased, with a large envelope in his hand.

"This is something for you," he said.

She quickly tore open the envelope and took from it a card on which were engraved the following words:

*The Minister of Public Instruction and
Mme Georges Ramponneau
request the pleasure
of the company of*

M. AND MME. LOISEL

*on Monday evening, the 18th of January
at the Ministry*

Instead of being overjoyed, as her husband had expected, she threw the card on the table in a pet, saying in a complaining voice:

"What use is this to me?"

"But, darling, I thought you would be pleased. You never go out, and this is a chance not to be missed. I had the greatest difficulty in getting an invitation. Everyone is longing to be asked. It is a very smart occasion, and not many of the staff have been invited. You will meet all the official world there!"

An angry look came into her eyes as she impatiently replied:

"And how do you expect me to dress for this smart occasion?"

This problem had not occurred to him.

"Why," he muttered, "that little frock, I suppose, which you put on when we go to the theatre: I must say, it always looks very nice to me..."

He stopped speaking, for his wife was crying. Two large tears were slowly moving down her cheeks, from the corners of her eyes to the corners of her mouth. At the sight of them he felt dumbfounded and bewildered.

"W...what's the matter?" he stammered.

By a violent effort she recovered her self-control, and answered in a calm voice while she dabbed at her tear-stained face:

"Nothing...except that I haven't a thing to wear. I can't possibly go to this party. You had better give the card to one of your colleagues whose wife has a more extensive wardrobe than mine."

He was miserable.

"Look here, Mathilde," he said: "how much would the right kind of dress cost, something simple, I mean, which you could wear on other occasions?"

She thought for a while, totting up figures in her head, and wondering how much she could ask for without meeting with an immediate refusal and an exclamation of horror from her cheese-paring clerk of a husband.

At last, with some hesitation, she replied:

"I can't tell to a penny, but I think I could manage with four hundred francs."

His face went slightly pale, for he had been keeping in reserve precisely that sum with the object of buying a gun, so as to be able to treat himself to a few outings next summer in the plain of Nanterre, with a few friends who went there for the lark-shooting.

Nevertheless, he said:

"Right: you shall have your four hundred francs. But try to make it a really nice dress."

The day of the party was approaching, but there was something depressed, uneasy, and anxious about Madame Loisel, though her dress was ready. One evening her husband said:

"What's wrong? You have been acting very strangely for the last few days."

"It vexes me," she answered, "to think that I have no jewellery, not a single thing to wear with my dress. I shall look like a poor relation. I would rather stay away from the party than go like that."

"You can wear flowers," he said. "It's very much the thing this season. For ten francs you can get two or three really magnificent roses."

But she was not to be convinced. "No...There is nothing more humiliating than to be the one poor little guest among a lot of rich women."

"Why!" he exclaimed, "what a silly you are! How about that friend of yours, Madame Forestier? Why not ask her to lend you something? You know her quite well enough for that."

She uttered a joyful cry.

"Of course! Why did I never think of it?"

Next day she went to see her friend and told her of her trouble.

Madame Forestier went to her wardrobe with a looking-glass front, took from it a large locked box, opened it, and said:

"Take what you like, my dear."

First of all she saw several bracelets, then a string of pearls, then a Venetian cross in gold and gems, of beautiful workmanship. She tried them on before the glass, unable to make up her mind, reluctant to take them off, to give them back. And all the time she kept on asking:

"Have you nothing else?"

"Why, of course. Look and see what you can find. You must know what you would like best."

Suddenly, Mathilde came upon a black satin case with, in it, a superb diamond *rivière*. Her heart began to beat faster, and she was filled with a mad longing. With trembling fingers she fastened it round her throat against her high-necked dress, and looked at her reflection in a kind of ecstasy.

Then, with considerable hesitation, as though fearing a refusal, she said:

"Would you really lend me this? I don't want anything else."

"Why, certainly."

She flung her arms round her friend's neck, kissed her in a transport of affection, and fled away with her treasure.

The great day came. Madame Loisel was a tremendous success. She was the prettiest woman there, elegant, graceful, smiling, and wildly happy. The men all looked at her, asked who she was and tried hard to be introduced to her. All the Secretaries wanted to waltz with her. The Minister noticed her.

She danced madly. Pleasure had gone to her head like wine. She had no thought for anything but the triumph of her beauty, the splendour of her success. She moved in a happy mist made up of homage, admiration, awakened desires, and that sense of undisputed victory which is so dear to the female heart.

She stayed until four in the morning. Ever since midnight her husband had been fast asleep in a small, deserted *salon*, in the company of three other gentlemen whose wives were thoroughly enjoying themselves.

He put round her shoulders the wrap he had brought for this purpose, a shabby reminder of their day-to-day existence, the poverty of which was at odds with the beauty of her ball-dress. She was conscious of the contrast, and would have liked to slip away unnoticed by the other women wrapped in rich furs.

Loisel held her back.

"You'll catch cold outside. Wait here while I go and look for a cab."

But she would not listen, and hurried down the stairs. When they got into the street, there was no cab to be found. They looked everywhere, calling to the drivers of those they saw at a distance.

In this way they walked on in the direction of the Seine, hopeless and with chattering teeth. At last, on the Quai, they came upon one of those ancient nocturnal prowlers which are never to be seen in Paris except after dark, as though they are too much ashamed of their poverty-stricken appearance to venture out in the daylight.

It took them to their door in the Rue des Martyrs, and gloomily they climbed up to their home. It was all over now, she was thinking, and he, that he must be at the Ministry by ten.

She took off her wrap in front of the glass, that she might once more see herself in all her glory. But, suddenly, she uttered a cry. The *rivière* was no longer round her neck.

Her husband, half undressed, asked her what the matter was.

She turned to him in a panic: "I've...I've...not got Madame

Forestier's necklace!" Distractedly, he jumped to his feet.

"But...that's not possible!" he exclaimed.

They hunted in the folds of her dress, of her cloak, in every available pocket. They could find it nowhere.

"You're sure you still had it when we started home?" he asked.

"Quite sure; I touched it in the hall at the Ministry."

"But if you'd lost it in the street we should have heard it fall! It must be in the cab!"

"Yes, that's probably where it is. Did you take the number?"

"No. You didn't happen to notice it, I suppose?"

"No."

They looked at one another in consternation. At last, Loisel began to put on his clothes again.

"I'll go over the part of the way we came on foot, just to see..."

He went out. She remained slumped in an armchair, still in her ball-dress, without the strength to go to bed, without a fire to warm her, without the power to think.

Her husband came back about seven. He had found nothing.

They went to the Police Station, to a number of newspaper offices with an offer of a reward, to the hackney-coach companies, to any and every place that might offer them a gleam of hope.

She spent all that day in an unrelieved state of terror at the thought of the frightful disaster which had come upon them.

Loisel returned that evening, pale-faced and hollow-eyed. He had failed to discover anything.

"You must write to your friend," he said, "saying that you have broken the catch of her necklace, and that you are having it mended. That will give us time to have a further look round."

She wrote to his dictation.

By the end of the week they had given up all hope.

Loisel, who looked five years older, said:

"We shall have to see whether we can't replace it."

Next day they took the case to the jeweller whose name was inside it. He went through his books.

"It was not I, Madame, who sold this *rivière*; I only supplied the case."

They went from shop to shop, trying to find a necklace like the lost one, trying to remember it in detail, both of them sick with misery and distress.

In a small shop in the Palais-Royal, they found a string of diamonds which looked like the exact double of the necklace they had lost. Its price was forty thousand francs, but they could have it for thirty-six.

They begged the jeweller not to sell it for six days. They further made it a condition of purchase that he would buy it back for thirty-four thousand should the original be found before the end of February.

Loisel had inherited eighteen thousand francs from his father. The rest he would have to borrow.

And borrow he did, getting a thousand here, five hundred there, five louis from one man, three from another, backing bills, pledging objects at a ruinous rate of interest, dealing with professional money-lenders or with anyone who would advance him cash. He loaded himself with debts for the rest of his life, rashly affixed his signature to promissory notes without being sure that he could meet them. Terrified by the prospect of his future and the black penury which was to be his lot, by a future of physical privations and moral torment, he took delivery of the new necklace, and put down thirty-six thousand francs on the jeweller's counter.

When Madame Loisel carried the *rivière* to Madame Forestier, all the latter said, in a rather injured tone, was:

"You really ought to have let me have it sooner. I might have needed it."

She did not open the case, which was what her friend had feared she might do. What would she have thought if she had noticed the substitution? Might she not have taken her for a thief?

Madame Loisel's life, from then on, was one of miserable poverty. But she played her part, from the very first, heroically. The terrible debt had got to be settled, and settle it she would. The maidservant was given notice. They moved to a cheaper flat, in the attics.

She undertook all the heavy work of the household, all the odious cooking. She did all the washing-up, spoiling her pretty pink fingernails on greasy crockery and dirty saucepans. She scrubbed the dirty linen, shirts, and dish-clouts, and hung them on a line to dry. She carried the refuse down every morning to the street, and brought up the water, stopping on each landing to get her breath. Dressed like a woman of the people, she made the round of the greengrocer, the grocer, and the butcher with a basket on her arm, haggling over prices, putting up with abuse, doling out her miserable pittance penny by penny.

Each month there were bills to be paid, others to be renewed, and a constant begging for time.

Her husband spent his evenings auditing the accounts of various shopkeepers, and often worked far into the night, doing copying at five sous a page.

This life lasted for ten years. At the end of that time they had paid back every penny with interest, plus accumulated compound interest.

Madame Loisel now looked like an old woman. She had the typical appearance of the working-class housewife, strong, hard, and coarse. Her hair was all anyhow, her skirt awry, her hands red. She spoke in a loud voice, and splashed water all over the place when she scrubbed the floors. But sometimes, when her husband was at the office, she would sit down at the window and dream of the long-distant evening when she had been the Belle of the Ball.

What would have happened if she had not lost the necklace? Who could say? How strange life is, how changeable! What small things make the difference between safety and disaster!

One Sunday, when she had gone to the Champs-Elysées for a little relaxation from the labours of the week, she suddenly caught sight of a woman walking with a child. It was Madame Forestier, still young, still beautiful, still seductive.

Madame Loisel felt strangely excited. Should she speak to

her? Of course! And now that every debt was settled, she would tell her the whole story. Why not?

She went up to her.

"Good morning, Jeanne."

The other did not recognize her and seemed surprised at being addressed so familiarly by such a low-class creature.

"I don't think I know you, Madame…I fear you must have made a mistake."

"Oh no, I have not…I am Mathilde Loisel…"

Her friend uttered a cry:

"But, my poor Mathilde, how you have changed!"

"Yes, I have been through very hard times since I saw you last, and much unhappiness…all because of you!"

"Because of me?…How do you mean?"

"Do you remember the diamond necklace which you lent me for a party at the Ministry?"

"Certainly I do. What of it?"

"Only that I lost it."

"But you gave it back…"

"What I gave you back was another like it. For the last ten years we have been paying for it. You must realize that it was not easy for us to do that, for we had no money of our own…But it is all over now, and I am very happy to think that it is."

"Do you mean that you bought a diamond *rivière* to replace mine?"

"Yes. You didn't notice any difference, did you? They were exactly alike."

There was something at once simple and proud in her smile.

Madame Forestier, deeply moved, took both her friend's hands in hers.

"Oh, you poor, poor thing! Mine was imitation and worth, at most, five hundred francs!…"

BUTCH
MINDS THE BABY

Damon Runyon
(1880–1946)

Damon Runyon was quite a fellow. When I was reading about his life, I was particularly struck by the fact that in his later years he reportedly smoked three packs of cigarettes and drank sixty cups of coffee each day. All that caffeine gave him a lot of energy, too: he was a prolific journalist, a Hollywood scriptwriter, a racehorse owner and a fight promoter—all at the same time. When he died, his ashes were scattered over Broadway (at his request) from an airplane flown by a World War I ace, Eddie Rickenbacker.

Runyon liked to have a late breakfast every day at Lindy's restaurant on Broadway, which he called Mindy's in his stories. There he observed the underworld characters who frequented the place and listened to their lively vocabulary, which, with his reporter's ear, he faithfully and unforgettably reproduced in his stories.

ne evening along about seven o'clock I am sitting in Mindy's restaurant putting on the gefillte fish, which is a dish I am very fond of, when in comes three parties from Brooklyn wearing caps as follows: Harry the Horse, Little Isadore and Spanish John.

Now these parties are not such parties as I will care to have much truck with, because I often hear rumours about them that are very discreditable, even if the rumours are not true. In fact, I hear that many citizens of Brooklyn will be very glad indeed to see Harry the Horse, Little Isadore and

Spanish John move away from there, as they are always doing something that is considered a knock to the community, such as robbing people, or maybe shooting or stabbing them, and throwing pineapples, and carrying on generally.

I am really much surprised to see these parties on Broadway, as it is well known that the Broadway coppers just naturally love to shove such parties around, but here they are in Mindy's, and there I am, so of course I give them a very large hello, as I never wish to seem inhospitable, even to Brooklyn parties. Right away they come over to my table and sit down, and Little Isadore reaches out and spears himself a big hunk of my gefillte fish with his fingers, but I overlook this, as I am using the only knife on the table.

Then they all sit there looking at me without saying anything, and the way they look at me makes me very nervous indeed. Finally I figure that maybe they are a little embarrassed being in a high-class spot such as Mindy's, with legitimate people around and about, so I say to them, very polite: "It is a nice night."

"What is nice about it?" asks Harry the Horse, who is a thin man with a sharp face and sharp eyes.

Well, now that it is put up to me in this way, I can see there is nothing so nice about the night, at that, so I try to think of something else jolly to say, while Little Isadore keeps spearing at my gefillte fish with his fingers, and Spanish John nabs one of my potatoes.

"Where does Big Butch live?" Harry the Horse asks.

"Big Butch?" I say, as if I never hear the name before in my life, because in this man's town it is never a good idea to answer any question without thinking it over, as sometime you may give the right answer to the wrong guy, or the wrong answer to the right guy. "Where does Big Butch live?" I ask them again.

"Yes, where does he live?" Harry the Horse says, very impatient. "We wish you to take us to him."

"Now wait a minute, Harry," I say, and I am now more nervous than somewhat. "I am not sure I remember the exact house Big Butch lives in, and furthermore I am not sure Big Butch will care to have me bringing people to see him, especially three at a time, and especially from Brooklyn. You know Big Butch has a very bad disposition, and there is no telling what he may say to me if he does not like the idea of me taking you to him."

"Everything is very kosher," Harry the Horse says. "You need not be afraid of anything whatever. We have a business proposition for Big Butch. It means a nice score for him, so you take us to him at once, or the chances are I will have to put the arm on somebody around here."

Well, as the only one around there for him to put the arm on at this time seems to be me, I can see where it will be good policy for me to take these parties to Big Butch, especially as the last of my gefillte fish is just going down Little Isadore's gullet, and Spanish John is finishing up my potatoes, and is dunking a piece of rye bread in my coffee, so there is nothing more for me to eat.

So I lead them over into West Forty-ninth Street, near Tenth Avenue, where Big Butch lives on the ground floor of an old brownstone-front house, and who is sitting out on the stoop but Big Butch himself. In fact, everybody in the neighbourhood is sitting out on the front stoops over there, including women and children, because sitting out on the front stoops is quite a custom in this section.

Big Butch is peeled down to his undershirt and pants, and he has no shoes on his feet, as Big Butch is a guy who likes his comfort. Furthermore, he is smoking a cigar, and laid out on the stoop beside him on a blanket is a little baby with not much clothes on. This baby seems to be asleep, and every now and then Big Butch fans it with a folded newspaper to shoo away the mosquitoes that wish to nibble on the baby. These mosquitoes come across the river from the Jersey side on hot nights and they seem to be very fond of babies.

"Hello, Butch," I say, as we stop in front of the stoop.

"Sh-h-h-h!" Butch says, pointing at the baby, and making more noise with his shush than an engine blowing off steam. Then he gets up and tiptoes down to the sidewalk where we are standing, and I am hoping that Butch feels all right, because when Butch does not feel so good he is apt to be very short with one and all. He is a guy of maybe six foot two and a couple of feet wide, and he has big hairy hands and a mean look.

In fact, Big Butch is known all over this man's town as a guy you must not monkey with in any respect, so it takes plenty of weight off of me when I see that he seems to know the parties from Brooklyn, and nods at them very friendly, especially at Harry the Horse. And right away Harry states a most surprising proposition to Big Butch.

It seems that there is a big coal company which has an office in an old building down in West Eighteenth Street, and in this office is a safe, and in this safe is the company payroll of twenty thousand dollars cash money. Harry the Horse knows the money is there because a personal friend of his who is the paymaster for the company puts it there late this very afternoon.

It seems that the paymaster enters into a dicker with Harry the Horse and Little Isadore and Spanish John for them to slug him while he is carrying the payroll from the bank to the office in the afternoon, but something happens that they miss connections on the exact spot, so the paymaster has to carry the sugar on to the office without being slugged, and there it is now in two fat bundles.

Personally it seems to me as I listen to Harry's story that the paymaster must be a very dishonest character to be making deals to hold still while he is being slugged and the company's sugar taken away from him, but of course it is none of my business, so I take no part in the conversation.

Well, it seems that Harry the Horse and Little Isadore and Spanish John wish to get the money out of the safe, but none of them knows anything about opening safes, and while they are standing around over in Brooklyn talking over what is to be done in this emergency Harry suddenly remembers that Big Butch is once in the business of opening safes for a living.

In fact, I hear afterwards that Big Butch is considered the best safe opener east of the Mississippi River in his day, but the law finally takes to sending him to Sing Sing for opening these safes, and after he is in and out of Sing Sing three different times for opening safes Butch gets sick and tired of the place, especially as they pass what is called the Baumes Law in New York, which is a law that says if a guy is sent to Sing Sing four times hand running, he must stay there for the rest of his life, without any argument about it.

So Big Butch gives up opening safes for a living, and goes into business in a small way, such as running beer, and handling a little Scotch now and then, and becomes an honest citizen. Furthermore, he marries one of the neighbour's children over on the West Side by the name of Mary Murphy, and I judge the baby on this stoop comes of this marriage between Big Butch and Mary because I can see that it is a very homely baby, indeed. Still, I never see many babies that I consider rose geraniums for looks, anyway.

Well, it finally comes out that the idea of Harry the Horse and Little Isadore and Spanish John is to get Big Butch to open the coal company's safe and take the payroll money out, and they are willing to give him fifty per cent of the money for his bother, taking fifty per cent for themselves for finding the plant, and paying all the overhead, such as the paymaster, out of their bit, which strikes me as a pretty fair sort of deal for Big Butch. But Butch only shakes his head.

"It is old-fashioned stuff," Butch says. "Nobody opens pete boxes for a living any more. They make the boxes too good, and they are all wired up with alarms and are a lot of trouble generally. I am in a legitimate business now and going along. You boys know I cannot stand another fall, what with being away three times already, and in addition to this I must mind the baby. My old lady goes to Mrs. Clancy's wake tonight up in the Bronx, and the chances are she will be there all night, as she is very fond of wakes, so I must mind little John Ignatius Junior."

"Listen, Butch," Harry the Horse says, "this is a very soft pete. It is old-fashioned, and you can open it with a toothpick. There are no wires on it, because they never put more than a dime in it before in years. It just happens they have to put the twenty G's in it tonight because my pal the paymaster makes it a point not to get back from the jug with the scratch in time to pay off today, especially after he sees we miss out on him. It is the softest touch you will every know, and where can a guy pick up ten G's like this?"

I can see that Big Butch is thinking the ten G's over very seriously, at that, because in these times nobody can afford to pass up ten G's, especially a guy in the beer business, which is very, very tough just now. But finally he shakes his head again and says like this:

"No," he says, "I must let is go, because I must mind the baby. My old lady is very, very particular about this, and I dast not leave little John Ignatius Junior for a minute. If Mary comes home and finds I am not minding the baby she will put the blast on me plenty. I like to turn a few honest bobs now and then as well as anybody, but," Butch says, "John Ignatius Junior comes first with me."

Then he turns away and goes back to the stoop as much as to say he is through arguing, and sits down beside John Ignatius Junior again just in time to keep a mosquito from carrying off one of John's legs. Anybody can see that Big Butch is very fond of this baby, though personally I will not give you a dime a dozen for babies, male and female.

Well, Harry the Horse and Little Isadore and Spanish John are very much disappointed, and stand around talking among themselves, and paying no attention to me, when all of a sudden Spanish John, who never has much to say up to this time, seems to have a bright idea. He talks to Harry and Isadore, and they get all pleasured up over what he has to say, and finally Harry goes to Big Butch.

"Sh-h-h-h!" Big Butch says, pointing to the baby as Harry opens his mouth.

"Listen, Butch," Harry says in a whisper, "we can take the baby with us, and you can mind it and work, too."

"Why," Big Butch whispers back, "this is quite an idea indeed. Let us go into the house and talk things over."

So he picks up the baby and leads us into his joint, and gets out some pretty fair beer, though it is needled a little, at that, and we sit around the kitchen chewing the fat in whispers. There is a crib in the kitchen, and Butch puts the baby in his crib, and it keeps on snoozing away first rate while we are talking. In fact, it is sleeping so sound that I am commencing to figure that Butch must give it some of the needled beer he is feeding us, because I am feeling a little dopey myself.

Finally Butch says that as long as he can take John Ignatius Junior with him he sees no reason why he shall not go and open the safe for them, only he says he must have five per cent more to put in the baby's bank when he gets back, so as to round himself up with his ever-loving wife in case of a beef from her over keeping the baby out in the night air. Harry the Horse says he considers this extra five per cent a little strong, but Spanish John, who seems to be a very square guy, says that after all it is only fair to cut the baby in if it is to be with them when they are making the score, and Little Isadore seems to think this is all right, too. So Harry the Horse gives in, and says five per cent it is.

Well, as they do not wish to start out until after midnight, and as there is plenty of time, Big Butch gets out some more needled beer, and then he goes looking for the tools with which he opens safes, and which he says he does not see since the day John Ignatius Junior is born, and he gets them out to build the crib.

Now this is a good time for me to bid one and all farewell, and what keeps me there is something I cannot tell you to this day, because personally I never before have any idea of taking part in a safe opening, especially with a baby, as I consider such actions very dishonourable. When I come to think things over afterwards, the only thing I can figure is the needled beer, but I wish to say I am really very much surprised at myself when I find myself in a taxi-cab along about one o'clock in the morning with these Brooklyn parties and Big Butch and the baby.

Butch has John Ignatius Junior rolled up in a blanket, and John is still pounding his ear. Butch has a satchel of tools, and what looks to me like a big flat book, and just before we leave the house Butch hands me a package and tells me to be very careful with it. He gives Little Isadore a smaller package, which Isadore shoves into his pistol pocket, and when Isadore sits down in the taxi something goes wa-wa, like a sheep, and Big Butch becomes very indignant because it seems Isadore is sitting on John Ignatius Junior's doll, which says "Mamma" when you squeeze it.

It seems Big Butch figures that John Ignatius Junior may wish something to play with in case he wakes up, and it is a good thing for Little Isadore that the mamma doll is not squashed so it cannot say "Mamma" any more, or the chances are Little Isadore will get a good bust in the snoot.

We let the taxi-cab go a block away from the spot we are headed for in West Eighteenth Street, between Seventh and Eighth Avenues, and walk the rest of the way two by two. I walk with Big Butch, carrying my package, and Butch is lugging the baby and his satchel and the flat thing that looks like a book. It is so quiet down in West Eighteenth Street at such an hour that you can hear yourself think, and in fact I hear myself thinking very plain that I am a big sap to be on a job like this, especially with a baby, but I keep going just the same, which shows you what a very big sap I am, indeed.

There are very few people in West Eighteenth Street when we get there, and one of them is a fat guy who is leaning against a building almost in the centre of the block, and who takes a walk for himself as soon as he sees us. It seems that this fat guy is the watchman at the coal company's office and is also a personal friend of Harry the Horse, which is why he takes the walk when he sees us coming.

It is agreed before we leave Big Butch's house that Harry the Horse and Spanish John are to stay outside the place as lookouts, while Big Butch is inside opening the safe, and that Little Isadore is to go with Butch. Nothing whatever is said by anybody about where I am to be at any time, and I can see that, no matter where I am, I will still be an outsider, but, as Butch gives me the package to carry, I figure he wishes me to remain with him.

It is no bother at all getting into the office of the coal company, which is on the ground floor, because it seems the watchman leaves the front door open, this watchman being a most obliging guy, indeed. In fact he is so obliging that by and by he comes back and lets Harry the Horse and Spanish John tie him up good and tight, and stick a handkerchief in his mouth and chuck him in an areaway next to the office, so nobody will think he has anything to do with opening the safe in case anybody comes around asking.

The office looks out on the street, and the safe that Harry the Horse and Little Isadore and Spanish John wish Big Butch to open is standing up against the rear wall of the office facing the street windows. There is one little electric light burning very dim over the safe so that when anybody walks past the place outside, such as a watchman, they can look in through the window and see the safe at all times, unless they are blind. It is not a tall safe, and it is not a big safe, and I can see Big Butch grin when he sees it, so I figure this safe is not much of a safe, just as Harry the Horse claims.

Well, as soon as Big Butch and the baby and Little Isadore and me get into the office, Big Butch steps over to the safe and unfolds what I think is the big flat book, and what is it but a sort of screen painted on one side to look exactly like the front of a safe. Big Butch stands this screen up on the floor in front of the real safe, leaving plenty of space in between, the idea being that the screen will keep anyone passing in the street outside from see-ing Butch when he is opening the safe, because when a man is opening a safe he needs all the privacy he can get.

Big Butch lays John Ignatius Junior down on the floor on the blanket behind the phony safe front and takes his tools out of the satchel and starts to work opening the safe, while Little Isadore and me get back in a corner where it is dark, because there is not room for all of us back of the screen. However, we can see what Big Butch is doing, and I wish to say while I never before see a professional safe opener at work, and never wish to see another, this Butch handles himself like a real artist.

He starts drilling into the safe around the combination lock, working very fast and very quiet, when all of a sudden what hap-pens but John Ignatius Junior sits up on the blanket and lets out a squall. Naturally this is most disquieting to me, and personally I am in favour of beaning John Ignatius Junior with something to make him keep still, because I am nervous enough as it is. But the squalling does not seem to bother Big Butch. He lays down his tools and picks up John Ignatius Junior and starts whispering, "There, there, there, my itty oddleums. Da-dad is here."

Well, this sounds very nonsensical to me in such a situation, and it makes no impression whatever on John Ignatius Junior. He keeps on squalling, and I judge he is squalling pretty loud because I see Harry the Horse and Spanish John both walk past the window and look in very anxious. Big Butch jiggles John Ignatius Junior up and down and keeps whispering baby talk to him, which sounds very undignified coming from a high-class safe opener, and finally Butch whispers to me to hand him the package I am carrying.

He opens the package, and what is in it but a baby's nursing bottle full of milk. Moreover, there is a little tin stew pan, and Butch hands the pan to me and whispers to me to find a water tap somewhere in the joint and fill the pan with water. So I go stumbling around in the dark in a room behind the office and bark my shins several times before I find a tap and fill the pan. I take it back to Big Butch, and he squats there with the baby on one arm, and gets a tin of what is called canned heat out of the package, and lights this canned heat with his cigar lighter, and starts heating the pan of water with the nursing bottle in it.

Big Butch keeps sticking his finger in the pan of water while it is heating, and by and by he puts the rubber nipple of the nursing bottle in his mouth and takes a pull at it to see if the milk is warm enough, just like I see dolls who have babies do. Apparently the milk is OK, as Butch hands the bottle to John Ignatius Junior, who grabs hold of it with both hands and starts sucking on the business end. Naturally he has to stop squalling, and Big Butch goes to work on the safe again, with John Ignatius Junior sitting on the blanket, pulling on the bottle and looking wiser than a treeful of owls.

It seems the safe is either a tougher job than anybody figures, or Big Butch's tools are not so good, what with being old and rusty and used for building baby cribs, because he breaks a couple of drills and works himself up into quite a sweat without getting anywhere. Butch afterwards explains to me that he is one of the first guys in this country to open safes without explosives, but he says to do this work properly you have to know the safes so as to drill to the tumblers of the lock just right, and it seems that this particular safe is a new type to him, even if it is old, and he is out of practice.

Well, in the meantime John Ignatius Junior finishes his bottle and starts mumbling again, and Big Butch gives him a tool to play with, and finally Butch needs this tool and tries to take it away from John Ignatius Junior, and the baby lets out such a squawk that Butch has to let him keep it until he can sneak it away from him, and this causes more delay.

Finally Big Butch gives up trying to drill the safe open, and he whispers to us that he will have to put a little shot in it to loosen up the lock, which is all right with us, because we are getting tired of hanging around and listening to John Ignatius Junior's glug-glugging. As far as I am personally concerned, I am wishing I am home in bed.

Well, Butch starts pawing through his satchel looking for something and it seems that what he is looking for is a little bottle of some kind of explosive with which to shake the lock on the safe up some, and at first he cannot find this bottle, but finally he discovers that John Ignatius Junior has it and is gnawing at the cork, and Butch has quite a battle making John Ignatius Junior give it up.

Anyway, he fixes the explosive in one of the holes he drills near the combination lock on the safe, and then he puts in a fuse, and just before he touches off the fuse Butch picks up John Ignatius Junior and hands him to Little Isadore, and tells us to go into the room behind the office. John Ignatius Junior does not seem to care for Little Isadore, and I do not blame him, at that, because he starts to squirm around quite some in Isadore's arms and lets out a squall, but all of a sudden he becomes very quiet indeed, and, while I am not able to prove it, something tells me that Little Isadore has his hand over John Ignatius Junior's mouth.

Well, Big Butch joins us right away in the back room, and sound comes out of John Ignatius Junior again as Butch takes him from Little Isadore, and I am thinking that it is a good thing for Isadore that the baby cannot tell Big Butch what Isadore does to him.

"I put in just a little bit of a shot," Big Butch says, "and it will not make any more noise than snapping your fingers."

But a second later there is a big whoom from the office, and the whole joint shakes, and John Ignatius Junior laughs right out loud. The chances are he thinks it is the Fourth of July.

"I guess maybe I put in too big a charge," Big Butch says, and then he rushes into the office with Little Isadore and me after him, and John Ignatius Junior still laughing very heartily for a small baby. The door of the safe is swinging loose, and the whole joint looks somewhat wrecked, but Big Butch loses no time in getting his dukes into the safe and grabbing out two big bundles of cash money, which he sticks inside his shirt.

As we go into the street Harry the Horse and Spanish John come running up much excited, and Harry says to Big Butch like this:

"What are you trying to do," he says, "wake up the whole town?"

"Well," Butch says, "I guess maybe the charge is too strong, at that, but nobody seems to be coming, so you and Spanish John walk over to Eighth Avenue, and the rest of us will walk to Seventh, and if you go along quiet, like people minding their own business, it will be all right."

But I judge Little Isadore is tired of John Ignatius Junior's company by this time, because he says he will go with Harry the Horse and Spanish John, and this leaves Big Butch and John Ignatius Junior and me to go the other way. So we start moving, and all of a sudden two cops come tearing around the corner toward which Harry and Isadore and Spanish John are going. The chances are the cops hear the earthquake Big Butch lets off and are coming to investigate.

But the chances are, too, that if Harry the Horse and the other two keep on walking along very quietly like Butch tells them to, the coppers will pass them up entirely, because it is not likely that coppers will figure anybody to be opening safes with explosives in this neighbourhood. But the minute Harry the Horse sees the coppers he loses his nut, and he outs with the old equalizer and starts blasting away, and what does Spanish John do but get his out, too, and open up.

The next thing anybody knows, the two coppers are down on the ground with slugs in them, but other coppers are coming from every which direction, blowing whistles and doing a little blasting themselves, and there is plenty of excitement, especially when the coppers who are not chasing Harry the Horse and Little Isadore and Spanish John start poking around the neighbour-hood and find Harry's pal, the watchman, all tied up nice and tight where Harry leaves him, and the watchman explains that some scoundrels blow open the safe he is watching.

All this time Big Butch and me are walking in the other direc-tion toward Seventh Avenue, and Big Butch has John Ignatius in his arms, and John Ignatius is now squalling very loud, indeed. The chances are he is still thinking of the big whoom back there which tickles him so and is wishing to hear some more whooms. Anyway, he is beating his own best record for squalling, and as we go walking along Big Butch says to me like this:

"I dast not run," he says, "because if any coppers see me run-ning they will start popping at me and maybe hit John Ignatius Junior, and besides running will joggle the milk up in him and make him sick. My old lady always warns me never to joggle John Ignatius Junior when he is full of milk."

"Well, Butch," I say, "there is no milk in me, and I do not care if I am joggled up, so if you do not mind, I will start doing a piece of running at the next corner."

But just then around the corner of Seventh Avenue toward which we are headed comes two or three coppers with a big fat sergeant with them, and one of the coppers, who is half out of breath as if he has been doing plenty of sprinting, is explaining to the sergeant that somebody blows a safe down the street and shoots a couple of coppers in the getaway.

And there is Big Butch, with John Ignatius Junior in his arms and twenty G's in his shirt-front and a tough record behind him, walking right up to them.

I am feeling very sorry, indeed, for Big Butch, and very sorry for myself, too, and I am saying to myself that if I get out of this I will never associate with anyone but ministers of the gospel as long as I live. I can remember thinking that I am getting a better break than Butch, at that, because I will not have to go to Sing Sing for the rest of my life, like him, and I also remember wondering what they will give John Ignatius Junior, who is still tearing off these squalls, with Big Butch saying: "There, there, there, Daddy's itty woogleums." Then I hear one of the coppers say to the fat sergeant: "We better nail these guys. They may be in on this."

Well, I can see it is goodbye to Butch and John Ignatius Junior and me, as the fat sergeant steps up to Big Butch, but instead of putting the arm on Butch, the fat sergeant only points at John Ignatius Junior and asks very sympathetic: "Teeth?"

"No," Big Butch says. "Not teeth. Colic. I just get the doctor here out of bed to do something for him, and we are going to a drugstore to get some medicine."

Well, naturally I am very much surprised at this statement, because of course I am not a doctor, and if John Ignatius Junior has colic it serves him right, but I am only hoping they do not ask for my degree, when the fat sergeant says: "Too bad. I know what it is. I got three of them at home. But," he says, "it acts more like it is teeth than colic."

Then as Big Butch and John Ignatius Junior and me go on about our business I hear the fat sergeant say to the copper, very sarcastic: "Yea, of course a guy is out blowing safes with a baby in his arms! You will make a great detective, you will!"

I do not see Big Butch for several days after I learn that Harry the Horse and Little Isadore and Spanish John get back to Brooklyn all right, except they are a little nicked up here and there from the slugs the coppers toss at them, while the coppers they clip are not damaged so very much. Furthermore, the chances are I will not see Big Butch for several years, if it is left to me, but he comes looking for me one night, and he seems to be all pleasured up about something.

"Say," Big Butch says to me, "you know I never give a copper credit for knowing any too much about anything, but I wish to say that this fat sergeant we run into the other night is a very, very smart duck. He is right about it being teeth that is ailing John Ignatius Junior, for what happens yesterday but John cuts in his first tooth."

A
Tradition of
Eighteen Hundred
and Four

Thomas Hardy
(1840–1928)

For the next story, it's important to be in the right frame of mind. So imagine yourself sitting with friends in the low-ceilinged parlour of an old, half-timbered pub in the West Country of England. Outside the wind is screeching, and the rain is lashing the windows, but you are being warmed by a roaring, crackling fire. Delicious smells, of roasting beef and Yorkshire pudding, bring pleasant reminders of the dinner you've just enjoyed, as you raise your brimming glass of foamy dark-brown ale. On a night like this, time stands still, and there's nothing more enjoyable than to lean back into your wing-chair and listen to old Solomon Selby's tale of his youth.

he widely discussed possibility of an invasion of England through a Channel tunnel has more than once recalled old Solomon Selby's story to my mind.

The occasion on which I numbered myself among his audience was one evening when he was sitting in the yawning chimney-corner of the inn-kitchen, with some others who had gathered there, and I entered for shelter from the rain. Withdrawing the stem of his pipe from the dental notch in which it habitually rested, he leaned back in the recess behind him and smiled into the fire. The smile was neither mirthful nor sad, not precisely humorous nor altogether thoughtful. We who knew him recognized it in a moment: it was his narrative smile. Breaking off our few desultory remarks we drew up closer, and he thus began:

"My father, as you mid know, was a shepherd all his life, and lived out by the Cove four miles yonder, where I was born and lived likewise, till I moved here shortly afore I was married. The cottage that first knew me stood on the top of the down, near the sea; there was no house within a mile and a half of it; it was built o' purpose for the farm-shepherd, and had no other use. They tell me that it is now pulled down, but that you can see where it stood by the mounds of earth and a few broken bricks that are still lying about. It was a bleak and dreary place in wintertime, but in summer it was well enough, though the garden never came to much, because we could not get up a good shelter for the vegetables and currant bushes; and where there is much wind they don't thrive.

"Of all the years of my growing up the ones that bide clearest in my mind were eighteen hundred and three, four, and five. This was for two reasons: I had just then grown to an age when a child's eyes and ears take in and note down everything about him, and there was more at that date to bear in mind than there ever has been since with me. It was, as I need hardly tell ye, the time after the first peace, when Bonaparte was scheming his descent upon England. He had crossed the great Alp mountains, fought in Egypt, drubbed the Turks, the Austrians, and the Proossians, and now thought he'd have a slap at us. On the other side of the Channel, scarce out of sight and hail of a man standing on our English shore, the French army of a hundred and sixty thousand men and fifteen thousand horses had been brought together from all parts, and were drilling every day. Bonaparte had been three years a-making his preparations; and to ferry these soldiers and cannon and horses across he had contrived a couple of thousand flat-bottomed boats. These boats were small things, but wonderfully built. A good few of 'em were so made as to have a little stable on board each for the two horses that were to haul the cannon carried at the stern. To get in order all these, and other things required, he had assembled there five or six thousand fellows that worked at trades—carpenters, blacksmiths, wheelwrights, saddlers, and whatnot. O 'twas a curious time!

"Every morning Neighbour Boney would muster his multitude of soldiers on the beach, draw 'em up in line, practise 'em in the manoeuvre of embarking, horses and all, till they could do it without a single hitch. My father drove a flock of ewes up into Sussex that year, and as he went along the drover's track over the high downs thereabout he could see this drilling actually going on—the accoutrements of the rank and file glittering in the sun like silver. It was thought and always said by my uncle Job, sergeant of foot (who used to know all about these matters), that Bonaparte meant to cross with oars on a calm night. The grand query with us was, Where would my gentleman land? Many of the common people thought it would be at Dover; others, who knew how unlikely it was that any skilful general would make a business of landing just where he was expected, said he'd go either east into the River Thames, or west'ard to some convenient place, most likely one of the little bays inside the Isle of Portland, between the Beal and St. Alban's Head—and for choice the three-quarter-round Cove, screened from every mortal eye, that seemed made o' purpose, out by where we lived, and which I've climmed up with two tubs of brandy across my shoulders on scores o' dark nights in my younger days. Some had heard that a part o' the French fleet would sail right round Scotland, and come up the Channel to a suitable haven. However, there was much doubt upon the matter; and no wonder, for after-years proved that Bonaparte himself could hardly make up his mind upon that great and very particular point, where to land. His uncertainty came about in this wise, that he could get no news as to where and how our troops lay in waiting, and that his knowledge of possible places where flat-bottomed boats might be quietly run ashore, and the men they brought marshalled in order, was dim to the last degree. Being flat-bottomed, they didn't require a harbour for unshipping their cargo of men, but a good shelving beach away from sight, and with a fair open road toward London. How the question posed that great Corsican tyrant (as we used to call him), what pains he took to settle it, and, above all, what a risk he ran on one particular night in trying to do so, were known only to one man here and there; and certainly to no maker of newspapers or printer of books, or my account o't would not have had so many heads shaken over it as it has by gentry who only believe what they see in printed lines.

"The flocks my father had charge of fed all about the downs near our house, overlooking the sea and shore each way for miles. In winter and early spring father was up a deal at nights, watching and tending the lambing. Often he'd go to bed early, and turn out at twelve or one; and on the other hand, he'd sometimes stay up till twelve or one, and then turn in to bed. As soon as I was old enough I used to help him, mostly in the way of keeping an eye upon the ewes while he was gone home to rest. This is what I was doing in a particular month in either the year four or five—I can't certainly fix which, but it was long before I was took away from the sheepkeeping to be bound prentice to a trade. Every night at that time I was at the fold, about half a mile, or it may be a little more, from our cottage, and no living thing at all with me but the ewes and young lambs. Afeard? No; I was never afeard of being alone at these times; for I had been reared in such an out-step place that the lack o' human beings at night made me less fearful than the sight of 'em. Directly I saw a man's shape after dark in a lonely place I was frightened out of my senses.

"One day in that month we were surprised by a visit from my uncle Job, the sergeant in the Sixty-first foot, then in camp on the downs above King George's watering-place, several miles to the west yonder. Uncle Job dropped in about dusk, and went up with my father to the fold for an hour or two. Then he came home, had a drop to drink from the tub of sperrits that the smugglers kept us in for housing their liquor when they'd made a run, and for burning 'em off when there was danger. After that he stretched himself out on the settle to sleep. I went to bed: at one o'clock father came home, and waking me to go and take his place, according to custom, went to bed himself. On my way out of the house I passed Uncle Job on the settle. He opened his eyes, and upon my telling him where I was going he said it was a shame that such a youngster as I should go up there all alone; and when he had fastened up his stock and waist-belt he set off along with me, taking a drop from the sperrit-tub in a little flat bottle that stood in the corner-cupboard.

"By and by we drew up to the fold, saw that all was right, and then, to keep ourselves warm, curled up in a heap of straw that lay inside the thatched hurdles we had set up to break the stroke of the wind when there was any. Tonight, however, there was none. It was one of those very still nights when, if you stand on the high hills anywhere within two or three miles of the sea, you can hear the rise and fall of the tide along the shore, coming and going every few moments like a sort of great snore of the sleeping world. Over the lower ground there was a bit of a mist, but on the hill where we lay the air was clear, and the moon, then in her last quarter, flung a fairly good light on the grass and scattered straw.

"While we lay there Uncle Job amused me by telling me strange stories of the wars he had served in and the wownds he had got. He had already fought the French in the Low Countries, and hoped to fight 'em again. His stories lasted so long that at last I was hardly sure that I was not a soldier myself, and had seen such service as he told of. The wonders of his tales quite bewildered my mind, till I fell asleep and dreamed of battle, smoke, and flying soldiers, all of a kind with the doings he had been bringing up to me.

"How long my nap lasted I am not prepared to say. But some faint sounds over and above the rustle of the ewes in the straw, the bleat of the lambs, and the tinkle of the sheep-bell brought me to my waking senses. Uncle Job was still beside me; but he too had fallen asleep. I looked out from the straw, and saw what it was that had aroused me. Two men, in boat-cloaks, cocked hats, and swords, stood by the hurdles about twenty yards off.

"I turned my ear thitherward to catch what they were saying, but though I heard every word o't, not one did I understand. They spoke in a tongue that was not ours—in French, as I afterward found. But if I could not gain the meaning of a word, I was shrewd boy enough to find out a deal of the talkers' business. By the light o' the moon I could see that one of 'em carried a roll of paper in his hand, while every moment he spoke quick to his comrade, and pointed right and left with the other hand to spots along the shore. There was no doubt that he was explaining to the second gentleman the shapes and features of the coast. What happened soon after made this still clearer to me.

"All this time I had not waked Uncle Job, but now I began to be afeared that they might light upon us, because uncle breathed so heavily through's nose. I put my mouth to his ear and whispered, 'Uncle Job.'

"'What is it, my boy?' he said, just as if he hadn't been asleep at all.

"'Hush!' says I. 'Two French generals—'

"'French?' says he.

"'Yes,' says I. 'Come to see where to land their army!'

"I pointed 'em out; but I could say no more, for the pair were coming at that moment much nearer to where we lay. As soon as they got as near as eight or ten yards, the officer with a roll in his hand stooped down to a slanting hurdle, unfastened his roll upon it, and spread it out. Then suddenly he sprung a dark lantern open on the paper, and showed it to be a map.

"'What be they looking at?' I whispered to Uncle Job.

"'A chart of the Channel,' says the sergeant (knowing about such things).

"The other French officer now stooped likewise, and over the map they had a long consultation, as they pointed here and there on the paper, and then hither and thither at places along the shore beneath us. I noticed that the manner of one officer was very respectful toward the other, who seemed much his superior, the second in rank calling him by a sort of title that I did not know the sense of. The head one, on the other hand, was quite familiar with his friend, and more than once clapped him on the shoulder.

"Uncle Job had watched as well as I, but though the map had been in the lantern-light, their faces had always been in shade. But when they rose from stooping over the chart the light flashed upward, and fell smart upon one of 'em's features. No sooner had this happened than Uncle Job gasped, and sank down as if he'd been in a fit.

"'What is it—what is it, Uncle Job?' said I.

"'O good God!' says he, under the straw.

"'What?' says I.

"'Boney!' he groaned out.

"'Who?' says I.

"'Bonaparty,' he said. 'The Corsican ogre. O that I had got but my new-flinted firelock, that there man should die! But I haven't got my new-flinted firelock, and that there man must live. So lie low, as you value your life!'

"I did lie low, as you mid suppose. But I couldn't help peeping. And then I too, lad as I was, knew that it was the face of Bonaparte. Not know Boney? I should think I did know Boney. I should have known him by half the light o' that lantern. If I had seen a picture of his features once, I had seen it a hundred times. There was his bullet head, his short neck, his round yaller cheeks and chin, his gloomy face, and his great glowing eyes. He took off his hat to blow himself a bit, and there was the forelock in the middle of his forehead, as in all the draughts of him. In moving, his cloak fell a little open, and I could see for a moment his white-fronted jacket and one of his epaulettes.

"But none of this lasted long. In a minute he and his general had rolled up the map, shut the lantern, and turned to go down toward the shore.

"Then Uncle Job came to himself a bit. 'Slipped across in the night-time to see how to put his men ashore,' he said. 'The like o' that man's coolness eyes will never again see! Nephew, I must act in this, and immediate, or England's lost!'

"When they were over the brow, we crope out, and went some little way to look after them. Halfway down they were joined by two others, and six or seven minutes brought them to the shore. Then, from behind a rock, a boat came out into the weak moonlight of the Cove, and they jumped in; it put off instantly, and vanished in a few minutes between the two rocks that stand at the mouth of the Cove as we all know. We climmed back to where we had been before, and I could see, a short way out, a larger vessel, though still not very large. The little boat drew up alongside, was made fast at the stern as I suppose, for the largest sailed away, and we saw no more.

"My uncle Job told his officers as soon as he got back to

camp; but what they thought of it I never heard—neither did he. Boney's army never came, and a good job for me; for the Cove below my father's house was where he meant to land, as this secret visit showed. We coast-folk should have been cut down one and all, and I should not have sat here to tell this tale."

We who listened to old Selby that night have been familiar with his simple gravestone for these ten years past. Thanks to the incredulity of the age his tale has been seldom repeated. But if anything short of the direct testimony of his own eyes could persuade an auditor that Bonaparte had examined these shores for himself with a view to a practicable landing-place, it would have been Solomon Selby's manner of narrating the adventure which befell him on the down.

Rip Van Winkle

Washington Irving
(1783–1859)

Like Rip Van Winkle, Washington Irving was not overly fond of hard work. He was lucky to have six adoring older siblings who were prepared to indulge his taste for trips to the Old World, where he would spend hours— well, years actually—wandering around museums, art galleries, ancient ruins and English country churches. From these peregrinations he produced The Sketch Book *in 1820, which was a huge success on both sides of the Atlantic. Most of the sketches deal with English life, but the two most famous—"Rip Van Winkle" and "The Legend of Sleepy Hollow"—are based in New York State, and these, I'm told, are both inspired by German folktales. There is a sense of optimism and goodwill in Irving's writing that I always enjoy returning to. And I never tire of the tale of Rip and his very long sleep.*

hoever has made a voyage up the Hudson must remember the Kaatskill mountains. They are a dismembered branch of the great Appalachian family, and are seen away to the west of the river, swelling up to a noble height, and lording it over the surrounding country. Every change of season, every change of weather, indeed, every hour of the day, produces some change in the magical hues and shapes of these mountains, and they are regarded by all the good wives, far and near, as perfect barometers. When the weather is fair and settled, they are clothed

in blue and purple, and print their bold outlines on the clear evening sky; but sometimes, when the rest of the landscape is cloudless, they will gather a hood of grey vapours about their summits, which, in the last rays of the setting sun, will glow and light up like a crown of glory.

At the foot of these fairy mountains, the voyager may have descried the light smoke curling up from a village, whose shingle-roofs gleam among the trees, just where the blue tints of the upland melt away into the fresh green of the nearer landscape. It is a little village, of great antiquity, having been founded by some of the Dutch colonists, in the early times of the province, just about the beginning of the government of the good Peter Stuyvesant (may he rest in peace!) and there were some of the houses of the original settlers standing within a few years, built of small yellow bricks brought from Holland, having latticed windows and gable fronts, surmounted with weathercocks.

In that same village and in one of these very houses (which, to tell the precise truth, was sadly time-worn and weather-beaten), there lived many years since, while the country was yet a province of Great Britain, a simple good-natured fellow, of the name of Rip Van Winkle. He was a descendant of the Van Winkles who figured so gallantly in the chivalrous days of Peter Stuyvesant, and accompanied him to the siege of Fort Christina. He inherited, however, but little of the martial character of his ancestors. I have observed that he was a simple good-natured man; he was, moreover, a kind neighbour, and an obedient hen-pecked husband. Indeed, to the latter circumstance might be owing that meekness of spirit which gained him such universal popularity; for those men are most apt to be obsequious and con-ciliating abroad, who are under the discipline of shrews at home. Their tempers, doubtless, are rendered pliant and malleable in the fiery furnace of domestic tribulation, and a curtain lecture is worth all the sermons in the world for teaching the virtues of patience and long-suffering. A termagant wife may, therefore, in some respects, be considered a tolerable blessing; and if so, Rip Van Winkle was thrice blessed.

Certain it is that he was a great favourite among all the good wives of the village, who, as usual with the amiable sex, took his part in all family squabbles; and never failed, whenever they talked those matters over in their evening gossipings, to lay all the blame on Dame Van Winkle. The children of the village, too, would shout with joy whenever he approached. He assisted at their sports, made their playthings, taught them to fly kites and shoot marbles, and told them long stories of ghosts, witches, and Indians. Whenever he went dodging about the village, he was surrounded by a troop of them hanging on his skirts, clambering on his back, and playing a thousand tricks on him with impunity; and not a dog would bark at him throughout the neighbourhood.

The great error in Rip's composition was an insuperable aversion to all kinds of profitable labour. It could not be from the want of assiduity or perseverance; for he would sit on a wet rock, with a rod as long and heavy as a Tartar's lance, and fish all day without a murmur, even though he should not be encouraged by a single nibble. He would carry a fowling-piece on his shoulder for hours together, trudging through woods and swamps, and up hill and down dale, to shoot a few squirrels or wild pigeons. He would never refuse to assist a neighbour even in the roughest toil, and was a foremost man at all country frolics for husking Indian corn, or building stone fences; the women of the village, too, used to employ him to run their errands, and to do such little odd jobs as their less obliging husbands would not do for them. In a word, Rip was ready to attend to anybody's business but his own; but as to doing family duty, and keeping his farm in order, he found it impossible.

In fact, he declared it was of no use to work on his farm; it was the most pestilent little piece of ground in the whole country; everything about it went wrong, and would go wrong, in spite of him. His fences were continually falling to pieces; his cow would either go astray, or get among the cabbages; weeds were sure to grow quicker in his fields than anywhere else; the rain always made a point of setting in just as he had some outdoor work to do; so that though his patrimonial estate had dwindled away under his management, acre by acre, until there was little more left than a mere patch of Indian corn and potatoes, yet it was the worst conditioned farm in the neighbourhood.

His children, too, were as ragged and wild as if they belonged to nobody. His son Rip, an urchin begotten in his own likeness, promised to inherit the habits, with the old clothes, of his father. He was generally seen trooping like a colt at his mother's heels, equipped in a pair of his father's cast-off galligaskins which he had much ado to hold up with one hand, as a fine lady does her train in bad weather.

Rip Van Winkle, however, was one of those happy mortals, of foolish, well-oiled dispositions, who take the world easy, eat white bread or brown, whichever can be got with least thought or trouble, and would rather starve on a penny than work for a pound. If left to himself, he would have whistled life away in perfect contentment; but his wife kept continually dinning in his ears about his idleness, his carelessness, and the ruin he was bringing on his family. Morning, noon, and night, her tongue was incessantly going, and everything he said or did was sure to produce a torrent of household eloquence. Rip had but one way of replying to all lectures of the kind, and that, by frequent use, had grown into a habit. He shrugged his shoulders, shook his head, cast up his eyes, but said nothing. This, however, always provoked a fresh volley from his wife; so that he was fain to draw off his forces, and take to the outside of the house—the only side which, in truth, belongs to a henpecked husband.

Rip's sole domestic adherent was his dog Wolf, who was as much henpecked as his master; for Dame Van Winkle regarded them as companions in idleness, and even looked upon Wolf with an evil eye, as the cause of his master's going so often astray. True it is, in all points of spirit, befitting an honourable dog, he was as courageous an animal as ever scoured the woods—but what courage can withstand the ever-during and all-besetting terrors of a woman's tongue? The moment Wolf entered the house, his crest fell, his tail drooped to the ground, or curled between his legs, he sneaked about with a gallows air, casting many a sidelong glance at Dame Van Winkle, and at the least flourish of a broomstick or ladle, he would fly to the door with yelping precipitation.

Times grew worse and worse with Rip Van Winkle as years of

matrimony rolled on; a tart temper never mellows with age, and a sharp tongue is the only edged tool that grows keener with constant use. For a long while he used to console himself, when driven from home, by frequenting a kind of perpetual club of the sages, philosophers, and other idle personages of the village; which held its sessions on a bench before a small inn, designated by a rubicund portrait of His Majesty George the Third. Here they used to sit in the shade through a long lazy summer's day, talking listlessly over village gossip, or telling endless sleepy stories about nothing. But it would have been worth any statesman's money to have heard the profound discussions that sometimes took place, when by chance an old newspaper fell into their hands from some passing traveller. How solemnly they would listen to the contents, as drawled out by Derrick Van Bummel, the schoolmaster, a dapper learned little man, who was not to be daunted by the most gigantic word in the dictionary; and how sagely they would deliberate upon public events some months after they had taken place.

The opinions of this junto were completely controlled by Nicholas Vedder, a patriarch of the village, and landlord of the inn, at the door of which he took his seat from morning till night, just moving sufficiently to avoid the sun and keep in the shade of a large tree; so that the neighbours could tell the hour by his movements as accurately as by a sundial. It is true he was rarely heard to speak, but smoked his pipe incessantly. His adherents, however (for every great man has his adherents), perfectly understood him, and knew how to gather his opinions. When anything that was read or related displeased him, he was observed to smoke his pipe vehemently, and to send forth short, frequent, and angry puffs, but when pleased he would inhale the smoke slowly and tranquilly, and emit it in light and placid clouds; and sometimes, taking the pipe from his mouth, and letting the fragrant vapour curl about his nose, would gravely nod his head in token of perfect approbation.

From even this stronghold the unlucky Rip was at length routed by his termagant wife, who would suddenly break in upon the tranquillity of the assemblage and call the members all to naught;

nor was that august personage, Nicholas Vedder himself, sacred from the daring tongue of this terrible virago, who charged him outright with encouraging her husband in habits of idleness.

Poor Rip was at last reduced almost to despair; and his only alternative, to escape from the labour of the farm and clamour of his wife, was to take gun in hand and stroll away into the woods. Here he would sometimes seat himself at the foot of a tree, and share the contents of his wallet with Wolf, with whom he sympathized as a fellow-sufferer in persecution. "Poor Wolf," he would say, "thy mistress leads thee a dog's life of it; but never mind, my lad, whilst I live thou shalt never want a friend to stand by thee!" Wolf would wag his tail, look wistfully in his master's face, and if dogs can feel pity, I verily believe he reciprocated the sentiment with all his heart.

In a long ramble of the kind on a fine autumnal day, Rip had unconsciously scrambled to one of the highest parts of the Kaatskill mountains. He was after his favourite sport of squirrel-shooting, and the still solitudes had echoed and re-echoed with the reports of his gun. Panting and fatigued, he threw himself, late in the afternoon, on a green knoll, covered with mountain herbage, that crowned the brow of a precipice. From an opening between the trees he could overlook all the lower country for many a mile of rich woodland. He saw at a distance the lordly Hudson, far, far below him, moving on its silent but majestic course, with the reflection of a purple cloud, or the sail of a lagging bark, here and there sleeping on its glassy bosom, and at last losing itself in the blue highlands.

On the other side he looked down into a deep mountain glen, wild, lonely, and shagged, the bottom filled with fragments from the impending cliffs, and scarcely lighted by the reflected rays of the setting sun. For some time Rip lay musing on this scene; evening was gradually advancing; the mountains began to throw their long blue shadows over the valleys; he saw that it would be dark long before he could reach the village, and he heaved a heavy sigh when he thought of encountering the terrors of Dame Van Winkle.

As he was about to descend, he heard a voice from a distance, hallooing, "Rip Van Winkle! Rip Van Winkle!" He looked round, but could see nothing but a crow winging its solitary flight across the mountain. He thought his fancy must have deceived him, and turned again to descend, when he heard the same cry ring through the still evening air: "Rip Van Winkle! Rip Van Winkle!" At the same time Wolf bristled up his back, and, giving a loud growl, skulked to his master's side, looking fearfully down into the glen. Rip now felt a vague apprehension stealing over him; he looked anxiously in the same direction, and perceived a strange figure slowly toiling up the rocks, and bending under the weight of something he carried on his back. He was surprised to see any human being in this lonely and unfrequented place; but supposing it to be someone of the neighbourhood in need of his assistance, he hastened down to yield it.

On nearer approach he was still more surprised at the singularity of the stranger's appearance. He was a short, square-built old fellow, with thick bushy hair and a grizzled beard. His dress was of the antique Dutch fashion—a cloth jerkin, strapped round the waist—several pair of breeches, the outer one of ample volume, decorated with rows of buttons down the sides, and bunches at the knees. He bore on his shoulder a stout keg, that seemed full of liquor, and made signs for Rip to approach and assist him with the load. Though rather shy and distrustful of this new acquaintance, Rip complied with his usual alacrity; and mutually relieving each other, they clambered up a narrow gully, apparently the dry bed of a mountain torrent. As they ascended, Rip every now and then heard long rolling peals, like distant thunder, that seemed to issue out of a deep ravine, or rather cleft, between lofty rocks, towards which their rugged path conducted. He paused for an instant, but supposing it to be the muttering of one of those transient thunder-showers which often take place in mountain heights, he proceeded. Passing through the ravine, they came to a hollow, like a small amphitheatre, surrounded by perpendicular precipices, over the brinks of which impending trees shot their branches, so that you only caught glimpses of the azure sky and the bright evening cloud. During the whole time Rip and his companion had laboured on in silence, for though the former marvelled greatly what could be the object of carrying a keg of liquor up this wild mountain; yet there was something strange and incomprehensible about the unknown, that inspired awe and checked familiarity.

On entering the amphitheatre, new objects of wonder presented themselves. On a level spot in the centre was a company of odd-looking personages playing at ninepins. They were dressed in a quaint outlandish fashion; some wore short doublets, others jerkins, with long knives in their belts, and most of them had enormous breeches, of similar style with that of the guide's. Their visages, too, were peculiar; one had a large head, broad face, and small piggish eyes; the face of another seemed to consist entirely of nose, and was surmounted by a white sugar-loaf hat, set off with a little red cock's tail. They all had beards, of various shapes and colours. There was one who seemed to be the commander. He was a stout old gentleman, with a weather-beaten countenance; he wore a laced doublet, broad belt and hanger, high-crowned hat and feather, red stockings, and high-heeled shoes, with roses in them. The whole group reminded Rip of the figures in an old Flemish painting, in the parlour of Dominie Van Shaick, the village parson, and which had been brought over from Holland at the time of the settlement.

What seemed particularly odd to Rip was, that though these folks were evidently amusing themselves, yet they maintained the gravest faces, the most mysterious silence, and were, withal, the most melancholy party of pleasure he had ever witnessed. Nothing interrupted the stillness of the scene but the noise of the balls, which, whenever they were rolled, echoed along the mountains like rumbling peals of thunder.

As Rip and his companion approached them, they suddenly desisted from their play, and stared at him with such fixed, statue-like gaze, and such strange, uncouth, lacklustre countenances, that his heart turned within him, and his knees smote together. His companion now emptied the contents of the keg into large flagons, and made signs to him to wait upon the company. He obeyed with fear and trembling; they quaffed the liquor in profound silence, and then returned to their game.

By degrees Rip's awe and apprehension subsided. He even

ventured, when no eye was fixed upon him, to taste the beverage, which he found had much of the flavour of excellent Hollands. He was naturally a thirsty soul, and was soon tempted to repeat the draught. One taste provoked another; and he reiterated his visits to the flagon so often, that at length his senses were over-powered, his eyes swam in his head, his head gradually declined, and he fell into a deep sleep.

On waking, he found himself on the green knoll whence he had first seen the old man of the glen. He rubbed his eyes—it was a bright sunny morning. The birds were hopping and twittering among the bushes, and the eagle was wheeling aloft, and breast-ing the pure mountain breeze. "Surely," thought Rip, "I have not slept here all night." He recalled the occurrences before he fell asleep. The strange man with a keg of liquor—the mountain ravine—the wild retreat among the rocks—the woebegone party at ninepins—the flagon—"Oh! that flagon! that wicked flagon!" thought Rip; "what excuse shall I make to Dame Van Winkle?"

He looked round for his gun, but in place of the clean, well-oiled fowling-piece, he found an old firelock lying by him, the barrel incrusted with rust, the lock falling off, and the stock worm-eaten. He now suspected that the grave roysters of the mountain had put a trick upon him, and, having dosed him with liquor, had robbed him of his gun. Wolf, too, had disappeared, but he might have strayed away after a squirrel or partridge. He whistled after him, and shouted his name, but all in vain; the echoes repeated his whistle and shout, but no dog was to be seen.

He determined to revisit the scene of the last evening's gam-bol, and, if he met with any of the party, to demand his dog and gun. As he rose to walk he found himself stiff in the joints, and wanting in his usual activity. "These mountain beds do not agree with me," thought Rip; "and if this frolic should lay me up with a fit of the rheumatism, I shall have a blessed time with Dame Van Winkle." With some difficulty he got down into the glen: he found the gully up which he and his companion had ascended the preceding evening; but, to his astonishment, a mountain stream was now foaming down it—leaping from rock to rock, and fill-ing the glen with babbling murmurs. He, however, made shift to scramble up its sides, working his toilsome way through thickets of birch, sassafras, and witch-hazel, and sometimes tripped up or entangled by the wild grapevines that twisted their coils or tendrils from tree to tree, and spread a kind of network in his path.

At length he reached to where the ravine had opened through the cliffs to the amphitheatre; but no traces of such opening remained. The rocks presented a high impenetrable wall, over which the torrent came tumbling in a sheet of feathery foam, and fell into a broad, deep basin, black from the shadows of the surrounding forest. Here, then, poor Rip was brought to a stand. He again called and whistled after his dog; he was only answered by the cawing of a flock of idle crows, sporting high in air about a dry tree that overhung a sunny precipice; and who, secure in their elevation, seemed to look down and scoff at the poor man's perplexities. What was to be done?—the morning was passing away, and Rip felt famished for want of his breakfast. He grieved to give up his dog and his gun; he dreaded to meet his wife; but it would not do to starve among the mountains. He shook his head, shouldered the rusty firelock, and, with a heart full of trouble and anxiety, turned his steps homeward.

As he approached the village he met a number of people, but none whom he knew, which somewhat surprised him, for he had thought himself acquainted with everyone in the country round. Their dress, too, was of a different fashion from that to which he was accustomed. They all stared at him with equal marks of surprise, and, whenever they cast their eyes upon him, invariably stroked their chins. The constant recurrence of this gesture induced Rip, involuntarily, to do the same—when, to his astonishment, he found his beard had grown a foot long!

He had now entered the skirts of the village. A troop of strange children ran at his heels, hooting after him, and pointing at his grey beard. The dogs, too, not one of which he recognized for an old acquaintance, barked at him as he passed. The very village was altered; it was larger and more populous. There were rows of houses which he had never seen before, and those which had been his familiar haunts had disappeared. Strange names were over the doors—strange faces at the windows—everything was strange. His mind now misgave him; he began to doubt whether both he and the world around him were not bewitched. Surely this was his native village, which he had left but the day before. There stood the Kaatskill mountains—there ran the silver Hudson at a distance—there was every hill and dale precisely as it had always been. Rip was sorely perplexed. "That flagon last night," thought he, "has addled my poor head sadly!"

It was with some difficulty that he found the way to his own house, which he approached with silent awe, expecting every moment to hear the shrill voice of Dame Van Winkle. He found the house gone to decay—the roof fallen in, the windows shattered, and the doors off the hinges. A half-starved dog that looked like Wolf, was skulking about it. Rip called him by name, but the cur snarled, showed his teeth, and passed on. This was an unkind cut indeed—"My very dog," sighed poor Rip, "has forgotten me!"

He entered the house, which, to tell the truth, Dame Van Winkle had always kept in neat order. It was empty, forlorn, and apparently abandoned. The desolateness overcame all his connubial fears—he called loudly for his wife and children—the lonely chambers rang for a moment with his voice, and then all again was silence.

He now hurried forth, and hastened to his old resort, the village inn—but it too was gone. A large, rickety, wooden building stood in its place, with great gaping windows, some of them broken and mended with old hats and petticoats, and over the door was painted, "The Union Hotel, by Jonathan Doolittle." Instead of the great tree that used to shelter the quiet little Dutch inn of yore, there was now reared a tall naked pole, with something on the top that looked like a red nightcap, and from it was fluttering a flag, on which was a singular assemblage of stars and stripes—all this was strange and incomprehensible. He recognized on the sign, however, the ruby face of King George, under which he had smoked so many a peaceful pipe; but even this was singularly metamorphosed. The red coat was changed for one of blue and buff, a sword was held in the hand instead of a sceptre, the head was decorated with a cocked hat, and underneath was painted in large characters, GENERAL WASHINGTON.

There was, as usual, a crowd of folks about the door, but none that Rip recollected. The very character of the people seemed changed. There was a busy, bustling, disputatious tone about it, instead of the accustomed phlegm and drowsy tranquillity. He looked in vain for the sage Nicholas Vedder, with his broad face, double chin, and fair long pipe, uttering clouds of tobacco-smoke instead of idle speeches; or Van Bummel, the schoolmaster, doling forth the contents of an ancient newspaper. In place of these, a lean, bilious-looking fellow, with his pockets full of handbills, was haranguing vehemently about rights of citizens—elections—members of Congress—liberty—Bunker's Hill—heroes of seventy-six—and other words, which were a perfect Babylonish jargon to the bewildered Van Winkle.

The appearance of Rip, with his long grizzled beard, his rusty fowling-piece, his uncouth dress, and an army of women and children at his heels, soon attracted the attention of the tavern politicians. They crowded round him, eyeing him from head to foot with great curiosity. The orator bustled up to him, and, drawing him partly aside, inquired "on which side he voted?" Rip stared in vacant stupidity. Another short but busy little fellow pulled him by the arm, and, rising on tiptoe, inquired in his ear, "Whether he was Federal or Democrat?" Rip was equally at a loss to comprehend the question; when a knowing, self-important old gentleman, in a sharp cocked hat, made his way through the crowd, putting them to the right and left with his elbows as he passed, and planting himself before Van Winkle, with one arm akimbo, the other resting on his cane, his keen eyes and sharp hat penetrating, as it were, into his very soul, demanded in an austere tone, "What brought him to the election with a gun on his shoulder, and a mob at his heels, and whether he meant to breed a riot in the village?"—"Alas! gentlemen," cried Rip, somewhat dismayed, "I am a poor quiet man, a native of the place, and a loyal subject of the king, God bless him!"

Here a general shout burst from the bystanders—"A tory! a tory! a spy! a refugee! hustle him! away with him!" It was with great difficulty that the self-important man in the cocked hat restored order; and, having assumed a tenfold austerity of brow, demanded again of the unknown culprit, what he came there for, and whom he was seeking? The poor man humbly assured him that he meant no harm, but merely came there in search of some of his neighbours, who used to keep about the tavern.

"Well—who are they?—name them."

Rip bethought himself a moment, and inquired, "Where's Nicholas Vedder?"

There was a silence for a little while, when an old man replied in a thin piping voice, "Nicholas Vedder! Why, he is dead and gone these eighteen years! There was a wooden tombstone in the church-yard that used to tell all about him, but that's rotten and gone too."

"Where's Brom Dutcher?"

"Oh, he went off to the army in the beginning of the war; some say he was killed at the storming of Stony Point—others say he was drowned in a squall at the foot of Antony's Nose. I don't know—he never came back again."

"Where's Van Bummel, the schoolmaster?"

"He went off to the wars too, was a great militia general, and is now in Congress."

Rip's heart died away at hearing of these sad changes in his home and friends, and finding himself thus alone in the world. Every answer puzzled him too, by treating of such enormous lapses of time, and of matters which he could not understand: war—Congress—Stony Point. He had no courage to ask after any more friends, but cried out in despair, "Does nobody here know Rip Van Winkle?"

"Oh, Rip Van Winkle!" exclaimed two or three. "Oh, to be sure! that's Rip Van Winkle yonder, leaning against the tree."

Rip looked, and beheld a precise counterpart of himself, as he went up the mountain: apparently as lazy, and certainly as ragged. The poor fellow was now completely confounded. He doubted his own identity, and whether he was himself or another man. In the midst of his bewilderment, the man in the cocked hat demanded who he was, and what was his name?

"God knows," exclaimed he, at his wits' end; "I'm not myself—I'm somebody else—that's me yonder—no—that's some-body else got into my shoes—I was myself last night, but I fell asleep on the mountain, and they've changed my gun, and everything's changed, and I'm changed, and I can't tell what's my name, or who I am!"

The bystanders began now to look at each other, nod, wink significantly, and tap their fingers against their foreheads. There was a whisper, also, about securing the gun, and keeping the old fellow from doing mischief, at the very suggestion of which the self-important man in the cocked hat retired with some precipitation. At this critical moment a fresh comely woman pressed through the throng to get a peep at the grey-bearded man. She had a chubby child in her arms, which, frightened at his looks, began to cry. "Hush, Rip," cried she, "hush, you little fool; the old man won't hurt you." The name of the child, the air of the mother, the tone of her voice, all awakened a train of recollections in his mind.

"What is your name, my good woman?" asked he.

"Judith Gardenier."

"And your father's name?"

"Ah, poor man, Rip Van Winkle was his name, but it's twenty years since he went away from home with his gun, and never has been heard of since—his dog came home without him; but whether he shot himself, or was carried away by the Indians, nobody can tell. I was then but a little girl."

Rip had but one question to ask; but he put it with a faltering voice:

"Where's your mother?"

"Oh, she too had died but a short time since; she broke a blood-vessel in a fit of passion at a New England pedlar."

There was a drop of comfort, at least, in this intelligence. The honest man could contain himself no longer. He caught his daughter and her child in his arms. "I am your father!" cried he— "Young Rip Van Winkle once—old Rip Van Winkle now!—Does nobody know poor Rip Van Winkle?"

All stood amazed, until an old woman, tottering out from among the crowd, put her hand to her brow, and peering under it in his face for a moment, exclaimed, "Sure enough! it is Rip Van Winkle—it is himself! Welcome home again, old neighbour—Why, where have you been these twenty long years?"

Rip's story was soon told, for the whole twenty years had been to him but as one night. The neighbours stared when they heard it; some were seen to wink at each other, and put their tongues in their cheeks: and the self-important man in the cocked hat, who, when the alarm was over, had returned to the field, screwed down the corners of his mouth, and shook his head—upon which there was a general shaking of the head throughout the assemblage.

It was determined, however, to take the opinion of old Peter Vanderdonk, who was seen slowly advancing up the road. He was a descendant of the historian of that name, who wrote one of the earliest accounts of the province. Peter was the most ancient inhabitant of the village, and well versed in all the wonderful events and traditions of the neighbourhood. He recollected Rip at once, and corroborated his story in the most satisfactory manner. He assured the company that it was a fact, handed down from his ancestor the historian, that the Kaatskill mountains had always been haunted by strange beings. That it was affirmed that the great Hendrick Hudson, the first discoverer of the river and country, kept a kind of vigil there every twenty years, with his crew of the *Half-moon*; being permitted in this way to revisit the scenes of his enterprise, and keep a guardian eye upon the river, and the great city called by his name. That his father had once seen them in their old Dutch dresses playing at ninepins in a hollow of the mountain; and that he himself had heard, one summer afternoon, the sound of their balls, like distant peals of thunder.

To make a long story short, the company broke up, and returned to the more important concerns of the election. Rip's daughter took him home to live with her; she had a snug, well-furnished house, and a stout cheery farmer for her husband, whom Rip recollected for one of the urchins that used to climb upon his back. As to Rip's son and heir, who was the ditto of himself, seen leaning against the tree, he was employed to work on the farm; but evinced an hereditary disposition to attend to anything else but his business.

Rip now resumed his old walks and habits; he soon found many of his former cronies, though all rather the worse for the wear and tear of time; and preferred making friends among the rising generation, with whom he soon grew into great favour.

Having nothing to do at home, and being arrived at that happy age when a man can be idle with impunity, he took his place once more on the bench at the inn door, and was reverenced as one of the patriarchs of the village, and a chronicle of the old times "before the war." It was some time before he could get into the regular track of gossip, or could be made to comprehend the strange events that had taken place during his torpor. How that there had been a revolutionary war—that the country had thrown off the yoke of Old England—and that, instead of being a subject of His Majesty George the Third, he was now a free citizen of the United States. Rip, in fact, was no politician; the changes of states and empires made but little impression on him; but there was one species of despotism under which he had long groaned, and that was—petticoat government. Happily that was at an end; he had got his neck out of the yoke of matrimony, and could go in and out whenever he pleased without dreading the tyranny of Dame Van Winkle. Whenever her name was mentioned, however, he shook his head, shrugged his shoulders, and cast up his eyes; which might pass either for an expression of resignation to his fate, or joy at his deliverance.

He used to tell his story to every stranger that arrived at Mr. Doolittle's hotel. He was observed at first to vary on some points every time he told it, which was, doubtless, owing to his having so recently awaked. It at last settled down precisely to the tale I have related, and not a man, woman, or child in the neighbourhood but knew it by heart. Some always pretended to doubt the reality of it, and insisted that Rip had been out of his head, and that this was one point on which he always remained flighty. The old Dutch inhabitants, however, almost universally gave it full credit. Even to this day they never hear a thunderstorm of a summer afternoon about the Kaatskill, but they say Hendrick Hudson and his crew are at their game of ninepins; and it is a common wish of all henpecked husbands in the neighbourhood, when life hangs heavy on their hands, that they might have a quieting draught out of Rip Van Winkle's flagon.

MICHAEL

A Pastoral Poem
by William Wordsworth
(1770–1850)

Unlike his poetic forebears, William Wordsworth chose not to write about kings and queens, dashing warriors, and the heroes of myth and legend. Instead, he created deeply felt, often tragic poetry about the lives of the farmers, shepherds and itinerant poor of England's Lake District, where he lived.

When I was preparing materials for this collection, I reread "Michael" for the first time in a number of years, and it occurred to me that this is a poem that has a particular resonance today. In difficult economic times, many people are forced to uproot themselves and seek a livelihood in the cities. "Michael" is first and foremost a poem about the people who are left behind.

 f from the public way you
     turn your steps
Up the tumultuous brook
     of Green-head Gill,
You will suppose that with
     an upright path
Your feet must struggle; in
     such bold ascent
The pastoral Mountains front you, face to face.
But, courage! For beside that boisterous Brook
The mountains have all opened out themselves,
And made a hidden valley of their own.

No habitation there is seen; but such
As journey thither find themselves alone
With a few sheep, with rocks and stones, and kites
That overhead are sailing in the sky.
It is in truth an utter solitude,
Nor should I have made mention of this Dell
But for one object which you might pass by,
Might see and notice not. Beside the brook
There is a straggling heap of unhewn stones!
And to that place a story appertains,
Which, though it be ungarnished with events,
Is not unfit, I deem, for the fireside,
Or for the summer shade. It was the first,
The earliest of those tales that spake to me
Of Shepherds, dwellers in the valleys, men
Whom I already loved, not verily
For their own sakes, but for the fields and hills
Where was their occupation and abode.
And hence this Tale, while I was yet a boy
Careless of books, yet having felt the power
Of Nature, by the gentle agency
Of natural objects led me on to feel
For passions that were not my own, and think
At random and imperfectly indeed
On man; the heart of man and human life.
Therefore, although it be a history
Homely and rude, I will relate the same
For the delight of a few natural hearts,
And with yet fonder feeling, for the sake
Of youthful Poets, who among these Hills
Will be my second self when I am gone.

Upon the Forest-side in Grasmere Vale
There dwelt a Shepherd, Michael was his name,
An old man, stout of heart, and strong of limb.
His bodily frame had been from youth to age
Of an unusual strength: his mind was keen,

Intense and frugal, apt for all affairs,
And in his Shepherd's calling he was prompt
And watchful more than ordinary men.
Hence he had learned the meaning of all winds,
Of blasts of every tone, and oftentimes
When others heeded not, He heard the South
Make subterraneous music, like the noise
Of Bagpipers on distant Highland hills;
The Shepherd, at such warning, of his flock
Bethought him, and he to himself would say
The winds are now devising work for me!
And truly at all times the storm, that drives
The Traveller to a shelter, summoned him
Up to the mountains: he had been alone
Amid the heart of many thousand mists
That came to him and left him on the heights.
So lived he till his eightieth year was passed.

And grossly that man errs, who should suppose
That the green Valleys, and the Streams and Rocks
Were things indifferent to the Shepherd's thoughts.
Fields, where with cheerful spirits he had breathed
The common air; the hills, which he so oft
Had climbed with vigorous steps; which had impressed
So many incidents upon his mind
Of hardship, skill or courage, joy or fear;
Which like a book preserved the memory
Of the dumb animals, whom he had saved,
Had fed or sheltered, linking to such acts,
So grateful in themselves, the certainty
Of honourable gains; these fields, these hills
Which were his living Being, even more
Than his own Blood—what could they be less? had laid
Strong hold on his affections, were to him
A pleasurable feeling of blind love,
The pleasure which there is in life itself.

He had not passed his days in singleness.
He had a Wife, a comely Matron, old
Though younger than himself full twenty years.
She was a woman of a stirring life
Whose heart was in her house: two wheels she had
Of antique form, this large for spinning wool,
That small for flax, and if one wheel had rest,
It was because the other was at work.
The Pair had but one Inmate in their house,
An only Child, who had been born to them
When Michael telling o'er his years began
To deem that he was old, in Shepherd's phrase,
With one foot in the grave. This only son,
With two brave sheep dogs tried in many a storm,
The one of an inestimable worth,
Made all their Household. I may truly say,
That they were as a proverb in the vale
For endless industry. When day was gone,
And from their occupations out of doors
The Son and Father were come home, even then
Their labour did not cease, unless when all
Turned to their cleanly supper-board, and there
Each with a mess of pottage and skimmed milk,
Sat round their basket piled with oaten cakes,
And their plain home-made cheese. Yet when their meal
Was ended, Luke (for so the Son was named)
And his old Father, both betook themselves
To such convenient work, as might employ
Their hands by the fireside; perhaps to card
Wool for the Housewife's spindle, or repair
Some injury done to sickle, flail, or scythe,
Or other implement of house or field.

Down from the ceiling by the chimney's edge,
Which in our ancient uncouth country style
Did with a huge projection overbrow
Large space beneath, as duly as the light

Of day grew dim, the Housewife hung a lamp;
An aged utensil, which had performed
Service beyond all others of its kind.
Early at evening did it burn and late,
Surviving Comrade of uncounted Hours
Which going by from year to year had found
And left the Couple neither gay perhaps
Nor cheerful, yet with objects and with hopes
Living a life of eager industry.
And now, when Luke was in his eighteenth year,
There by the light of this old lamp they sat,
Father and Son, while late into the night
The Housewife plied her own peculiar work,
Making the cottage through the silent hours
Murmur as with the sound of summer flies.
Not with a waste of words, but for the sake
Of pleasure, which I know that I shall give
To many living now, I of this Lamp
Speak thus minutely: for there are no few
Whose memories will bear witness to my tale.
The Light was famous in its neighbourhood,
And was a public Symbol of the life
The thrifty Pair had lived. For, as it chanced,
Their Cottage on a plot of rising ground
Stood single, with large prospect North and South,
High into Easedale, up to Dunmal-Raise,
And Westward to the village near the Lake.
And from this constant light so regular
And so far seen, the House itself by all
Who dwelt within the limits of the vale,
Both old and young, was named the Evening Star.

Thus living on through such a length of years,
The Shepherd, if he loved himself, must needs
Have loved his Helpmate; but to Michael's heart
This Son of his old age was yet more dear—
Effect which might perhaps have been produced

By that instinctive tenderness, the same
Blind Spirit, which is in the blood of all,
Or that a child, more than all other gifts,
Brings hope with it, and forward-looking thoughts,
And stirrings of inquietude, when they
By tendency of nature needs must fail.
From such, and other causes, to the thoughts
Of the old Man his only Son was now
The dearest object that he knew on earth.
Exceeding was the love he bare to him,
His Heart and his Heart's joy! For oftentimes
Old Michael, while he was a babe in arms,
Had done him female service, not alone
For dalliance and delight, as is the use
Of Fathers, but with patient mind enforced
To acts of tenderness; and he had rocked
His cradle with a woman's gentle hand.

And in a later time, ere yet the Boy
Had put on Boy's attire, did Michael love,
Albeit of a stern unbending mind,
To have the young one in his sight, when he
Had work by his own door, or when he sat
With sheep before him on his Shepherd's stool,
Beneath that large old Oak, which near their door
Stood, and from its enormous breadth of shade
Chosen for the Shearer's covert from the sun,
Thence in our rustic dialect was called
The CLIPPING TREE, a name which yet it bears.
There, while they two were sitting in the shade,
With others round them, earnest all and blithe,
Would Michael exercise his heart with looks
Of fond correction and reproof bestowed
Upon the child, if he disturbed the sheep
By catching at their legs, or with his shouts
Scared them, while they lay still beneath the shears.

And when by Heaven's good grace the Boy grew up
A healthy Lad, and carried in his cheek
Two steady roses that were five years old,
The Michael from a winter coppice cut
With his own hand a sapling, which he hooped
With iron, making it throughout in all
Due requisites a perfect Shepherd's Staff,
And gave it to the Boy; wherewith equipped
He as a Watchman oftentimes was placed
At gate or gap, to stem or turn the flock,
And to his office prematurely called
There stood the urchin, as you will divine,
Something between a hindrance and a help,
And for this cause not always, I believe,
Receiving from his Father hire of praise.
Thought nought was left undone, which staff or voice,
Or looks, or threatening gestures could perform.
   But soon as Luke, full ten years old, could stand
Against the mountain blasts, and to the heights,
Not fearing toil, nor length of weary ways,
He with his Father daily went, and they
Were as companions, why should I relate
That objects which the Shepherd loved before
Were dearer now? that from the Boy there came
Feelings and emanations, things which were
Light to the sun and music to the wind;
And that the Old Man's heart seemed born again.
   Thus in his Father's sight the Boy grew up:
And now when he had reached his eighteenth year,
He was his comfort and his daily hope.

While this good household thus were living on
From day to day, to Michael's ear there came
Distressful tidings. Long before the time
Of which I speak, the Shepherd had been bound
In surety for his Brother's Son, a man
Of an industrious life, and ample means,

But unforeseen misfortunes suddenly
Had pressed upon him, and old Michael now
Was summoned to discharge the forfeiture,
A grievous penalty, but little less
Than half his substance. This unlooked-for claim
At the first hearing, for a moment took
More hope out of his life than he supposed
That any old man ever could have lost.
As soon as he had gathered so much strength
That he could look his trouble in the face,
It seemed that his sole refuge was to sell
A portion of his patrimonial fields.
Such was his first resolve; he thought again,
And his heart failed him. "Isabel," said he,
Two evenings after he had heard the news,
"I have been toiling more than seventy years,
And in the open sunshine of God's love
Have we all lived, yet if these fields of ours
Should pass into a Stranger's hand, I think
That I could not lie quiet in my grave.
Our lot is a hard lot; the Sun itself
Has scarcely been more diligent than I,
And I have lived to be a fool at last
To my own family. An evil Man
That was, and made an evil choice, if he
Were false to us; and if he were not false,
There are ten thousand to whom loss like this
Had been no sorrow. I forgive him—but
'Twere better to be dumb than to talk thus.
When I began, my purpose was to speak
Of remedies and of a cheerful hope.
Our Luke shall leave us, Isabel; the land
Shall not go from us, and it shall be free,
He shall possess it, free as is the wind
That passes over it. We have, thou knowest,
Another Kinsman, he will be our friend
In this distress. He is a prosperous man,

Thriving in trade, and Luke to him shall go,
And with his Kinsman's help and his own thrift,
He quickly will repair this loss, and then
May come again to us. If here he stay,
What can be done? Where everyone is poor
What can be gained?" At this, the old man paused,
And Isabel sat silent, for her mind
Was busy, looking back into past times.
There's Richard Bateman, thought she to herself,
He was a parish-boy—at the church-door
They made a gathering for him, shillings, pence,
And halfpennies, wherewith the Neighbours bought
A Basket, which they filled with Pedlar's wares,
And with this Basket on his arm, the Lad
Went up to London, found a Master there,
Who out of many chose the trusty Boy
To go and overlook his merchandise
Beyond the seas, where he grew wondrous rich,
And left estates and monies to the poor,
And at his birthplace built a Chapel, floored
With Marble, which he sent from foreign lands.
These thoughts, and many others of like sort,
Passed quickly through the mind of Isabel,
And her face brightened. The Old Man was glad,
And thus resumed. "Well! Isabel, this scheme
These two days has been meat and drink to me.
Far more than we have lost is left us yet.
—We have enough—I wish indeed that I
Were younger, but this hope is a good hope.
—Make ready Luke's best garments, of the best
Buy for him more, and let us send him forth
Tomorrow, or the next day, or tonight:
—If he could go, the Boy should go tonight."
Here Michael ceased, and to the fields went forth
With a light heart. The Housewife for five days
Was restless morn and night, and all day long
Wrought on with her best fingers to prepare

Things needful for the journey of her Son.
But Isabel was glad when Sunday came
To stop her in her work; for, when she lay
By Michael's side, she for the two last nights
Heard him, how he was troubled in his sleep:
And when they rose at morning she could see
That all his hopes were gone. That day at noon
She said to Luke, while they two by themselves
Were sitting at the door, "Thou must not go,
We have no other Child but thee to lose,
None to remember—do not go away,
For if thou leave thy Father he will die."
The Lad made answer with a jocund voice,
And Isabel, when she had told her fears,
Recovered heart. That evening her best fare
Did she bring forth, and all together sat
Like happy people round a Christmas fire.

Next morning Isabel resumed her work,
And all the ensuing week the house appeared
As cheerful as a grove in Spring: at length
The expected letter from their Kinsman came,
With kind assurances that he would do
His utmost for the welfare of the Boy,
To which requests were added that forthwith
He might be sent to him. Ten times or more
The letter was read over; Isabel
Went forth to shew it to the neighbours round:
Nor was there at that time on English Land
A prouder heart than Luke's. When Isabel
Had to her house returned, the Old Man said
"He shall depart tomorrow." To this word
The Housewife answered, talking much of things
Which, if at such short notice he should go,
Would surely be forgotten. But at length
She gave consent, and Michael was at ease.

Near the tumultuous brook of Green-head Gill,
In that deep Valley, Michael had designed
To build a Sheepfold, and, before he heard
The tidings of his melancholy loss,
For this same purpose he had gathered up
A heap of stones, which close to the brook side
Lay thrown together, ready for the work.
With Luke that evening thitherward he walked;
And soon as they had reached the place he stopped
And thus the Old Man spake to him. "My Son,
Tomorrow thou wilt leave me; with full heart
I look upon thee, for thou art the same
That wert a promise to me ere thy birth,
And all thy life has been my daily joy.
I will relate to thee some little part
Of our two histories; 'twill do thee good
When thou art from me, even if I should speak
Of things thou canst not know of.—After thou
First cam'st into the world, as it befalls
To newborn infants, thou didst sleep away
Two days, and blessings from thy Father's tongue
Then fell upon thee. Day by day passed on,
And still I loved thee with increasing love.
Never to living ear came sweeter sounds
Than when I heard thee by our own fireside
First uttering without words a natural tune,
When thou, a feeding babe, didst in thy joy
Sing at thy Mother's breast. Month followed month,
And in the open fields my life was passed
And in the mountains, else I think that thou
Hadst been brought up upon thy father's knees.
—But we were playmates, Luke; among these hills,
As well thou know'st, in us the old and young
Have played together, nor with me didst thou
Lack any pleasure which a boy can know."
Luke had a manly heart; but at these words
He sobbed aloud; the Old Man grasped his hand,

And said, "Nay do not take it so—I see
That these are things of which I need not speak.
—Even to the utmost I have been to thee
A kind and a good Father: and herein
I but repay a gift which I myself
Received at others' hands, for, though now old
Beyond the common life of man, I still
Remember them who loved me in my youth.
Both of them sleep together: here they lived
As all their Forefathers had done, and when
At length their time was come, they were not loath
To give their bodies to the family mould.
I wished that thou should'st live the life they lived.
But 'tis a long time to look back, my Son,
And see so little gain from sixty years.
These fields were burthened when they came to me;
'Till I was forty years of age, not more
Than half of my inheritance was mine.
I toiled and toiled; God blessed me in my work,
And 'till these three weeks past the land was free.
—It looks as if it never could endure
Another Master. Heaven forgive me, Luke,
If I judge ill for thee, but it seems good
That thou should'st go." At this the Old Man paused,
Then, pointing to the Stones near which they stood,
Thus, after a short silence, he resumed:
"This was a work for us, and now, my Son,
It is a work for me. But, lay one Stone—
Here, lay it for me, Luke, with thine own hands.
I for the purpose brought thee to this place.
Nay, Boy, be of good hope:—we both may live
To see a better day. At eighty-four
I still am strong and stout;—do thou thy part,
I will do mine.—I will begin again
With many tasks that were resigned to thee;
Up to the heights, and in among the storms,
Will I without thee go again, and do

All works which I was wont to do alone,
Before I knew thy face.—Heaven bless thee, Boy!
Thy heart these two weeks has been beating fast
With many hopes—it should be so—yes—yes—
I knew that thou could'st never have a wish
To leave me, Luke, thou has been bound to me
Only by links of love, when thou art gone
What will be left to us!—But, I forget
My purposes. Lay now the cornerstone,
As I requested, and hereafter, Luke,
When thou art gone away, should evil men
Be thy companions, let this Sheepfold be
Thy anchor and thy shield; amid all fear
And all temptation, let it be to thee
An emblem of the life thy Fathers lived,
Who, being innocent, did for that cause
Bestir them in good deeds. Now, fare thee well—
When thou return'st, thou in this place wilt see
A work which is not here, a covenant
'Twill be between us—but whatever fate
Befall thee, I shall love thee to the last,
And bear thy memory with me to the grave."

The Shepherd ended here; and Luke stooped down,
And as his Father had requested, laid
The first stone of the Sheepfold; at the sight
The Old Man's grief broke from him, to his heart
He pressed his Son, he kissed him and wept;
And to the House together they returned.
Next morning, as had been resolved, the Boy
Began his journey, and when he had reached
The public Way, he put on a bold face;
And all the Neighbours as he passed their doors
Came forth, with wishes and with farewell prayers,
That followed him 'till he was out of sight.
A good report did from their Kinsman come,
Of Luke and his well-doing; and the Boy

Wrote loving letters, full of wondrous news,
Which, as the Housewife phrased it, were throughout
The prettiest letters that were ever seen.
Both parents read them with rejoicing hearts.
So, many months passed on: and once again
The Shepherd went about his daily work
With confident and cheerful thoughts; and now
Sometimes when he could find a leisure hour
He to that valley took his way, and there
Wrought at the Sheepfold. Meantime Luke began
To slacken in his duty, and at length
He in the dissolute city gave himself
To evil courses: ignominy and shame
Fell on him, so that he was driven at last
To seek a hiding-place beyond the seas.

There is a comfort in the strength of love;
'Twill make a thing endurable, which else
Would break the heart:—Old Michael found it so.
I have conversed with more than one who well
Remember the Old Man, and what he was
Years after he had heard this heavy news.
His bodily frame had been from youth to age
Of an unusual strength. Among the rocks
He went, and still looked up upon the sun,
And listened to the wind; and as before
Performed all kinds of labour for his Sheep,
And for the land his small inheritance.
And to that hollow Dell from time to time
Did he repair, to build the Fold of which
His flock had need. 'Tis not forgotten yet
The pity which was then in every heart
For the Old Man—and 'tis believed by all
That many and many a day he thither went,
And never lifted up a single stone.
There, by the Sheepfold, sometimes was he seen
Sitting alone, with that his faithful Dog,

Then old, beside him, lying at his feet.
The length of full seven years from time to time
He at the building of the Sheepfold wrought,
And left the work unfinished when he died.

Three years, or little more, did Isabel
Survive her Husband: at her death the estate
Was sold, and went into a Stranger's hand.
The Cottage which was named The Evening Star
Is gone, the ploughshare has been through the ground
On which it stood; great changes have been wrought
In all the neighbourhood, yet the Oak is left
That grew beside their Door; and the remains
Of the unfinished Sheepfold may be seen
Beside the boisterous brook of Green-head Gill.

To Build a Fire

Jack London
(1876–1916)

"It certainly was cold." This sentence is repeated over and over again in this story, and it's something every Canadian can relate to. The narrator mentions that the temperature is actually minus 75°F, which is a good deal colder even than the coldest winter's day here in Mahone Bay, I'm pleased to report. By the way, according to my calculation, minus 75 degrees Fahrenheit is about minus 60 degrees Celsius. But when it gets that cold, does it really matter?

ay had broken cold and grey, exceedingly cold and grey, when the man turned aside from the main Yukon trail and climbed the high earth-bank, where a dim and little-travelled trail led eastward through the fat spruce timberland. It was a steep bank, and he paused for breath at the top, excusing the act to himself by looking at his watch. It was nine o'clock. There was no sun nor hint of sun, though there was not a cloud in the sky. It was a clear day, and yet there seemed an intangible pall over the face of things, a subtle gloom that made the day dark, and that was due to the absence of sun. This fact did not worry the man. He was used to the lack of sun. It had been days since he had seen the sun, and he knew that a few more days must pass before that cheerful orb, due south, would just peep above the skyline and dip immediately from view.

The man flung a look back along the way he had come. The Yukon lay a mile wide and hidden under three feet of ice. On top of this ice were as many feet of snow. It was all pure white, rolling in gentle undulations where the ice-jams of the freeze-up had formed. North and south, as far as his eye could see, it was unbroken white, save for a dark hairline that curved and twisted from around the spruce-covered island to the south, and that curved and twisted away into the north, where it disappeared behind another spruce-covered island. This dark hairline was the trail—the main trail—that led south five hundred miles to the Chilcoot Pass, Dyea, and salt water; and that led north seventy miles to Dawson, and still on to the north a thousand miles to Nulato, and finally to St. Michael on Bering Sea, a thousand miles and half a thousand more.

But all this—the mysterious, far-reaching hairline trail, the absence of sun from the sky, the tremendous cold, and the strangeness and weirdness of it all—made no impression on the man. It was not because he was long used to it. He was a new-comer in the land, a *chechaquo*, and this was his first winter. The trouble with him was that he was without imagination. He was quick and alert in the things of life, but only in the things, and not in the significances. Fifty degrees below zero meant eighty-odd degrees of frost. Such fact impressed him as being cold and uncomfortable, and that was all. It did not lead him to meditate upon his frailty as a creature of temperature, and upon man's frailty in general, able only to live within certain narrow limits of heat and cold; and from there on it did not lead him to the con-jectural field of immortality and man's place in the universe. Fifty degrees below zero stood for a bite of frost that hurt and must be guarded against by the use of mittens, ear-flaps, warm moccasins, and thick socks. Fifty degrees below zero was to him just pre-cisely fifty degrees below zero. That there should be anything more to it than that was a thought that never entered his head.

As he turned to go on, he spat speculatively. There was a sharp, explosive crackle that startled him. He spat again. And again, in the air, before it could fall to the snow, the spittle crack-led. He knew that at fifty below spittle crackled on the snow, but this spittle had crackled in the air. Undoubtedly it was colder than fifty below—how much colder he did not know. But the temper-

ature did not matter. He was bound for the old claim on the left
fork of Henderson Creek, where the boys were already. They had
come over across the divide from the Indian Creek country, while
he had come the roundabout way to take a look at the possibilities of getting out logs in the spring from the islands in the
Yukon. He would be in to camp by six o'clock; a bit after dark,
it was true, but the boys would be there, a fire would be going,
and a hot supper would be ready. As for lunch, he pressed his
hand against the protruding bundle under his jacket. It was also
under his shirt, wrapped up in a handkerchief and lying against
the naked skin. It was the only way to keep the biscuits from
freezing. He smiled agreeably to himself as he thought of those
biscuits, each cut open and sopped in bacon grease, and each
enclosing a generous slice of fried bacon.

He plunged in among the big spruce trees. The trail was faint.
A foot of snow had fallen since the last sled had passed over, and
he was glad he was without a sled, travelling light. In fact, he carried nothing but the lunch wrapped in the handkerchief. He was
surprised, however, at the cold. It certainly was cold, he concluded, as he rubbed his numb nose and cheek-bones with his
mittened hand. He was a warm-whiskered man, but the hair on
his face did not protect the high cheek-bones and the eager nose
that thrust itself aggressively into the frosty air.

At the man's heels trotted a dog, a big native husky, the
proper wolf-dog, grey-coated and without any visible or tem-
peramental difference from its brother, the wild wolf. The animal
was depressed by the tremendous cold. It knew that it was no
time for travelling. Its instinct told it a truer tale than was told to
the man by the man's judgment. In reality, it was not merely
colder than fifty below zero; it was colder than sixty below, than
seventy below. It was seventy-five below zero. Since the freezing
point is thirty-two above zero, it meant that one hundred and
seven degrees of frost obtained. The dog did not know anything
about thermometers. Possibly in its brain there was no sharp consciousness of a condition of very cold such as was in the man's
brain. But the brute had its instinct. It experienced a vague but
menacing apprehension that subdued it and made it slink along

at the man's heels, and that made it question eagerly every un-wonted movement of the man as if expecting him to go into camp or to seek shelter somewhere and build a fire. The dog had learned fire, and it wanted fire, or else to burrow under the snow and cuddle its warmth away from the air.

The frozen moisture of its breathing had settled on its fur in a fine powder of frost, and especially were its jowls, muzzle, and eyelashes whitened by its crystalled breath. The man's red beard and moustache were likewise frosted, but more solidly, the deposit taking the form of ice and increasing with every warm, moist breath he exhaled. Also, the man was chewing tobacco, and the muzzle of ice held his lips so rigidly that he was unable to clear his chin when he expelled the juice. The result was that a crystal beard of the colour and solidity of amber was increasing its length on his chin. If he fell down it would shatter itself, like glass, into brittle fragments. But he did not mind the appendage. It was the penalty all tobacco-chewers paid in that country, and he had been out before in two cold snaps. They had not been so cold as this, he knew, but by the spirit thermometer at Sixty Mile he knew they had been registered at fifty below and at fifty-five.

He held on through the level stretch of woods for several miles, crossed a wide flat of nigger-heads, and dropped down a bank to the frozen bed of a small stream. This was Henderson Creek, and he knew he was ten miles from the forks. He looked at his watch. It was ten o'clock. He was making four miles an hour, and he cal-culated that he would arrive at the forks at half-past twelve. He decided to celebrate that event by eating his lunch there.

The dog dropped in again at his heels, with a tail drooping discouragement, as the man swung along the creek-bed. The fur-row of the old sled-trail was plainly visible, but a dozen inches of snow covered the marks of the last runners. In a month no man had come up or down that silent creek. The man held steadily on. He was not much given to thinking, and just then particularly he had nothing to think about save that he would eat lunch at the forks and that at six o'clock he would be in camp with the boys. There was nobody to talk to; and, had there been, speech would have been impossible because of the ice-muzzle on his mouth. So he continued monotonously to chew tobacco and to increase the length of his amber beard.

Once in a while the thought reiterated itself that it was very cold and that he had never experienced such cold. As he walked along he rubbed his cheek-bones and nose with the back of his mittened hand. He did this automatically, now and again changing hands. But rub as he would, the instant he stopped his cheek-bones went numb, and the following instant the end of his nose went numb. He was sure to frost his cheeks; he knew that, and experienced a pang of regret that he had not devised a nose-strap of the sort Bud wore in cold snaps. Such a strap passed across the cheeks, as well, and saved them. But it didn't matter much, after all. What were frosted cheeks? A bit painful, that was all; they were never serious.

Empty as the man's mind was of thoughts, he was keenly observant, and he noticed the changes in the creek, the curves and bends and timber-jams, and always he sharply noted where he placed his feet. Once, coming around a bend, he shied abruptly, like a startled horse, curved away from the place where he had been walking, and retreated several paces back along the trail. The creek he knew was frozen clear to the bottom—no creek could contain water in that arctic winter—but he knew also that there were springs that bubbled out from the hillsides and ran along under the snow and on top the ice of the creek. He knew that the coldest snaps never froze these springs, and he knew likewise their danger. They were traps. They hid pools of water under the snow that might be three inches deep, or three feet. Sometimes a skin of ice half an inch thick covered them, and in turn was covered by the snow. Sometimes there were alternate layers of water and ice-skin, so that when one broke through he kept on breaking through for a while, sometimes wetting himself to the waist.

That was why he had shied in such panic. He had felt the give under his feet and heard the crackle of a snow-hidden ice-skin. And to get his feet wet in such a temperature meant trouble and danger. At the very least it meant delay, for he would be forced to stop and build a fire, and under its protection to bare his feet while he dried his socks and moccasins. He stood and studied the creek-bed and its banks, and decided that the flow of water came from the right. He reflected a while, rubbing his nose and cheeks, then skirted to the left, stepping gingerly and testing the footing for each step. Once clear of the danger, he took a fresh chew of tobacco and swung along at his four-mile gait.

In the course of the next two hours he came upon several similar traps. Usually the snow above the hidden pools had a sunken, candied appearance that advertised the danger. Once again, however, he had a close call; and once, suspecting danger, he compelled the dog to go on in front. The dog did not want to go. It hung back until the man shoved it forward, and then it went quickly across the white, unbroken surface. Suddenly it broke through, floundered to one side, and got away to firmer footing. It had wet its forefeet and legs, and almost immediately the water that clung to it turned to ice. It made quick efforts to lick the ice off its legs, then dropped down in the snow and began to bite out the ice that had formed between the toes. This was a matter of instinct. To permit the ice to remain would mean sore feet. It did not know this. It merely obeyed the mysterious prompting that arose from the deep crypts of its being. But the man knew, having achieved a judgment on the subject, and he removed the mitten from his right hand and helped tear out the ice-particles. He did not expose his fingers more than a minute, and was astonished at the swift numbness that smote them. It certainly was cold. He pulled on the mitten hastily, and beat the hand savagely across his chest.

At twelve o'clock the day was at its brightest. Yet the sun was too far south on its winter journey to clear the horizon. The bulge of the earth intervened between it and Henderson Creek, where the man walked under a clear sky at noon and cast no shadow. At half-past twelve, to the minute, he arrived at the forks of the creek. He was pleased at the speed he had made. If he kept it up, he would certainly be with the boys by six. He unbuttoned his jacket and shirt and drew forth his lunch. The action consumed no more than a quarter of a minute, yet in that brief moment the numbness laid hold of the exposed fingers. He did not put the mitten on, but, instead, struck the fingers a dozen sharp smashes against his leg. Then he sat down on a snow-covered log to eat. The sting that followed upon the striking of his fingers against his leg ceased so quickly that he was startled. He had had no chance to take a bite of biscuit. He struck the fingers repeatedly and returned them to the mitten, baring the other hand for the purpose of eating. He tried to take a mouthful, but the ice-muzzle prevented. He had forgotten to build a fire and thaw out. He chuckled at his foolishness, and as he chuckled he noted the numbness creeping into the exposed fingers. Also, he noted that the stinging which had first come to his toes when he sat down was already passing away. He wondered whether the toes were warm or numb. He moved them inside the moccasins and decided that they were numb.

He pulled the mitten on hurriedly and stood up. He was a bit frightened. He stamped up and down until the stinging returned into the feet. It certainly was cold, was his thought. That man from Sulphur Creek had spoken the truth when telling how cold it sometimes got in the country. And he had laughed at him at the time! That showed one must not be too sure of things. There was no mistake about it, it *was* cold. He strode up and down, stamping his feet and threshing his arms, until reassured by the returning warmth. Then he got out matches and proceeded to make a fire. From the undergrowth, where high water of the previous spring had lodged a supply of seasoned twigs, he got his firewood. Working carefully from a small beginning, he soon had a roaring fire, over which he thawed the ice from his face and in the protection of which he ate his biscuits. For the moment the cold of space was outwitted. The dog took satisfaction in the fire, stretching out close enough for warmth and far enough away to escape being singed.

When the man had finished, he filled his pipe and took his comfortable time over a smoke. Then he pulled on his mittens, settled the ear-flaps of his cap firmly about his ears, and took the creek trail up the left fork. The dog was disappointed and yearned back toward the fire. This man did not know cold. Possibly all the generations of his ancestry had been ignorant of cold, of real cold, of cold one hundred and seven degrees below freezing point. But the dog knew; all its ancestry knew, and it had inherited the knowledge. And it knew that it was not good to walk abroad in such fearful cold. It was the time to lie snug in a hole in the snow and wait for a curtain of cloud to be drawn across the face of outer space whence this cold came. On the other hand, there was no keen intimacy between the dog and the man. The one was the toil-slave of the other, and the only caresses it had ever received were the caresses of the whiplash and of harsh and menacing throat-sounds that threatened the whiplash. So the dog made no effort to communicate its apprehension to the man. It was not concerned in the welfare of the man; it was for its own sake that it yearned back toward the fire. But the man whistled, and spoke to it with the sound of whiplashes, and the dog swung in at the man's heel and followed after.

The man took a chew of tobacco and proceeded to start a new amber beard. Also, his moist breath quickly powdered with white his moustache, eyebrows, and lashes. There did not seem to be so many springs on the left fork of the Henderson, and for half an hour the man saw no signs of any. And then it happened. At a place where there were no signs, where the soft, unbroken snow seemed to advertise solidity beneath, the man broke through. It was not deep. He wet himself halfway to the knees before he floundered out to the firm crust.

He was angry, and cursed his luck aloud. He had hoped to get into camp with the boys at six o'clock, and this would delay him an hour, for he would have to build a fire and dry out his foot-gear. This was imperative at that low temperature—he knew that much; and he turned aside to the bank, which he climbed. On top, tangled in the underbrush about the trunks of several small spruce trees, was a high-water deposit of dry firewood—sticks and twigs, principally, but also larger portions of seasoned branches and fine, dry, last-year's grasses. He threw down several large pieces on top of the snow. This served for a foundation and prevented the young flame from drowning itself in the snow it otherwise would melt. The flame he got by touching a match to a small shred of birch-bark that he took from his pocket. This burned even more readily than paper. Placing it on the foundation, he fed the young flame with wisps of dry grass and with the tiniest of dry twigs.

He worked slowly and carefully, keenly aware of his danger. Gradually, as the flame grew stronger, he increased the size of the twigs with which he fed it. He squatted in the snow, pulling the twigs out from their entanglement in the brush and feeding directly to the flame. He knew there must be no failure. When it is seventy-five below zero, a man must not fail in his first attempt to build a fire—that is, if his feet are wet. If his feet are dry, and he fails, he can run along the trail for half a mile and restore his circulation. But the circulation of wet and freezing feet cannot be restored by running when it is seventy-five below. No matter how fast he runs, the wet feet will freeze the harder.

All this the man knew. The old-timer on Sulphur Creek had told him about it the previous fall, and now he was appreciating the advice. Already all sensation had gone out of his feet. To build a fire he had been forced to remove his mittens, and the fingers had quickly gone numb. His pace of four miles an hour had kept his heart pumping blood to the surface of his body and to all the extremities. But the instant he stopped, the action of the pump eased down. The cold of space smote the unprotected tip of the planet, and he, being on that unprotected tip, received the full force of the blow. The blood of his body recoiled before it. The blood was alive, like the dog, and like the dog it wanted to hide away and cover itself up from the fearful cold. So long as he walked four miles an hour, he pumped that blood, willy-nilly, to the surface; but now it ebbed away and sank down into the recesses of his body. The extremities were the first to feel its absence. His wet feet froze the faster, and his exposed fingers numbed the faster, though they had not yet begun to freeze. Nose and cheeks were already freezing, while the skin of all his body chilled as it lost its blood.

But he was safe. Toes and nose and cheeks would be only touched by the frost, for the fire was beginning to burn with strength. He was feeding it with twigs the size of his finger. In another minute he would be able to feed it with branches the size of his wrist, and then he could remove his wet foot-gear, and, while it dried, he could keep his naked feet warm by the fire, rubbing them at first, of course, with snow. The fire was a success. He was safe. He remembered the advice of the old-timer on Sulphur Creek, and smiled. The old-timer had been very serious in laying down the law that no man must travel alone in the Klondike after fifty below. Well, here he was; he had had the accident; he was alone; and he had saved himself. Those old-timers were rather womanish, some of them, he thought. All a man had to do was to keep his head, and he was all right. Any man who was a man could travel alone. But it was surprising, the rapidity with which his cheeks and nose were freezing. And he had not thought his fingers could go lifeless in so short a time. Lifeless they were, for he could scarcely make them move together to grip a twig, and they seemed remote from his body and from him. When he touched a twig, he had to look and see whether or not he had hold of it. The wires were pretty well down between him and his finger-ends.

All of which counted for little. There was the fire, snapping and crackling and promising life with every dancing flame. He started to untie his moccasins. They were coated with ice; the thick German socks were like sheaths of iron halfway to the knees; and the moccasin strings were like rods of steel all twisted and knotted as by some conflagration. For a moment he tugged with his numb fingers, then, realizing the folly of it, he drew his sheath-knife.

But before he could cut the strings, it happened. It was his own fault or, rather, his mistake. He should not have built the fire under the spruce tree. He should have built it in the open. But it had been easier to pull the twigs from the brush and drop them directly on the fire. Now the tree under which he had done this carried a weight of snow on its boughs. No wind had blown for weeks, and each bough was fully freighted. Each time he had pulled a twig he had communicated a slight agitation to the tree—an imperceptible agitation, so far as he was concerned, but an agitation sufficient to bring about the disaster. High up in the tree one bough capsized its load of snow. This fell on the boughs beneath, capsizing them. This process continued, spreading out and involving the whole tree. It grew like an avalanche, and it descended without warning upon the man and the fire, and the fire was blotted out! Where it had burned was a mantle of fresh and disordered snow.

The man was shocked. It was as though he had just heard his own sentence of death. For a moment he sat and stared at the spot where the fire had been. Then he grew very calm. Perhaps the old-timer on Sulphur Creek was right. If he had only had a trail-mate he would have been in no danger now. The trail-mate could have built the fire. Well, it was up to him to build the fire over again, and this second time there must be no failure. Even if he succeeded, he would most likely lose some toes. His feet must be badly frozen by now, and there would be some time before the second fire was ready.

Such were his thoughts, but he did not sit and think them. He was busy all the time they were passing through his mind. He made a new foundation for a fire, this time in the open, where no treacherous tree could blot it out. Next, he gathered dry grasses and tiny twigs from the high-water flotsam. He could not bring his fingers together to pull them out, but he was able to gather them by the handful. In this way he got many rotten twigs and bits of green moss that were undesirable, but it was the best he could do. He worked methodically, even collecting an armful of the larger branches to be used later when the fire gathered strength. And all the while the dog sat and watched him, a certain yearning wistfulness in its eyes, for it looked upon him as the fire-provider, and the fire was slow in coming.

When all was ready, the man reached in his pocket for a second piece of birch-bark. He knew the bark was there, and, though he could not feel it with his fingers, he could hear its crisp rustling as he fumbled for it. Try as he would, he could not clutch hold of it. And all the time, in his consciousness, was the knowledge that each instant his feet were freezing. This thought tended to put him in a panic, but he fought against it and kept calm. He pulled on his mittens with his teeth, and threshed his arms back and forth, beating his hands with all his might against his sides.

He did this sitting down, and he stood up to do it; and all the while the dog sat in the snow, its wolf-brush of a tail curled around warmly over its forefeet, its sharp wolf-ears pricked forward intently as it watched the man. And the man, as he beat and threshed with his arms and hands, felt a great surge of envy as he regarded the creature that was warm and secure in its natural covering.

After a time he was aware of the first far-away signals of sensation in his beaten fingers. The faint tingling grew stronger till it evolved into a stinging ache that was excruciating, but which the man hailed with satisfaction. He stripped the mitten from his right hand and fetched forth the birch-bark. The exposed fingers were quickly going numb again. Next he brought out his bunch of sulphur matches. But the tremendous cold had already driven the life out of his fingers. In his effort to separate one match from the others, the whole bunch fell in the snow. He tried to pick it out of the snow, but failed. The dead fingers could neither touch nor clutch. He was very careful. He drove the thought of his freezing feet, and nose, and cheeks, out of his mind, devoting his whole soul to the matches. He watched, using the sense of vision in place of that of touch, and when he saw his fingers on each side the bunch, he closed them—that is, he willed to close them, for the wires were down, and the fingers did not obey. He pulled the mitten on the right hand, and beat it fiercely against his knee. Then, with both mittened hands, he scooped the bunch of matches, along with much snow, into his lap. Yet he was no better off.

After some manipulation he managed to get the bunch between the heels of his mittened hands. In this fashion he carried it to his mouth. The ice crackled and snapped when by a violent effort he opened his mouth. He drew the lower jaw in, curled the upper lip out of the way, and scraped the bunch with his upper teeth in order to separate a match. He succeeded in getting one, which he dropped on his lap. He was no better off. He could not pick it up. Then he devised a way. He picked it up in his teeth and scratched it on his leg. Twenty times he scratched before he succeeded in lighting it. As it flamed he held it with his teeth to the birch-bark. But the burning brimstone went up his nostrils and into his lungs, causing him to cough spasmodically. The match fell into the snow and went out.

The old-timer on Sulphur Creek was right, he thought in the moment of controlled despair that ensued: after fifty below, a man should travel with a partner. He beat his hands, but failed in exciting any sensation. Suddenly he bared both hands, removing the mittens with his teeth. He caught the whole bunch between the heels of his hands. His arm-muscles not being frozen enabled him to press the hand-heels tightly against the matches. Then he scratched the bunch along his leg. It flared into flame, seventy sulphur matches at once! There was no wind to blow them out. He kept his head to one side to escape the strangling fumes, and held the blazing bunch to the birch-bark. As he so held it, he became aware of sensation in his hand. His flesh was burning. He could smell it. Deep down below the surface he could feel it. The sensation developed into pain that grew acute. And still he endured it, holding the flame of the matches clumsily to the bark that would not light readily because his own burning hands were in the way, absorbing most of the flame.

At last, when he could endure no more, he jerked his hands apart. The blazing matches fell sizzling into the snow, but the birch-bark was alight. He began laying dry grasses and the tiniest twigs on the flame. He could not pick and choose, for he had to lift the fuel between the heels of his hands. Small pieces of rotten wood and green moss clung to the twigs, and he bit them off as well as he could with his teeth. He cherished the flame carefully and awkwardly. It meant life, and it must not perish. The withdrawal of blood from the surface of his body now made him begin to shiver, and he grew more awkward. A large piece of green moss fell squarely on the little fire. He tried to poke it out with his fingers, but his shivering frame made him poke too far, and he disrupted the nucleus of the little fire, the burning grasses and tiny twigs separating and scattering. He tried to poke them together again, but in spite of the tenseness of the effort, his shivering got away with him, and the twigs were hopelessly scattered. Each twig gushed a puff of smoke and went out. The fire-provider had failed. As he looked apathetically about him, his eyes chanced on the dog, sitting across the ruins of the fire from him, in the snow, making restless, hunching movements, slightly lifting one forefoot and then the other, shifting its weight back and forth on them with wistful eagerness.

The sight of the dog put a wild idea into his head. He remembered the tale of the man, caught in a blizzard, who killed a steer and crawled inside the carcass, and so was saved. He would kill the dog and bury his hands in the warm body until the numbness went out of them. Then he could build another fire. He spoke to the dog, calling it to him; but in his voice was a strange note of fear that frightened the animal, who had never known the man to speak in such way before. Something was the matter, and its suspicious nature sensed danger—it knew not what danger, but somewhere, somehow, in its brain arose an apprehension of the man. It flattened its ears down at the sound of the man's voice, and its restless, hunching movements and liftings and shiftings of its forefeet became more pronounced; but it would not come to the man. He got on his hands and knees and crawled toward the dog. This unusual posture again excited suspicion, and the animal sidled mincingly away.

The man sat up in the snow for a moment and struggled for calmness. Then he pulled on his mittens, by means of his teeth, and got upon his feet. He glanced down at first in order to assure himself that he was really standing up, for the absence of sensation in his feet left him unrelated to the earth. His erect position in itself started to drive the webs of suspicion from the dog's mind; and when he spoke peremptorily, with the sound of whiplashes in his voice, the dog rendered its customary allegiance and came to him. As it came within reaching distance, the man lost his control. His arms flashed out to the dog, and he experienced genuine surprise when he discovered that his hands could not clutch, that there was neither bend nor feeling in the fingers. He had forgotten for the moment that they were frozen and that they were freezing more and more. All this happened quickly, and before the animal could get away, he encircled its body with his arms. He sat down in the snow, and in this fashion held the dog, while it snarled and whined and struggled.

But it was all he could do, hold its body encircled in his arms and sit there. He realized that he could not kill the dog. There was no way to do it. With his helpless hands he could neither draw nor hold his sheath-knife nor throttle the animal. He released it, and it plunged wildly away, with tail between its legs, and still snarling. It halted forty feet away and surveyed him curiously, with ears sharply pricked forward. The man looked down at his hands in order to locate them, and found them hanging on the ends of his arms. It struck him as curious that one should have to use his eyes in order to find out where his hands were. He began threshing his arms back and forth, beating the mittened hands against his sides. He did this for five minutes, violently, and his heart pumped enough blood up to the surface to put a stop to his shivering. But no sensation was aroused in the hands. He had an impression that they hung like weights on the ends of his arms, but when he tried to run the impression down, he could not find it.

A certain fear of death, dull and oppressive, came to him. This fear quickly became poignant as he realized that it was no longer a mere matter of freezing his fingers and toes, or of losing his hands and feet, but that it was a matter of life and death with the chances against him. This threw him into a panic, and he turned and ran up the creek-bed along the old, dim trail. The dog joined in behind and kept up with him. He ran blindly, without intention, in fear such as he had never known in his life. Slowly, as he plowed and floundered through the snow, he began to see things again—the banks of the creek, the old timber-jams, the leafless aspens, and the sky. The running made him feel better. He did not shiver. Maybe, if he ran on, his feet would thaw out; and, anyway, if he ran far enough, he would reach camp and the boys. Without doubt he would lose some fingers and toes and some of his face; but the boys would take care of him, and save the rest of him when he got there. And at the same time there was another thought in his mind that said he would never get to the camp and the boys; that it was too many miles away, that the freezing had too great a start on him, and that he would soon be stiff and dead. This thought he kept in the background and refused to consider. Sometimes it pushed itself forward and

demanded to be heard, but he thrust it back and strove to think
of other things.

It struck him as curious that he could run at all on feet so
frozen that he could not feel them when they struck the earth and
took the weight of his body. He seemed to himself to skim along
above the surface, and to have no connection with the earth.
Somewhere he had once seen a winged Mercury, and he wondered if Mercury felt as he felt when skimming over the earth.

His theory of running until he reached camp and the boys had
one flaw in it: he lacked the endurance. Several times he stumbled, and finally he tottered, crumpled up, and fell. When he tried
to rise, he failed. He must sit and rest, he decided, and next time
he would merely walk and keep on going. As he sat and regained
his breath, he noted that he was feeling quite warm and comfortable. He was not shivering, and it even seemed that a warm
glow had come to his chest and trunk. And yet, when he touched
his nose or cheeks, there was no sensation. Running would not
thaw them out. Nor would it thaw out his hands and feet. Then
the thought came to him that the frozen portions of his body
must be extending. He tried to keep this thought down, to forget
it, to think of something else; he was aware of the panicky feeling that it caused, and he was afraid of the panic. But the thought
asserted itself, and persisted, until it produced a vision of his
body totally frozen. This was too much, and he made another
wild run along the trail. Once he slowed down to a walk, but the
thought of the freezing extending itself made him run again.

And all the time the dog ran with him, at his heels. When he
fell down a second time, it curled its tail over its forefeet and sat
in front of him, facing him, curiously eager and intent. The
warmth and security of the animal angered him, and he cursed it
till it flattened down its ears appeasingly. This time the shivering
came more quickly upon the man. He was losing in his battle
with the frost. It was creeping into his body from all sides. The
thought of it drove him on, but he ran no more than a hundred
feet, when he staggered and pitched headlong. It was his last
panic. When he had recovered his breath and control, he sat up
and entertained in his mind the conception of meeting death with

dignity. However, the conception did not come to him in such terms. His idea of it was that he had been making a fool of himself, running around like a chicken with its head cut off—such was the simile that occurred to him. Well, he was bound to freeze anyway, and he might as well take it decently. With this new-found peace of mind came the first glimmerings of drowsiness. A good idea, he thought, to sleep off to death. It was like taking an anaesthetic. Freezing was not so bad as people thought. There were lots worse ways to die.

He pictured the boys finding his body next day. Suddenly he found himself with them, coming along the trail and looking for himself. And, still with them, he came around a turn in the trail and found himself lying in the snow. He did not belong with himself any more, for even then he was out of himself, standing with the boys and looking at himself in the snow. It certainly was cold, was his thought. When he got back to the States he could tell the folks what real cold was. He drifted on from this to a vision of the old-timer on Sulphur Creek. He could see him quite clearly, warm and comfortable, and smoking a pipe.

"You were right, old hoss; you were right," the man mumbled to the old-timer of Sulphur Creek.

Then the man drowsed off into what seemed to him the most comfortable and satisfying sleep he had ever known. The dog sat facing him and waiting. The brief day drew to a close in a long, slow twilight. There were no signs of a fire to be made, and, besides, never in the dog's experience had it known a man to sit like that in the snow and make no fire. As the twilight drew on, its eager yearning for the fire mastered it, and with a great lifting and shifting of forefeet, it whined softly, then flattened its ears down in anticipation of being chidden by the man. But the man remained silent. Later, the dog whined loudly. And still later it crept close to the man and caught the scent of death. This made the animal bristle and back away. A little longer it delayed, howling under the stars that leaped and danced and shone brightly in the cold sky. Then it turned and trotted up the trail in the direction of the camp it knew, where were the other food-providers and fire-providers.

THE CELEBRATED JUMPING FROG OF CALAVERAS COUNTY

Mark Twain
(1835–1910)

This is one of those stories where you hear the author's voice in your head as you read it, as if he is sitting with you in a boat on a glassy lake, eyes glued to his fishing-rod, spinning a tale, accompanied by the chirping of crickets and the croaking of frogs. A cosy and ingratiating story, as impossible to resist as a conversation that begins, "Did I ever tell you about the time..."

 n compliance with the request of a friend of mine, who wrote me from the East, I called on good-natured, garrulous old Simon Wheeler, and inquired after my friend's friend, *Leonidas W. Smiley,* as requested to do, and I hereunto append the result. I have a lurking suspicion that *Leonidas W. Smiley* is a myth; that my friend never knew such a personage; and that he only conjectured that, if I asked old Wheeler about him, it would remind him of his infamous *Jim* Smiley, and he would go to work and bore me nearly to death with some infernal reminiscence of him as long and tedious as it should be useless to me. If that was the design, it certainly succeeded.

I found Simon Wheeler dozing comfortably by the bar-room stove of the old, dilapidated tavern in the ancient mining camp of Angel's, and I noticed that he was fat and bald-headed, and had an expression of winning gentleness and simplicity upon his tranquil countenance. He roused up and gave me good-day. I told him a friend of mine had commissioned me to make some inquiries about a cherished companion of his boyhood named *Leonidas W. Smiley—Rev. Leonidas W.* Smiley—a young minister of the Gospel, who he had heard was at one time a resident of Angel's Camp. I added, that, if Mr. Wheeler could tell me anything about this Rev. Leonidas W. Smiley, I would feel under many obligations to him.

Simon Wheeler backed me into a corner and blockaded me there with his chair, and then sat me down and reeled off the monotonous narrative which follows this paragraph. He never smiled, he never frowned, he never changed his voice from the gentle-flowing key to which he tuned the initial sentence, he never betrayed the slightest suspicion of enthusiasm; but all through the interminable narrative there ran a vein of impressive earnestness and sincerity, which showed me plainly that, so far from his imagining that there was anything ridiculous or funny about his story, he regarded it as a really important matter, and admitted its two heroes as men of transcendent genius in *finesse.* To me, the spectacle of a man drifting serenely along through such a queer yarn without ever smiling, was exquisitely absurd. As I said before, I asked him to tell me what he knew of Rev. Leonidas W. Smiley, and he replied as follows. I let him go on in his own way, and never interrupted him once:

There was a feller here once by the name of *Jim* Smiley, in the winter of '49—or maybe it was the spring of '50—I don't recollect exactly, somehow, though what makes me think it was one or the other is because I remember the big flume wasn't finished when he first came to the camp; but anyway, he was the curiousest man about always betting on anything that turned up you ever see, if he could get anybody to bet on the other side; and if he couldn't, he'd change sides. Any way that suited the other man would suit him—any way just so's he got a bet, *he* was satisfied. But still he was lucky, uncommon lucky—he most always come out winner. He was always ready and laying for a chance; there couldn't be no solit'ry thing mentioned but that feller'd offer to bet on it, and take any side you please, as I was just telling you. If there was a horse-race, you'd find him flush, or you'd find him busted at the end of it; if there was a dog-fight, he'd bet on it; if there was a cat-fight, he'd bet on it; if there was a chicken-fight, he'd bet on it; why, if there was two birds setting on a fence, he would bet you which one would fly first; or if there was a camp meeting, he would be there reg'lar, to bet on Parson Walker, which he judged to be the best exhorter about here, and so he was, too, and a good man. If he even seen a straddle-bug start to go anywheres, he would bet you how long it would take him to get wherever he was going to, and if you took him up, he would foller that straddle-bug to Mexico but what he would find out where he was bound for and how long he was on the road. Lots of the boys here has seen that Smiley, and can tell you about him. Why, it never made no difference to *him*—he would bet on *any*-thing—the dangdest feller. Parson Walker's wife laid very sick once, for a good while, and it seemed as if they warn't going to save her; but one morning he came in, and Smiley asked how she was, and he said she was considerable better—thank the Lord for his inf'nit mercy—and coming on so smart that, with the blessing of Prov'dence, she'd get well yet; and Smiley, before he thought, says, "Well, I'll risk two-and-a-half that she don't, anyway."

Thish-yer Smiley had a mare—the boys called her the fifteen-minute nag, but that was only in fun, you know, because, of course, she was faster than that—and he used to win money on that horse, for all she was so slow and always had the asthma, or the distemper, or the consumption, or something of that kind. They used to give her two or three hundred yards start, and then pass her under way; but always at the fag-end of the race she'd get excited and desperate-like, and come cavorting and straddling up, and scattering her legs around limber, sometimes in the air, and sometimes out to one side amongst the fences, and kicking up m-o-r-e dust, and raising m-o-r-e racket with her coughing and sneezing and blowing her nose—and always fetch up at the stand just about a neck ahead, as near as you could cipher it down.

And he had a little small bull pup, that to look at him you'd think he wan't worth a cent but to set around and look ornery and lay for a chance to steal something. But as soon as money was up on him, he was a different dog; his under-jaw'd begin to stick out like the fo'castle of a steamboat, and his teeth would uncover, and shine savage like the furnaces. And a dog might tackle him, and bully-rag him, and bite him, and throw him over his shoulder two or three times, and Andrew Jackson—which was the name of the pup—Andrew Jackson would never let on but what *he* was satisfied, and hadn't expected nothing else—and the bets being doubled and doubled on the other side all the time, till the money was all up; and then all of a sudden he would grab that other dog jest by the j'int of his hind leg and freeze to it— not claw, you understand, but only jest grip and hang on till they throwed up the sponge, if it was a year. Smiley always come out winner on that pup, till he harnessed a dog once that didn't have no hind legs, because they'd been sawed off by a circular saw, and when the thing had gone along far enough, and the money was all up, and he come to make a snatch for his pet holt, he saw in a minute how he'd been imposed on, and how the other dog had him in the door, so to speak, and he 'peared surprised, and then he looked sorter discouraged-like, and didn't try no more to win the fight, and so he got shucked out bad. He give Smiley a look, as much to say his heart was broke and it was *his* fault for putting up a dog that hadn't no hind legs for him to take holt of, which was his main dependence in a fight, and then he limped off a piece and laid down and died. It was a good pup, was that Andrew Jackson, and would have made a name for hisself if he'd lived, for the stuff was in him, and he had genius—I know it, because he hadn't no opportunities to speak of, and it don't stand to reason that a dog could make such a fight as he could under them circumstances, if he hadn't no talent. It always makes me feel sorry when I think of that last fight of his'n, and the way it turned out.

Well, thish-yer Smiley had rat-tarriers, and chicken-cocks, and tom-cats, and all them kind of things, till you couldn't rest, and you couldn't fetch nothing for him to bet on but he'd match you. He ketched a frog one day, and took him home, and said he cal'klated to edercate him; and so he never done nothing for these three months but set in his back yard and learn that frog to jump. And you bet you he *did* learn him, too. He'd give him a little punch behind, and the next minute you'd see that frog whirling in the air like a doughnut—see him turn one summerset, or maybe a couple, if he got a good start, and come down flat-footed and all right, like a cat. He got him up so in the matter of catching flies, and kept him in practice so constant, that he'd nail a fly every time as far as he could see him. Smiley said all a frog wanted was education, and he could do most anything—and I believe him. Why, I've seen him set Dan'l Webster down here on this floor—Dan'l Webster was the name of the frog—and sing out, "Flies, Dan'l, flies!" and quicker'n you could wink, he'd spring straight up, and snake a fly off 'n the counter there, and flop down on the floor again as solid as a gob of mud, and fall to scratching the side of his head with his hind foot as indifferent as if he hadn't no idea he's been doin' any more'n any frog might do. You never see a frog so modest and straight-for'ard as he was, for all he was so gifted. And when it come to fair and square jumping on the dead level, he could get over more ground at one strad-dle than any animal of his breed you ever see. Jumping on a dead level was his strong suit, you understand; and when it come to that, Smiley would ante up money on him as long as he had a red. Smiley was monstrous proud of his frog, and well he might be, for fellers that had travelled and been everywhere all said he laid over any frog that ever *they* see.

Well, Smiley kept the beast in a little lattice box, and he used to fetch him downtown sometimes and lay for a bet. One day a feller—a stranger in the camp, he was—come across him with his box, and says:

"What might it be that you've got in the box?"

And Smiley says, sorter indifferent like, "It might be a parrot, or it might be a canary, maybe, but it ain't—it's only just a frog."

An' the feller took it, and looked at it careful, and turned it round this way and that, and says, "H'm—so 'tis. Well, what's *he* good for?"

"Well," Smiley says, easy and careless, "he's good enough for *one* thing, I should judge—he can outjump any frog in Calaveras county."

The feller took the box again, and took another long, partic-ular look, and give it back to Smiley, and says, very deliberate,

"Well, I don't see no p'ints about that frog that's any better'n any other frog."

"Maybe you don't," Smiley says. "Maybe you understand frogs, and maybe you don't understand 'em; maybe you've had experience, and maybe you ain't only a amature, as it were. Anyways, I've got *my* opinion, and I'll risk forty dollars that he can outjump any frog in Calaveras county."

And the feller studied a minute, and then says, kinder sad like, "Well, I'm only a stranger here, and I ain't got no frog; but if I had a frog, I'd bet you."

And then Smiley says, "That's all right—that's all right—if you'll hold my box a minute, I'll go and get you a frog." And so the feller took the box, and put up his forty dollars along with Smiley's, and set down to wait.

So he set there a good while thinking and thinking to hisself, and then he got the frog out and prized his mouth open and took a teaspoon and filled him full of quail shot—filled him pretty near up to his chin—and set him on the floor. Smiley he went to the swamp and slopped around in the mud for a long time, and finally he ketched a frog, and fetched him in, and give him to this feller, and says:

"Now, if you're ready, set him alongside of Dan'l, with his forepaws just even with Dan'l, and I'll give the word." Then he says, "One—two—three—jump!" and him and the feller touched up the frogs from behind, and the new frog hopped off, but Dan'l give a heave, and hysted up his shoulders—so—like a Frenchman, but it wasn't no use—he couldn't budge; he was planted as solid as an anvil, and he couldn't no more stir than if he was anchored out. Smiley was a good deal surprised, and he was disgusted too, but he didn't have no idea what the matter was, of course.

The feller took the money and started away; and when he was going out at the door, he sorter jerked his thumb over his shoulder—this way—at Dan'l, and says again, very deliberate, "Well, *I* don't see no p'ints about that frog that's any better'n any other frog."

Smiley he stood scratching his head and looking down at

Dan'l a long time, and at last he says, "I do wonder what in the nation that frog throw'd off for—I wonder if there ain't something the matter with him—he 'pears to look mighty baggy, somehow." And he ketched Dan'l by the nap of the neck, and lifted him up and says, "Why, blame my cats, if he don't weigh five pounds!" and turned him upside down, and he belched out a double handful of shot. And then he see how it was, and he was the maddest man—he set the frog down and took out after that feller, but he never ketched him. And—

(Here Simon Wheeler heard his name called from the front yard, and got up to see what was wanted.) And turning to me as he moved away, he said: "Just set where you are, stranger, and rest easy—I ain't going to be gone a second."

But, by your leave, I did not think that a continuation of the history of the enterprising vagabond *Jim* Smiley would be likely to afford me much information concerning the Rev. *Leonidas W.* Smiley, and so I started away.

At the door I met the sociable Wheeler returning, and he buttonholed me and recommenced:

"Well, thish-yer Smiley had a yeller one-eyed cow that didn't have no tail, only jest a short stump like a bannanner, and—"

"Oh, hang Smiley and his afflicted cow!" I muttered, good-naturedly, and bidding the old gentleman good-day, I departed.

THE SIGNALMAN

Charles Dickens
(1812–1870)

Charles Dickens was both fascinated and horrified by trains. Railways were being established all over England when Dickens was a young man, and he saw both their power and their potential for destruction.

"The Signalman" was one of a series of stories about a man who uses his retirement to explore the railway lines that radiate out from Mugby Junction. The year before it was published, in 1865, Dickens was himself involved in a horrific train crash. Although he was unhurt, his experience in tending to the wounded and dying passengers haunted him to the end of his life, with "sudden vague rushes of terror" overtaking him at times—rather like the lonely signalman in this story, who is troubled by apparently groundless apprehensions ...

alloa! Below there!"

When he heard a voice thus calling to him, he was standing at the door of his box, with a flag in his hand, furled round its short pole. One would have thought, considering the nature of the ground, that he could not have doubted from what quarter the voice came; but, instead of looking up to where I stood on the top of the steep cutting nearly over his head, he turned himself about and looked down the Line. There was something remarkable in his manner of doing so, though I could not have said for my life, what. But, I know it was remarkable enough to attract my notice, even though his figure was foreshortened and shadowed, down in the deep trench, and mine was high above him, so steeped in the glow of an angry sunset that I had shaded my eyes with my hand before I saw him at all.

"Halloa! Below!"

From looking down the Line, he turned himself about again, and, raising his eyes, saw my figure high above him.

"Is there any path by which I can come down and speak to you?"

He looked up at me without replying, and I looked down at him without pressing him too soon with a repetition of my idle question. Just then, there came a vague vibration in the earth and air, quickly changing into a violent pulsation, and an oncoming rush that caused me to start back, as though it had force to draw me down. When such vapour as rose to my height from this rapid train, had passed me and was skimming away over the landscape, I looked down again, and saw him re-furling the flag he had shown while the train went by.

I repeated my inquiry. After a pause, during which he seemed to regard me with fixed attention, he motioned with his rolled-up flag towards a point on my level, some two or three hundred yards distant. I called down to him, "All right!" and made for that point. There, by dint of looking closely about me, I found a rough zig-zag descending path notched out: which I followed.

The cutting was extremely deep, and unusually precipitate. It was made through a clammy stone that became oozier and wetter as I went down. For these reasons, I found the way long enough to give me time to recall a singular air of reluctance or compulsion with which he had pointed out the path.

When I came down low enough upon the zig-zag descent, to see him again, I saw that he was standing between the rails on the way by which the train had lately passed, in an attitude as if he were waiting for me to appear. He had his left hand at his chin, and that left elbow rested on his right hand crossed over his breast. His attitude was one of such expectation and watchfulness, that I stopped a moment, wondering at it.

I resumed my downward way, and, stepping out upon the

level of the railroad and drawing nearer to him, saw that he was a dark sallow man, with a dark beard and rather heavy eyebrows. His post was in as solitary and dismal a place as ever I saw. On either side, a dripping-wet wall of jagged stone, excluding all view but a strip of sky; the perspective one way, only a crooked prolongation of this great dungeon; the shorter perspective in the other direction, terminating in a gloomy red light, and the gloomier entrance to a black tunnel, in whose massive architecture there was a barbarous, depressing, and forbidding air. So little sunlight ever found its way to this spot, that it had an earthy deadly smell; and so much cold wind rushed through it, that it struck chill to me, as if I had left the natural world.

Before he stirred, I was near enough to him to have touched him. Not even then removing his eyes from mine, he stepped back one step, and lifted his hand.

This was a lonesome post to occupy (I said), and it had riveted my attention when I looked down from up yonder. A visitor was a rarity, I should suppose; not an unwelcome rarity, I hoped? In me, he merely saw a man who had been shut up within narrow limits all his life, and who, being at last set free, had a newly awakened interest in these great works. To such purpose I spoke to him; but I am far from sure of the terms I used, for, besides that I am not happy in opening any conversation, there was something in the man that daunted me.

He directed a most curious look towards the red light near the tunnel's mouth, and looked all about it, as if something were missing from it, and then looked at me.

That light was part of his charge? Was it not?

He answered in a low voice: "Don't you know it is?"

The monstrous thought came into my mind as I perused the fixed eyes and the saturnine face, that this was a spirit, not a man. I have speculated since, whether there may have been infection in his mind.

In my turn, I stepped back. But in making the action, I detected in his eyes some latent fear of me. This put the monstrous thought to flight.

"You look at me," I said, forcing a smile, "as if you had a

dread of me."

"I was doubtful," he returned, "whether I had seen you before."

"Where?"

He pointed to the red light he had looked at.

"There?" I said.

Intently watchful of me, he replied (but without sound), Yes.

"My good fellow, what should I do there? However, be that as it may, I never was there, you may swear."

"I think I may," he rejoined. "Yes. I am sure I may."

His manner cleared, like my own. He replied to my remarks with readiness, and in well-chosen words. Had he much to do there? Yes; that was to say, he had enough responsibility to bear; but exactness and watchfulness were what was required of him, and of actual work—manual labour—he had next to none. To change that signal, to trim those lights, and to turn this iron handle now and then, was all he had to do under that head. Regarding those many long and lonely hours of which I seemed to make so much, he could only say that the routine of his life had shaped itself into that form, and he had grown used to it. He had taught himself a language down here—if only to know it by sight, and to have formed his own crude ideas of its pronunciation, could be called learning it. He had also worked at fractions and decimals, and tried a little algebra; but he was, and had been as a boy, a poor hand at figures. Was it necessary for him when on duty, always to remain in that channel of damp air, and could he never rise into the sunshine from between those high stone walls? Why, that depended upon times and circumstances. Under some conditions there would be less upon the Line than under others, and the same held good as to certain hours of the day and night. In bright weather, he did choose occasions for getting a little above these lower shadows; but, being at all times liable to be called by his electric bell, and at such times listening for it with redoubled anxiety, the relief was less than I would suppose.

He took me into his box, where there was a fire, a desk for an official book in which he had to make certain entries, a telegraphic instrument with its dial face and needles, and the little bell of which he had spoken. On my trusting that he would excuse the remark that he had been well educated, and (I hoped I might say without offence), perhaps educated above that station, he observed that instances of slight incongruity in such-wise would rarely be found wanting among large bodies of men; that he had heard it was so in workhouses, in the police force, even in that last desperate resource, the army; and that he knew it was so, more or less, in any great railway staff. He had been, when young (if I could believe it, sitting in that hut; he scarcely could), a student of natural philosophy, and had attended lectures; but he had run wild, misused his opportunities, gone down, and never risen again. He had no complaint to offer about that. He had made his bed, and he lay upon it. It was far too late to make another.

All that I have here condensed, he said in a quiet manner, with his grave dark regards divided between me and the fire. He threw in the word "Sir," from time to time, and especially when he referred to his youth: as though to request me to understand that he claimed to be nothing but what I found him. He was several times interrupted by the little bell, and had to read off messages, and send replies. Once, he had to stand without the door, and display a flag as a train passed, and make some verbal communication to the driver. In the discharge of his duties I observed him to be remarkably exact and vigilant, breaking off his discourse at a syllable, and remaining silent until what he had to do was done.

In a word, I should have set this man down as one of the safest of men to be employed in that capacity, but for the circumstance that while he was speaking to me he twice broke off with a fallen colour, turned his face towards the little bell when it did NOT ring, opened the door of the hut (which was kept shut to exclude the unhealthy damp), and looked out towards the red light near the mouth of the tunnel. On both of those occasions, he came back to the fire with the inexplicable air upon him which I had remarked, without being able to define, when we were so far asunder.

Said I when I rose to leave him: "You almost make me think that I have met with a contented man."

(I am afraid I must acknowledge that I said it to lead him on.)

"I believe I used to be so," he rejoined, in the low voice in which he had first spoken; "but I am troubled, sir, I am troubled."

He would have recalled the words if he could. He had said them, however, and I took them up quickly.

"With what? What is your trouble?"

"It is very difficult to impart, sir. It is very, very difficult to speak of. If ever you make me another visit, I will try to tell you."

"But I expressly intend to make you another visit. Say, when shall it be?"

"I go off early in the morning, and I shall be on again at ten tomorrow night, sir."

"I will come at eleven."

He thanked me, and went out at the door with me. "I'll show my white light, sir," he said, in his peculiar low voice, "till you have found the way up. When you have found it, don't call out! And when you are at the top, don't call out!"

His manner seemed to make the place strike colder to me, but I said no more than "Very well."

"And when you come down tomorrow night, don't call out! Let me ask you a parting question. What made you cry 'Halloa! Below there!' tonight?"

"Heaven knows," said I. "I cried something to that effect—"

"Not to that effect, sir. Those were the very words. I know them well."

"Admit those were the very words. I said them, no doubt, because I saw you below."

"For no other reason?"

"What other reason could I possibly have!"

"You have no feeling that they were conveyed to you in any supernatural way?"

"No."

He wished me good night, and held up his light. I walked by the side of the down Line of rails (with a very disagreeable sensation of a train coming behind me), until I found the path. It was easier to mount than to descend, and I got back to my inn without any adventure.

Punctual to my appointment, I placed my foot on the first notch of the zig-zag next night, as the distant clocks were striking eleven. He was waiting for me at the bottom, with his white light on. "I have not called out," I said, when we came close together; "may I speak now?" "By all means, sir." "Good night then, and here's my hand." "Good night, sir, and here's mine." With that, we walked side by side to his box, entered it, closed the door, and sat down by the fire.

"I have made up my mind, sir," he began, bending forward as soon as we were seated, and speaking in a tone but a little above a whisper, "that you shall not have to ask me twice what troubles me. I took you for someone else yesterday evening. That troubles me."

"That mistake?"

"No. That someone else."

"Who is it?"

"I don't know."

"Like me?"

"I don't know. I never saw the face. The left arm is across the face, and the right arm is waved. Violently waved. This way."

I followed his action with my eyes, and it was the action of an arm gesticulating with the utmost passion and vehemence: "For God's sake clear the way!"

"One moonlight night," said the man, "I was sitting here, when I heard a voice cry 'Halloa! Below there!' I started up, looked from that door, and saw this Someone else standing by the red light near the tunnel, waving as I just now showed you. The voice seemed hoarse with shouting, and it cried, 'Look out! Look out!' And then again 'Halloa! Below there! Look out!' I caught up my lamp, turned it on red, and ran towards the figure, calling, 'What's wrong? What has happened? Where?' It stood just outside the blackness of the tunnel. I advanced so close upon it that I wondered at its keeping the sleeve across its eyes. I ran right up at it, and had my hand stretched out to pull the sleeve away, when it was gone."

"Into the tunnel," said I.

"No. I ran on into the tunnel, five hundred yards. I stopped and held my lamp above my head, and saw the figures of the measured distance, and saw the wet stains stealing down the walls and trickling through the arch. I ran out again, faster than I had run in (for I had a mortal abhorrence of the place upon me), and I looked all round the red light with my own red light, and I went up the iron ladder to the gallery atop of it, and I came down again, and ran back here. I telegraphed both ways: 'An alarm has been given. Is anything wrong?' The answer came back, both ways: 'All well.'"

Resisting the slow touch of a frozen finger tracing out my spine, I showed him how that this figure must be a deception of his sense of sight, and how that figures, originating in disease of the delicate nerves that minister to the functions of the eye, were known to have often troubled patients, some of whom had become conscious of the nature of their affliction, and had even proved it by experiments upon themselves. "As to an imaginary cry," said I, "do but listen for a moment to the wind in this unnatural valley while we speak so low, and to the wild harp it makes of the telegraph wires!"

That was all very well, he returned, after we had sat listening for a while, and he ought to know something of the wind and the wires, he who so often passed long winter nights there, alone and watching. But he would beg to remark that he had not finished.

I asked his pardon, and he slowly added these words, touching my arm:

"Within six hours after the Appearance, the memorable accident on this Line happened, and within ten hours the dead and wounded were brought along through the tunnel over the spot where the figure had stood."

A disagreeable shudder crept over me, but I did my best against it. It was not to be denied, I rejoined, that this was a remarkable coincidence, calculated deeply to impress his mind. But, it was unquestionable that remarkable coincidences did continually occur, and they must be taken into account in dealing with such a subject. Though to be sure I must admit, I added (for I thought I saw that he was going to bring the objection to bear upon me), men of common sense did not allow much for coincidences in making the ordinary calculations of life.

He again begged to remark that he had not finished.

I again begged his pardon for being betrayed into inter-ruptions.

"This," he said, again laying his hand upon my arm, and glancing over his shoulder with hollow eyes, "was just a year ago. Six or seven months passed, and I had recovered from the sur-prise and shock, when one morning, as the day was breaking, I, standing at that door, looked towards the red light, and saw the spectre again." He stopped, with a fixed look at me.

"Did it cry out?"

"No. It was silent."

"Did it wave its arm?"

"No. It leaned against the shaft of the light, with both hands before the face. Like this."

Once more, I followed his action with my eyes. It was an action of mourning. I have seen such an attitude in stone figures on tombs.

"Did you go up to it?"

"I came in and sat down, partly to collect my thoughts, partly because it had turned me faint. When I went to the door again, daylight was above me, and the ghost was gone."

"But nothing followed? Nothing came of this?"

He touched me on the arm with his forefinger twice or thrice, giving a ghastly nod each time:

"That very day, as a train came out of the tunnel, I noticed, at a carriage window on my side, what looked like a confusion of hands and heads, and something waved. I saw it, just in time to signal the driver, Stop! He shut off, and put his brake on, but the train drifted past here a hundred and fifty yards or more. I ran after it, and, as I went along, heard terrible screams and cries. A beautiful young lady had died instantaneously in one of the com-partments, and was brought in here, and laid down on this floor between us."

Involuntarily, I pushed my chair back, as I looked from the boards at which he pointed, to himself.

"True, sir. True. Precisely as it happened, so I tell it you."

I could think of nothing to say, to any purpose, and my mouth was very dry. The wind and the wires took up the story with a long lamenting wail.

He resumed. "Now, sir, mark this, and judge how my mind is troubled. The spectre came back, a week ago. Ever since, it has been there, now and again, by fits and starts."

"At the light?"

"At the Danger-light."

"What does it seem to do?"

He repeated, if possible with increased passion and vehemence, that former gesticulation of "For God's sake clear the way!"

Then, he went on. "I have no peace or rest for it. It calls to me, for many minutes together, in an agonized manner, 'Below there! Look out! Look out!' It stands waving to me. It rings my little bell—"

I caught at that. "Did it ring your bell yesterday evening when I was here, and you went to the door?"

"Twice."

"Why, see," said I, "how your imagination misleads you. My eyes were on the bell, and my ears were open to the bell, and if I am a living man, it did not ring at those times. No, nor at any other time, except when it was rung in the natural course of physical things by the station communicating with you."

He shook his head. "I have never made a mistake as to that, yet, sir. I have never confused the spectre's ring with the man's. The ghost's ring is a strange vibration in the bell that it derives from nothing else, and I have not asserted that the bell stirs to the eye. I don't wonder that you failed to hear it. But *I* heard it."

"And did the spectre seem to be there, when you looked out?"

"It WAS there."

"Both times?"

He repeated firmly: "Both times."

"Will you come to the door with me, and look for it now?"

He bit his under-lip as though he were somewhat unwilling, but arose. I opened the door, and stood on the step, while he stood in the doorway. There, was the Danger-light. There, was the dismal mouth of the tunnel. There, were the high wet stone walls of the cutting. There, were the stars above them.

"Do you see it?" I asked him, taking particular note of his face. His eyes were prominent and strained; but not very much more so, perhaps, than my own had been when I had directed them earnestly towards the same spot.

"No," he answered. "It is not there."

"Agreed," said I.

We went in again, shut the door, and resumed out seats. I was thinking how best to improve this advantage, if it might be called one, when he took up the conversation in such a matter of course way, so assuming that there could be no serious question of fact between us, that I felt myself in the weakest of positions.

"By this time you will fully understand, sir," he said, "that what troubles me so dreadfully, is the question, What does the spectre mean?"

I was not sure, I told him, that I did fully understand.

"What is its warning against?" he said, ruminating, with his eyes on the fire, and only by times turning them on me. "What is the danger? Where is the danger? There is danger overhanging, somewhere on the Line. Some dreadful calamity will happen. It is not to be doubted this third time, after what has gone before. But surely this is a cruel haunting of *me*. What can *I* do!"

He pulled out his handkerchief, and wiped the drops from his heated forehead.

"If I telegraph Danger, on either side of me, or on both, I can give no reason for it," he went on, wiping the palms of his hands. "I should get into trouble, and do no good. They would think I was mad. This is the way it would work: Message: 'Danger! Take care!' Answer: 'What Danger? Where?' Message: 'Don't know. But for God's sake take care!' They would displace me. What else could they do?"

His pain of mind was most pitiable to see. It was the mental torture of a conscientious man, oppressed beyond endurance by an unintelligible responsibility involving life.

"When it first stood under the Danger-light," he went on,

putting his dark hair back from his head, and drawing his hands outward across and across his temples in an extremity of feverish distress, "why not tell me where that accident was to happen—if it must happen? Why not tell me how it could be averted—if it could have been averted? When on its second coming it hid its face, why not tell me instead: 'She is going to die. Let them keep her at home'? If it came, on those two occasions, only to show me that its warnings were true, and so to prepare me for the third, why not warn me plainly now? And I, Lord help me! A mere poor signalman on this solitary station! Why not go to somebody with credit to be believed, and power to act!"

When I saw him in this state, I saw that for the poor man's sake, as well as for the public safety, what I had to do for the time was to compose his mind. Therefore, setting aside all question of reality or unreality between us, I represented to him that whoever thoroughly discharged his duty must do well, and that at least it was his comfort that he understood his duty, though he did not understand these confounding Appearances. In this effort I succeeded far better than in the attempt to reason him out of his conviction. He became calm; the occupations incidental to his post as the night advanced, began to make larger demands on his attention; and I left him at two in the morning. I had offered to stay through the night, but he would not hear of it.

That I more than once looked back at the red light as I ascended the pathway, that I did not like the red light, and that I should have slept but poorly if my bed had been under it, I see no reason to conceal. Nor, did I like the two sequences of the accident and the dead girl. I see no reason to conceal that, either.

But, what ran most in my thoughts was the consideration how ought I to act, having become the recipient of this disclosure? I had proved the man to be intelligent, vigilant, painstaking, and exact; but how long might he remain so, in his state of mind? Though in a subordinate position, still he held a most important trust, and would I (for instance) like to stake my own life on the chances of his continuing to execute it with precision?

Unable to overcome a feeling that there would be something treacherous in my communicating what he had told me, to his superiors in the Company, without first being plain with himself and proposing a middle course to him, I ultimately resolved to offer to accompany him (otherwise keeping his secret for the present) to the wisest medical practitioner we could hear of in those parts, and to take his opinion. A change in his time of duty would come round next night, he had apprised me, and he would be off an hour or two after sunrise, and on again soon after sunset. I had appointed to return accordingly.

Next evening was a lovely evening, and I walked out early to enjoy it. The sun was not yet quite down when I traversed the field-path near the top of the deep cutting. I would extend my walk for an hour, I said to myself, half an hour on and half an hour back, and it would then be time to go to my signalman's box.

Before pursuing my stroll, I stepped to the brink, and mechanically looked down, from the point from which I had first seen him. I cannot describe the thrill that seized upon me, when, close to the mouth of the tunnel, I saw the appearance of a man, with his left sleeve across his eyes, passionately waving his right arm.

The nameless horror that oppressed me passed in a moment, for in a moment I saw that this appearance of a man was a man indeed, and that there was a little group of other men standing at a short distance, to whom he seemed to be rehearsing the gesture he made. The Danger-light was not yet lighted. Against its shaft, a little low hut, entirely new to me, had been made of some wooden supports and tarpaulin. It looked no bigger than a bed.

With an irresistible sense that something was wrong—with a flashing self-reproachful fear that fatal mischief had come of my leaving the man there, and causing no one to be sent to overlook or correct what he did—I descended the notched path with all the speed I could make.

"What is the matter?" I asked the men.

"Signalman killed this morning, sir."

"Not the man belonging to that box?"

"Yes, sir."

"Not the man I know?"

"You will recognize him, sir, if you knew him," said the man who spoke for the others, solemnly uncovering his own head and raising an end of the tarpaulin, "for his face is quite composed."

"O! how did this happen, how did this happen?" I asked, turning from one to another as the hut closed in again.

"He was cut down by an engine, sir. No man in England knew his work better. But somehow he was not clear of the outer rail. It was just at broad day. He had struck the light, and had the lamp in his hand. As the engine came out of the tunnel, his back was towards her, and she cut him down. That man drove her, and was showing how it happened. Show the gentleman, Tom."

The man, who wore a rough dark dress, stepped back to his former place at the mouth of the tunnel:

"Coming round the curve in the tunnel, sir," he said, "I saw him at the end, like as if I saw him down a perspective-glass. There was no time to check speed, and I knew him to be very careful. As he didn't seem to take heed of the whistle, I shut it off when we were running down upon him, and called to him as loud as I could call."

"What did you say?"

"I said, Below there! Look out! Look out! For God's sake clear the way!"

I started.

"Ah! it was a dreadful time, sir. I never left off calling to him. I put this arm before my eyes, not to see, and I waved this arm to the last; but it was no use."

Without prolonging the narrative to dwell on any one of its curious circumstances more than on any other, I may, in closing it, point out the coincidence that the warning of the Engine-Driver included, not only the words which the unfortunate Signalman had repeated to me as haunting him, but also the words which I myself—not he—had attached, and that only in my own mind, to the gesticulation he had imitated.

COME AGAIN IN THE SPRING

Richard Kennedy
(1932–)

If you are looking for Richard Kennedy's stories, you will probably find them in the children's section of your library or bookstore. My local children's librarian tells me that she considers Kennedy's stories to be a fail-safe choice for reading to groups of kids, who are invariably enchanted by his delightful tales. But personally, I think it's a shame that he is characterized as a "children's author." Kennedy's stories have the universality and simplicity of folk-tales, rendered in a charmingly homespun American style, and adults love them as much as younger folk.

"Come Again in the Spring" is really too recent to be considered a genuine classic, but I'm willing to bet it will be before long.

now was on the ground. Old Hark was standing out to the side of his cabin, scattering handfuls of cracked corn and scratch to the birds all around him. Now and then he sniffed the air. It smelled like more snow was coming.

A solitary figure bundled in a great bearskin coat trudged along the forest path to the old man's cabin.

He stopped in front of the cabin and shifted a large ledger out from under his arm. The burly figure opened it to a page, looked at the cabin and then to the page again, and walked out toward the old man.

"Good day," said the stranger.

"Howdy," said Old Hark, brushing his hand on his coat. "Your face is easy, but I can't recollect the name. We met?"

"Not in any formal way,", said the stranger. "But I've passed this way before. Maybe you've caught a glimpse of me. I'm Death."

The old man straightened his back and held the feed bag a little closer to his chest.

"Death, eh? Well, you got the wrong place."

"No," Death said, opening the ledger. "You're Old Hark, aren't you?"

"Maybe, and maybe not," said Old Hark, turning his back and scattering a handful of feed.

"Well, certainly you *are*," Death said, taking a pen from his pocket. "It's all right here in the book."

"Don't give a dang what's in the book," said Old Hark. "I ain't going. Come again in the spring."

Death sighed, and took the cap off the pen. "How tiresome," he said. "Everyone tries to put it off, and all it amounts to is making a little check mark after your name." He poised the pen above the book.

Old Hark turned. "I ain't afraid of you."

"No?" Death said, looking up.

"Come again in the spring. I won't hinder you none then. But you see all these birds? Come wintertime, they depend on me to feed them. They naturally ought to fly south in the fall but don't, reason that I been feeding 'em all winter since I was no bigger 'an a skip bug. They'd die if I was gone—they ain't real wintering birds. But you come back in the spring, and they'll know I won't be here next winter and have enough sense to go south."

"Oh, that wouldn't do at all," Death said. "The book is all made up in advance. Why, rescheduling you into the springtime would take a good week's work. Erasures would have to be made, new entries, changes of address, causes of departure...very complicated, no trifling matter at all, I assure you. No, it really won't do at all."

"Don't know about that," Old Hark said, "but I ain't going."

He took a few steps away. Death followed him.

"See here," Death said persuasively, "you're really getting quite old and feeble, you know, quite past the age I usually visit people."

"Ain't going," Old Hark said.

Death saw that the old man was resolute, not at all in the correct state of mind for the business at hand. He considered that he might cause a tree to fall on the old man's head. He consulted his book. Next to Old Hark's name was written: "Means of departure: Quiet, gentle, peaceful." So violence was out of the question.

Death turned a page in the book and studied the entries.

"Now, look," Death said. "I can give you another day. I can fit you in for tomorrow, but then you'll have to come quietly, gently, and peacefully. Even so I'll have to stay up half the night juggling these entries, but I'll do it as a special favour."

"Not tomorrow, either," said Old Hark. "Come again in the spring."

Death was getting impatient. "You're so old now and so feeble and your memory is so shabby you won't even remember me by then, and we'll have to go through all this again."

"There ain't nothing wrong with my memory."

"Isn't there, now?"

"It's perfect."

Death smiled. "If you think so, let me make you a wager."

"Let's hear it," said Old Hark.

"It's this," said Death. "Just so I can be sure you'll remember me next spring, let's make a test. If I can ask you a question about something that happened in your life and you can't remember, then you must come with me tomorrow."

"Agreed," said Old Hark. "Ask away."

Death closed the ledger and put his pen away. He smiled again and asked, "On your second birthday, your mother baked up a special treat. What was it?" Then Death turned and walked off toward the forest path. "Good day," he called. "I'll see you tomorrow."

It began to snow. Old Hark returned to his cabin, kicked the snow off his boots and went inside. He put on some coffee to perking and sat back in his rocking chair. He sat there for hours, remembering many things, many smells, and tastes, and sounds, and people, but of course he couldn't remember what his mother baked special on his second birthday.

Some birds chirped outside the door. The snow had stopped. Old Hark got a handful of feed, opened the door and chucked it out. The birds made a fuss of noise, but just as Old Hark closed the door, he heard one chirp above and unlike any of the others, a very strange chirp.

It sounded exactly as if one of the birds had said, "Plumcakes."

It snowed most of the night. Next morning, Old Hark made his rounds to the bird feeders and scattered plenty of feed. He got his shovel and a ladder out then and climbed up to shove some of the snow off the roof of the cabin.

While he was up there, Death came around with his ledger under his arm. He stood next to the ladder and shouted out a cheery "Good morning!" Old Hark looked down. He put a finger to one of his nostrils, blew his nose in the snow, and then said, "Plumcakes," and turned back to his work.

That was a surprise for Death. He had spent half the night working on the book. He was tired, and now he was angry and was tempted to pull the ladder out from the old man. But he remembered the words in the book, "Quiet, gentle, peaceful," and he got hold of himself.

"Very good," Death said. "I don't think there's one man in a thousand who could have remembered that far back. But of course it might have been luck. Perhaps you just made a guess at it."

"I didn't guess," Old Hark said.

"But you couldn't do it again," Death said.

"I reckon I could."

"Then just to be absolutely positive it wasn't a guess, let's try it one more time."

"One more time," Hark agreed. "Ask away."

"Very well," said Death. "The question is this: On your first birthday, your mother picked some wild flowers and put them in your crib with you. What kind of flowers were they?" And he walked away up the forest path.

After clearing the roof, Old Hark took his shovel to work on some drift that was leaning on to his fence. Now and then he threw some feed out of his pocket to the birds that followed him about. They were singing and chirping around the fence, and as he finished up and headed back to the cabin, Old Hark heard in back of him an unusual chirp, loud and clear.

It sounded exactly as if one of the birds had said, "Buttercups."

Next morning when Death came around, Old Hark was under his lean-to splitting wood.

"Good morning," Death said lightly, although actually he was feeling grouchy because he had been up half the night fixing his book to fit the old man into a new place.

Old Hark spit on his hands and took a fresh grip on his splitting maul. "Buttercups," he said, and swung the maul.

Death swallowed hard to keep from crying out. It was impossible. He would have liked to have Old Hark's wedge jump up and crack his skull, but of course that wasn't in the book. Slowly, Death got control of himself.

"Amazing," Death said. "I can scarcely believe it. What a memory. I'm astounded, really I am. You don't *suppose* you could possibly do that again? I hardly *believe* you could."

Old Hark took a breath and leaned on the butt of his splitting maul. "I reckon I just might," he said. "But supposing I do? Then you got to let me be all the way into next spring."

"Agreed," Death said. "Agreed. Then it's a wager. One more question. If you can answer, then I won't come again until next spring. If you can't answer...well, then..." Death made a check mark in the air.

"Ask away," said Old Hark.

"The question is this," said Death. "On the day you were born, when the midwife held you up in the air, what were the first words your father said?" Death cocked his head, smiled, and walked away.

After splitting the wood, Old Hark filled all the bird feeders and broke up the ice in the cistern. All the while he was paying close attention to the birds which always fluttered nearby, but he heard nothing out of the ordinary in their chirping. Then he went inside. He stoked up the fire, made coffee, took a nap and puttered with some harness. But every now and then he opened the door and threw out some feed, and listened carefully. Just ordinary singing and chirping. He was feeling especially tired and went to bed early with no answer to the question.

Now the reason the birds could tell him nothing was this. Old Hark had been born in that very cabin, and generations of birds had known him and everything about him, and because of their love for the old man they had passed on many memories of him, and so they knew the answers to the other questions.

But on the day the old man was born, in the very bed in which he now lay, the window was closed and the curtain was drawn, so the birds knew nothing of what his father's first words were upon seeing his newborn son. They could not help him.

Old Hark woke late, which wasn't like him. His bones hurt, and he felt tired. It took him much longer than usual to get his chores done, and the wind seemed to chill him to the heart. Still, he listened carefully to the birds. They said nothing special. Early in the afternoon, without coffee or even a bite to eat, he undressed and got back into bed. He had never felt quite so tired in his life. Through his half-closed eyes, he watched the birds on his window-sill hopping about, but he was too tired even to crack the window a bit so he could hear them sing. Now and then he fell asleep.

Death knocked on the door in the late afternoon.

"Come in," Old Hark whispered.

"Hello?" Death said, opening the door. Then he saw Old Hark laid out in the bed and understood at once that the old man had no answer to the question.

"Well, well," Death said, taking a chair next to the old man's bed and opening his book on his lap. "Now isn't that more like it, yes indeed. Ha, ha. You old rascal, I've been up half the night again on your account, you know, but it's quite all right now, yes indeed. It's good to see you lying there so quiet and gentle and…" Death glanced at the book. "…so peaceful."

Old Hark paid him no attention. He was watching the birds playing on the window-sill.

"Now," said Death, taking out his pen. "I've managed to fit you in for sunset. Oh, you should appreciate that. It's a choice spot, really. Very appropriate, very…*fitting* to the occasion, you know. Daylight ending, the sun going down, darkness coming on …Ah, yes, a choice spot—we usually reserve it for poets." Death ran a finger down the page. "Here we are," he said cheerfully. He took the cap off his pen and moved to make a check mark after Old Hark's name. Then he paused.

"Oh, yes," Death said. "It's a formality, but I must ask you so as to make it all strictly legal. As I recall then, the question was this: On the day you were born, when the midwife held you up in the air, what were the first words your father said?"

But Old Hark had not even been listening. He was looking at the birds, and he said to Death, "Open the window."

Death thrust his head forward and clutched at his pen.

"What did you say?"

"Let the birds sing."

"NOOOOOooooooooo!" Death bellowed. He flung his arms about hysterically, splattering ink, then screamed out again and fell off his chair in a fit. He got up in a rage and pitched his book through the window.

Birds flew in, singing. Death grabbed a handful of his coat-front and threw himself out the window and went stumbling up the forest path.

Old Hark leaped out of bed and watched Death disappear into the forest. He was feeling much better. He put on a wool shirt and got some coffee to perking, then cut himself some cheese and bread. In a short time he figured out what all the commotion had been about.

Of course what it was, is this: Death had lost the wager and must leave Old Hark to live until spring, for his father's first words on seeing his newborn son had been "Open the window! Let the birds sing!"

IN MY INDOLENCE

Italo Svevo
(1861–1928)

Now we move to the bright, sun-washed colours of Italy in the company of Italo Svevo, one of the major Italian writers of this century. I always think this story captures something quintessentially and uniquely Italian—an enjoyment of the good life, of fine wines and beautifully prepared food, and a relaxed attitude towards life's mysteries.

"In My Indolence" was written towards the end of Svevo's life, and is actually a fragment of a novel, not completed at the time of Svevo's death. In this story, the central character is an old man who wishes to partake of life's pleasures as long as he can. Old age was a recurrent theme in Svevo's work, and he wrote about it with great sensitivity and empathy. Ironically, he never actually experienced old age himself: he was killed in an automobile accident at the age of sixty-seven.

t is no good looking for the present in calendars or clocks; one consults them merely to establish one's relationship with the past or to move with some semblance of consciousness into the future. It is I and the things and people round me that constitute the true present.

What is more, my present itself consists of various tenses. To begin with there is one major, and interminable present, my retirement from business. A pathetic spectacle of inertia! Then there are a few important events that break it up, like my daughter's marriage: an event long passed and one that is becoming a part of another protracted present, interrupted—or perhaps renewed or, better, rectified—by her husband's death. The birth of my little grandson is now distant too, because the real present as far as Umbertino is concerned is my affection for him and his winning of it. He is not aware of this since he believes it his birthright. (Or does that small soul believe anything in general?) His present, and mine in relation to him, are merely his confident little steps, interrupted by painful moments of fear which, however, are relieved by the company of dolls when he can't have that of his mother or me, his grandfather. My present is also Augusta (poor woman!), reduced now to her animals—dogs, cats, birds— and her eternal unwellness which she hasn't the energy to cure. She does the little prescribed by Dr. Raulli, but refuses to listen to me—who by superhuman effort managed to overcome a similar tendency to heart trouble—nor to Carlo, who is just out of the university and so knows the most up-to-date medicines.

Unquestionably, a great part of my present is provided by medicine. I can't recall exactly when this present began, but it has been constantly punctuated by new medicines and theories. Where now is the time when I believed I was doing all my organism required by gulping down every evening a good dose of licorice compound, or a simple bromide (powdered or liquid)? Now, with Carlo's help, I command very different weapons against disease. Carlo tells me all he knows, but I, on the other hand, don't reveal everything I am imagining, because I am afraid he may not agree with me and, with his objections, may demolish the castle which I put such effort into seeking and which gives me a measure of tranquillity and security which people at my age don't normally have. A real castle it is! Carlo believes I accept all his suggestions so readily out of faith in him. Not quite! I am aware that he knows a great deal, and try to pick it up and apply it, but always with reservations. My arteries are not what they ought to be; about that there is no doubt. Last summer I reached a blood pressure of 240. Whether because of that or something else, I was very depressed altogether just then. Then generous doses of iodide and another drug, the name of which I never remember, brought the pressure down to 160, where it has remained till now…(I have just now interrupted my writing to measure it at the machine I keep ready on my table. It is exactly 160!). Before that, I felt threatened all the time by an apoplectic stroke, which I could feel coming nearer and nearer. The presence of death did not make me a kinder and better man, as I disliked everyone who wasn't threatened by a stroke; they had the disgustingly comfortable manner of people who sympathize, commiserate, and enjoy life.

But guided by Carlo, I even treated some organs which were in no need of help. But no doubt all organs must feel exhausted after so many years of work and are benefited by assistance. I sent them it unasked for. So often when disease strikes, the doctor sighs: "I've been called in too late!" So it is better to look ahead.

I cannot initiate cures for the liver when it shows no sign of malfunctioning, but, all the same, I must not risk an end like that of a son of a friend of mine who, one fine day, at the age of thirty-two and in full health, turned yellow as a melon with a violent attack of jaundice and expired within forty-eight hours.

"He had never been ill," his poor father told me: "He was a giant, yet he had to die."

Many giants come to a bad end. I've noticed this and am quite happy not to be one.

But prudence is a fine thing. So every Monday I donate a pill to my liver, and this protects it from violent and sudden maladies, at least until the following Monday. I watch over my kidneys with periodic analysis, and until now they have shown no sign of malfunctioning. But I know they can stand some help. My exclusively milk diet on Tuesdays affords me a certain security for the rest of the week. It would be a fine thing if others, who never give a thought to their kidneys, should be allowed to keep them running merrily, whilst I, who make a weekly sacrifice to them, should be rewarded by a surprise like the one that befell poor Copler!

About five years ago I was disturbed by chronic bronchitis. It interfered with my sleep and every now and then had me jumping out of bed at night to spend hours sitting in an armchair. The doctor did not see fit to tell me so, but no doubt some heart trouble was involved. Raulli prescribed that I should give up smoking, lose some weight, and eat very little meat. As giving up smoking was very difficult, I tried to fulfil the prescription by giving up meat altogether. But even losing weight was not easy. At the time, I had a net weight of ninety-four kilos. In three years I succeeded in losing two kilos, so at that rate, to reach the weight Raulli wanted, another eighteen years would have been needed. But it was difficult to eat moderately when one was abstaining from meat.

And here I must confess that I really owe my loss of weight to Carlo. It was one of his first medical successes. He proposed that I should give up one of my three daily meals; and I resolved to sacrifice supper, which we Triestines take at eight in the evening, as distinguished from other Italians, who have lunch at noon and dinner at seven. Every day I fast uninterruptedly for eighteen hours.

I soon found I slept better. I felt at once that my heart, no longer assisting in digestive work, could devote every beat to filling the veins, to carrying waste matter from the organism, and, above all, to nourishing the lungs. I who had once suffered from terrible periods of insomnia—that great agitation of longing for rest and, for that very reason, not being able to procure it— would lie there quite still, calmly awaiting the approach of warmth and sleep: a genuine parenthesis in an exhausting life. Sleep after a sumptuous dinner is something quite different: the heart concentrates on digestion and neglects all its other duties.

What all this proved, in the first place, was that I was better adapted to abstinence than to moderation. It was easier not to eat supper at all than to limit the amount one eats at lunch-time and breakfast. On these occasions there were no limitations. Twice a day I could gorge myself. And there was no harm in it, because eighteen hours of autophagy followed. In the beginning, the midday meal of *pasta asciutta* and vegetables was topped off with some eggs. Then I gave up even these, not because Raulli or Carlo asked me to, but in accordance with the judicious advice of a philosopher, Herbert Spencer, who discovered some law or other to the effect that organs which developed too fast—through overnourishment—are less strong than those taking a longer time to grow. The law, naturally, pertained to children, but I am convinced that returning to it is a step forward—that even a seventy-year-old child would do well to starve his organs rather than overnourish them. Carlo, moreover, agreed with my theory, and sometimes wanted people to believe that he had formulated it himself.

In this effort to renounce supper, I received great assistance from smoking, to which, for the first time in my life, I was reconciled even in theory. The smoker can fast better than others. A good smoke numbs whatever appetite there is. It is to smoking that I believe I owe reducing my weight to eighty kilos. It is a great relief to have hygienic reasons for smoking. One smokes rather more and with a perfectly clear conscience.

At bottom, health is a truly miraculous condition. Being the result of the interworking of various organs, whose functions we never completely know (as even Carlo, who understands the whole science, including the science of our ignorance, admitted), perfect health can probably never exist. Otherwise, its termination would be even more miraculous. Moving things ought to move for ever. Why not? Isn't this the law in the heavens, where surely the same laws apply as on earth? But I know that diseases are predestined and prepared from birth. From the very beginning, some organs start out weaker than others, overexerting themselves and driving related organs to greater effort; and wherever there is effort, fatigue results, and from it, ultimately, death.

For that reason, and only for that reason, a malady followed by death does not reveal any basic disorder in our nature. I am too ignorant to know whether in the heavens, as down here on earth, there exists the possibility of death and reproduction. All I know is that some stars, and even some planets, have less complete movements than others. It must be that a planet which does not rotate on itself is either lame, blind or hunchbacked.

But among our organs there is one that is the centre, a kind of sun in a solar system. Up until a few years ago this organ was thought to be the heart. At the moment everybody knows that our entire life turns on the sexual organs. Carlo turns up his nose at rejuvenation operations, but still, he doffs his cap when sexual organs are mentioned. He says: If the sexual organs could be rejuvenated, they would naturally rejuvenate the whole organism. This was nothing new to me. I would have known that without his telling me. But it will never come to pass. It's impossible. God only knows what the effects of monkey glands are. Perhaps a rejuvenated man on seeing a beautiful woman will be driven to climb the nearest tree. (Even so, this is a pretty juvenile act.)

One must accept the fact, Mother Nature is a maniac. That is to say, she has the reproduction mania. She maintains life within an organism so long as there is hope of its reproducing itself. Then she kills it off, and does so in the most diverse ways because of her other mania, that for remaining mysterious. She doesn't want to give herself away by always resorting to the same malady to kill off old people—a malady that would make the reason for death clear, a little tumour always in the same place, say.

I have always been very enterprising. And without resorting to an operation I decided to hoodwink Mother Nature into believing I was still fit for reproduction. So I took a mistress. It was the least disturbing affair I have ever had in my life. To begin with, I considered it neither a lapse of character nor a betrayal of Augusta. What I did feel was rather odd; it was as if taking a mistress was a decision equivalent to going to the chemist's.

Then, of course, matters complicated themselves a little. One finds out in the end that a whole person cannot be used as a medicine: or rather, another person is a complex medicine, containing a substantial proportion of poison. The episode occurred three years ago, when I was sixty-seven. I was not yet a very old man. Consequently, my heart, which was an organ of secondary importance in the affair and should not have had to figure in it, ended by taking part. And it so happened that on some days even Augusta profited from my liaison and was caressed, fondled, and rewarded, as she had been when I had had Carla. The curious thing was that it did not surprise her and that she was not even aware of the novelty. She inhabits her great calm and finds it only natural that I should occupy myself with her less than in the past; still, our present inertia does not weaken the bond between us, which is knotted with caresses and affectionate words. These caresses and words do not have to be repeated in order to endure, to exist somewhere, to remain alive always and always just as intimate. When, one day, seeking to salve my conscience, I placed two fingers underneath her chin and gazed at length into her faithful eyes, she abandoned herself to me, offering up her lips: "You have always stayed affectionate," she said.

At the moment I was a little taken aback. Then, examining the past, I realized I had never in fact been so wanting in affection as to deny my old love for her. I had even hugged her (a little absent-mindedly) every evening before closing my eyes in sleep.

It was somewhat difficult to find the right woman. There was no one in the house suited for such a role; nor was I eager to sully my own home. Still I would have done so, given the need to hoodwink Mother Nature, to stop her thinking the moment had arrived for my final illness, and given the enormous task of finding someone outside who would do for me, an old man occupied with political economy. But, really, there was no chance. The best-looking woman in the house was Augusta herself. There was also a little fourteen-year-old girl whom Augusta made use of for various household chores. But I knew that if I were to accost this child, Mother Nature, not believing me, would have struck me down at once with one of those thunderbolts she keeps at her disposal.

There is not much point in relating how I came to find Felicita. Out of sheer devotion to hygiene, I used, every day, to go some distance beyond the Piazza Unità to buy myself cigarettes, which meant a walk of half an hour or so. The shop assistant was an old woman, but the actual owner of the shop, who spent several hours every day there supervising, was Felicita, a girl about twenty-four years old. At first I had the impression she had inherited the shop; much later I learned that she had bought it with her own money. It was there that I came to know her.

We soon came to an understanding. She attracted me. She was a blonde who dressed in a variety of colours, in materials which I guessed were not expensive but always new-looking and showy. She took pride in her beauty: the small head puffed out on the sides with close-cropped, very curly hair, and the elegant body, very erect, as if carried on a pole, and with a slight backwards tilt. I noticed at once her liking for bright colours. In her house, this taste was revealed everywhere. Sometimes the house was not very well heated, and on one of these occasions I took special note of the colours she was wearing: a red kerchief knotted round her head in the style of a peasant woman, a yellow brocaded shawl round her shoulders, a quilted apron in red, yellow, and green over her blue skirt, and a pair of multicoloured quilted slippers on her feet. She was a real oriental figurine; but her pale face belonged unmistakably to our regions, with its eyes that scrutinized things and people, calculating what she could get out of them.

A monthly allowance was agreed upon from the outset; and, quite frankly, it was so high that I could not help comparing it with regret with the much lower ones of pre-war days. And as early as the twentieth of the month, Felicita, the dear girl, began to talk about the stipend that was falling due, thereby casting a cloud over a good part of the month. She was sincere, indeed transparently so. I was less so, and she never learned that I had come to her as a result of studying medical textbooks.

I soon forgot it too. I must say I still look back nostalgically at that house, so humble apart from the one room furnished with good taste and luxury corresponding to what I was paying—very soberly coloured and dimly lighted—in which Felicita appeared like some variegated flower.

She had a brother living in the same house—an honest, hardworking electrician whose daily wages were more than enough for him. He was extremely lean, but that had nothing to do with his not being married; on the contrary, as one could easily see, it was due to his tight-fistedness. I spoke to him when Felicita called him in to examine the fuses in our room. I discovered that brother and sister, being set on making themselves some money as soon as possible, had become business partners. Felicita carried on a very serious life between the tobacconist's shop and the house, and Gastone between his repair-shop and the house. Felicita must have been making more than Gastone, but that did not matter, since—as I was later to learn—she needed her brother's help. It was he who had organized the tobacco-stall business, which was proving such a sound investment. And he was so convinced that he was leading the life of an upright man as to speak scornfully of workers who frittered their earnings away with never a thought for the morrow.

All in all, we got on rather well together. The room, so soberly and meticulously kept, smacked of a doctor's consulting room. Only Felicita was a slightly sharp medicine that had to be gulped down without the palate's having leisure to savour it.

At the very beginning—before drawing up the agreement, indeed, and to encourage me to do so—she threw her arms round me and said: "You know, I don't find you repulsive, really I don't."

It was really quite nice, because said so nicely; but it gave me a shock. I had never really thought of myself as repulsive. On the contrary, I had believed I was returning to love, from which I had so long abstained through a misinterpretation of the laws of hygiene, in order to surrender, to offer myself up, to whoever wanted me. This would have been the true health-regimen I was after; any other form would have been incomplete and ineffectual. But despite the money I was paying for the cure, I did not dare explain to Felicita how I wanted her to be. And she, very frequently, in giving herself to me, would spoil the treatment with her naïvety: "Isn't it queer! I don't find you repulsive at all."

One day, with the brutality I am capable of on certain occasions, I murmured gently in her ear: "Isn't it queer! I don't find you repulsive, either." This made her giggle so much that the cure was interrupted.

And occasionally, in my mind, I even dare to boast—so as to encourage myself, to feel more confident, worthier, loftier, and so as to forget having dedicated part of my life to the effort of not being repulsive—that Felicita, in one or two brief moments during our long relationship, actually loved me. And looking for a genuine expression of her affection, I find it neither in the never-changing sweetness with which she invariably greeted me, nor in the maternal care with which she protected me from draughts, nor in the solicitude with which she once wrapped me in one of her brother's overcoats and lent me an umbrella, because a storm had blown up while I was at her place. What I remember is her murmuring, sincerely for once: "Oh, how I loathe you! You're repulsive!"

One day when as usual I was talking with Carlo about medicine, he remarked: "What you need is a girl given to gerontophilia."

Who knows? I did not confess to Carlo, but perhaps once I found and then lost just such a girl. Except that I do not believe Felicita was a thoroughgoing gerontophile. She got too much money out of me for me to think she really loved me for what I am.

She was certainly the most expensive woman I have ever known in my life. She studied me quietly with those cool, serene eyes of hers, often narrowing them to decide how far I would let myself be exploited. In the beginning, and for a long time afterwards, she was quite content with her allowance, because I, not yet a slave to habit, intimated it was all she would get. On several occasions she made a reach for my money but withdrew her hand from my pocket for fear of exposing herself to the risk of losing me. Once, though, she did bring it off. She got money out of me to buy a rather expensive fur, which I never laid eyes on. Another time, she got me to pay for an entire Parisian ensemble and then let me see it: but for one even as blind as I was, her multicoloured clothes were unforgettable and I found I had seen her in that suit before. She was an economy-minded woman who pretended to caprice only because she thought a man understood caprice in a woman more easily than avarice.

And this is how, against my will, the affair came to an end.

I used to visit her at set hours twice a week. Then, one Tuesday after I had started for her house, it occurred to me halfway there that I would be better off on my own. I returned to my study and quietly devoted myself to Beethoven's *Ninth Symphony* on the gramophone.

On Wednesday I should still not have felt such a strong craving for Felicita; it was really my avarice that drove me to her. I was paying a substantial allowance, and somehow, by not taking advantage of what was due to me, I felt as if I were paying too much. One must remember that when I undergo treatment, I pursue it conscientiously with the most scientific exactitude. Only by dint of doing so can one decide, at the end, if the cure was a good or a bad one.

As fast as my legs would carry me, I was in that room which I believed to be ours. For the moment it belonged to another. Fat old Misceli, a man about my age, was sitting in an easy chair in a corner while Felicita lounged comfortably on the couch, concentrating on the flavour of a long and very choice cigarette—a brand which was not to be had in her shop. Essentially, it was the very same position in which Felicita and I found ourselves when we were left together, the only difference being that, whereas Misceli was not smoking, I joined Felicita in doing so.

"What can I do for you?" Felicita asked icily, studying the fingernails of the hand that was holding the cigarette aloft.

Words failed me. Presently I found it easier to speak, because to tell the truth, I did not feel the least resentment towards Misceli. This fat man, who was old as I, looked considerably older because of his tremendous weight. He eyed me warily over the top of the shiny spectacles he wore perched on the tip of his nose. I always feel other old men to be older than I am.

"Oh, Misceli," I said forthrightly, fully resolved not to make a scene, "it's a long time since we've seen each other."

And I offered him my hand. He laid his ham of a hand in mine without returning my clasp. Still he said nothing. He was indeed showing himself—older than me.

By now, with the objectivity of the experienced man, I understood very clearly that my position and Misceli's were identical. I felt that, this being the case, we were in no position to resent each other. After all, our meeting here amounted to no more than a collision on the pavement. However painful it may be, one goes on one's way mumbling "Sorry."

With this thought, the gentleman innate in me asserted itself. I even felt called upon to make Felicita's situation more tolerable. And I said to her, "Signorina, I must have a hundred packets of 'Sport' cigarettes, top quality, as I have to give someone a present. The very freshest ones, if possible. The shop's a little too far so I took the liberty of dropping in here for an instant."

Felicita stopped examining her nails and became very gracious. She even got up and walked with me to the door. In a low voice, with intense reproach, she managed to say: "Why didn't you come yesterday?" And then, quickly, "And what have you come today for?"

I was offended. It was intolerable to be limited to fixed days, particularly at the price I was paying. I relieved myself by giving vent to my annoyance: "I've only come here today to let you know that I never want to see you any more! We're not going to see each other again!"

She stared at me astonished, and to look at me better stepped away from me, leaning even further back than usual. To be frank it was an odd pose, but it lent her a certain grace, that of a self-assured person capable of maintaining the most difficult equilibrium.

"As you like," she said shrugging. Then, to be sure she had understood me perfectly, just as she opened the door, she asked me: "Then we're not going to see any more of each other?"

And she searched my face.

"Certainly not!" said I a little querulously.

I was just starting down the stairs when fat old Misceli came bumbling to the door, yelling, "Wait! wait! I'm coming with you too. I've already told the Signorina how many 'Sports' I need. A hundred. Just like you."

We descended the stairs together while Felicita closed the door after a long pause, a pause that gave me pleasure.

We went down the long slope that leads into the Piazza Unità, slowly, careful where we placed our feet. Lumbering along on the slope, he certainly appeared older than I. Once he even stumbled and almost fell. I helped him promptly. He did not thank me. He was panting a little, and the effort to be made on the slope was still not over. Because of that, and only because of that, he did not speak. This is borne out by the fact that when we reached the level area behind the town hall, he relaxed and started talking.

"I never smoke 'Sports,'" he said. "But working-class people always prefer them. I have to give a present to my carpenter. And I wanted to buy the good ones Signorina Felicita always stocks." Now that he was talking he could only take short steps. He stopped altogether to rummage about in a trouser pocket. He pulled out a gold cigarette case, pressed a little button and the case flew open: "Would you like one?" he asked. "They're denicotinized."

I accepted one and also stopped, in order to light it. He stood there stock-still, waiting to put the case back in his pocket. And I thought, "At least she could have given me a more virile rival." In fact, I handled myself better than he both on the slope and on the flat. Compared with him, I was really a youngster. He even smoked denicotinized cigarettes, which have no flavour. I was more a man because, though I had always tried not to smoke, I had never stooped to the poltroonery of denicotinized cigarettes.

As God would have it, we arrived at the gate of the Tergesteo where we had to part. Misceli was now talking about other things: affairs on the Exchange, on which he was an expert. He seemed a bit excited to me, even a little distraught. In a word, it seemed as though he were talking without listening to himself. He was like me, who was not listening to him but studying him instead, trying to guess exactly what he was not saying.

I did not want to part from him without having tried to find out what was really in his mind. With this in view, I began by giving myself away completely. I burst out: "Felicita is nothing but a whore!"

Misceli provided a fresh spectacle, that of his embarrassment. His fat lower jaw began to move like that of a ruminant. Was this what he did when he didn't know what to say? Presently he said: "She doesn't seem so to me. She has excellent 'Sports.'"

He wanted to prolong this stupid comedy for ever.

I became angry: "Then, in other words, you intend to go on

seeing Signorina Felicita?"

Another pause. His jaw jutted out, swung to the left, returned to the right before fixing itself. Then, for the first time betraying an impulse to laugh, he said: "I'll be going back as soon as I need some 'Sports' again."

I laughed, myself. But I wanted further explanations: "Well, why did you leave her today?"

He hesitated, and in his darkened eyes, focused on the far end of the road, I detected signs of great sadness.

"I'm a little superstitious," he said. "When I'm interrupted in something, I believe in immediately recognizing the hand of Providence, and drop everything I'm doing. Once I had to go to Berlin on important business but I went no further than Sessana, after the train was held up there for several hours, I don't know exactly why. I don't believe one should force things—especially at our age."

This was still not enough for me, and I asked: "You didn't mind when you saw me going to Signorina Felicita for 'Sports' too, did you?"

He answered with such decisiveness that his jaw did not have time to swivel: "What difference could it make to me? Me jealous? Certainly not! We two are old. We're old. There's no harm in our making love occasionally; but we mustn't become jealous, that way one starts to look ridiculous. We ought never to get jealous. Listen to me, don't ever let people see you jealous; they would laugh at you."

His words sound friendly enough on paper, but in fact they were said in a tone full of anger and scorn. His fat face flaming, he approached me; being smaller than myself, he looked up at me as though trying to find the weakest point to strike. Why was he angry with me at the very moment of preaching against jealousy? What else had I done to him? Perhaps he was angry with me because I had held his train up at Sessana when he should have been arriving in Berlin.

But I was not jealous. I should, however, have liked to know how much he paid Felicita monthly. I felt if I could know—as seemed fitting to me—that he paid more than I did, I would have been satisfied.

But I didn't have time to investigate. All of a sudden Misceli became gentler and addressed himself to my discretion. His gentleness changed into a threat when he reminded me we were in each other's hands. I reassured him: I was married too and was aware of the danger of an imprudent word from either of us.

"Oh," he said, with an offhand gesture, "I don't ask for discretion because of my wife. There are certain things that haven't interested her for years. But I know you're under Dr. Raulli's care too. He threatened to leave me if I didn't follow his prescriptions—if I drank just one glass of wine, if I smoked more than ten cigarettes a day, even denicotinized ones, if I didn't give up...well, all the rest. He says that at our age a man's body maintains its equilibrium only because it can't decide in which direction to collapse. So you shouldn't suggest to it which part to choose, because then the decision would be easy." He went on, self-pityingly: "After all, it's easy prescribing for someone else, saying don't do this or that or the other. One might reply that rather than live like that it would be better to face dying a few months sooner."

He stayed with me a few moments longer, questioning me about my health. I told him I had once reached a blood pressure of 240, which pleased him enormously, because he had reached only 220. With one foot on the step that leads into the Tergesteo, he gave me a friendly wave and added: "Now, please, don't breathe a word about it."

I was obsessed for some days by Raulli's rhetorical figure of an old man's body that stays on its feet because it does not know in which direction to collapse. Of course, when the old doctor spoke of a "part" he meant *organ*. And "equilibrium" also had its meaning for him. Raulli must have known what he was talking about. With us old men, health can only mean a gradual and simultaneous weakening of all organs. Woe to us if one of them should lag behind, that is to say, stay too young! I suspect that then their interdependence changes into a conflict, and that the weak organs get bullied, with magnificent results for the general economy, one can imagine. Misceli's intervention must, therefore, have been desired by Providence, who guards over my life and even sent word how I was to behave by way of that mouth with the wandering jaw.

And I returned, pensively, to my gramophone. In the *Ninth Symphony* I encountered my organs again, collaborating and quarrelling. Working in concert during the first movements—particularly in the *scherzo*, when even the tympani, with their two notes, are allowed to synthetize what all the instruments are murmuring round them. The joy of the last movement seemed rebellion to me; crude, with a strength which is violence, with only slight brief gestures of regret and hesitation. Not for nothing does the human voice, the least rational of all sounds in nature, enter into the last movement. I admit that on other occasions I had interpreted this symphony otherwise—as the most intense representation of harmony between the most divergent of forces, into which, finally, even the human voice is received and fused. But that day the symphony, played by the same records, appeared as I say.

"Farewell, Felicita," I whispered when the music faded away. There was no need to think of her any longer.

She was not worth risking a sudden collapse for. There were so many medical theories in the world that it was hard to be ruled by them. Those rascally doctors' only contribution to life was to make it more difficult. The simplest things are too complicated. To abstain from drinking alcohol is a prescription of self-evident logic. Yet all the same, it is known that alcohol can sometimes have curative properties. Must I wait for the doctor, then, to allow myself the comfort of this potent medicine? There is no doubt that death sometimes results from a brief and sudden caprice on an organ's part, or a casual and momentary coincidence of different weaknesses. I mean, it would be momentary if it were not followed by death. Things must be so managed as to make the coincidence remain momentary. So aid has to be at hand, to stave off the cramps produced by overexertion or the collapse induced by inertia. So why wait for the doctor, who comes running merely to scribble out his bill? Only I am able to tell in time when I need something, by a feeling of discomfort.

Doctors, unfortunately, have not studied what can help in a case like that. I take various things, therefore, for instance a purgative and a sip of wine; and then I study myself. I might need something else: a glass of milk—with a drop of digitalis. And all taken in the most minute quantities, as recommended by the great Hahnemann. The mere presence of these minute quantities is enough to produce the reactions necessary for the activation of life, just as though an organ wants, not so much to be stimulated, but to be reminded. Seeing a drop of calcium, it exclaims: "Oh, look! I'd forgotten. I'm supposed to be working."

That is what was fatal about Felicita. It was impossible to take her in doses.

That evening Felicita's brother came to call on me. On seeing him I was seized with panic, particularly as Augusta herself showed him to my study. Fearing what he had to say to me, I was very happy when Augusta promptly withdrew.

He unknotted a handkerchief from which he took a parcel: one hundred packets of "Sports" cigarettes. He broke them down into five stacks, each of twenty packets, and it was therefore easy to verify the quantity. Then he had me feel how soft each packet was. They had been selected one by one from a large stock. He was sure I would be pleased.

And I certainly was pleased, feeling quite reassured, after having been so frightened. I at once paid the 160 lire I owed him and cheerfully thanked him. Cheerfully, because in fact I felt like laughing. A queer woman, Felicita. She might be jilted, but she didn't neglect her tobacconist's shop.

But the pale, lean man, after stuffing the lire he had received into his pocket, still made no move to leave. He hardly seemed to be Felicita's brother. I had seen him before, on other occasions, but better dressed. Now he was without a collar, and his clothes, though neat enough, were utterly threadbare. Strange that he felt he even had to have a special hat for workdays; the one he had on was positively filthy and misshapen from long wear.

He looked at me intently, hesitating to speak. It seemed that his slightly sombre look, rather out of place in the brightly lit room, was inviting me to guess what was on his mind. When he finally spoke, his look became even more imploring, so much so that it almost seemed like a threat. Intense supplications border on threats. I can very well understand that there are peasants who end up punishing the images they have prayed to by hurling them under their beds.

Finally, in a steady voice, he said to me: "Felicita says we have reached the tenth of the month."

I glanced at the calendar, from which I tore a sheet every day, and said: "She's quite right. We *have* reached the tenth. There's no doubt about it."

"But then," he said hesitantly, "you owe her for the whole month."

A second before he spoke I understood why he had got me to look at the calendar. I believe I blushed at the moment of discovering that between brother and sister everything was frank and honest where money was concerned. The only thing that really surprised me was the out-and-out request for the whole month's allowance. I was, in fact, not sure whether I might not be owed something. In my relations with Felicita, I had not kept very accurate accounts. But hadn't I always paid in advance? So shouldn't the last payment cover this fraction of the month? And I sat there, with my mouth somewhat agape, having to look into those strange eyes, trying to determine whether they were imploring or threatening. It is precisely the man of wide and long experience like myself who does not know how to behave: knowing as he does that a single word of his, a single deed, may lead to the most unforeseen consequences. One has only to read history to learn that causes and effects can stand in the most peculiar relations with each other. During my hesitation I took out my wallet and counted and sorted my money, so as not to mistake a 100-lira note for a 500 one. And when I had counted the notes, I gave them over. Thus the thing was done while I thought I was merely gaining time. And I said to myself: "I'll pay now and think later."

Felicita's brother himself had obviously stopped thinking about it, for his eye was no longer fixed on me and lost all its intentness. He put the money in a different pocket from the one in which he had deposited the 160 lire. He kept accounts and monies separate. He bowed to me, saying: "Good evening, Signor," and left. But in a moment or two he was back, because he had forgotten another parcel similar to the one he had given me. By way of excusing himself for returning, he said to me: "This is another hundred packets of 'Sports' I have to deliver to another gentleman."

They were, of course, for poor Misceli, who couldn't stand them either. I smoked all of mine, however, except for some packets I gave to my chauffeur Fortunato. When I have paid for something, sooner or later I finish up using it. It is a proof of my sense of thrift. And every time I had that taste of musty straw in my mouth I remembered Felicita and her brother vividly. By thinking about it, I finally remembered with absolute certainty that I had, in fact, not paid the allowance in advance. After thinking I had been cheated on a serious scale, I was relieved to find they had only been paid for twenty days extra.

I think I must have returned to see Felicita once again, before the twenty days I had paid for had elapsed, and purely because of my famous sense of economy—the habit of thrift which made me smoke up my "Sports." I said to myself: "Now that I have paid, I'd like to risk just once more—for the last time—the danger of showing my organism which direction it ought to collapse in. Just once! It will never notice the chance it's getting."

The door to her flat opened just as I was about to ring. Startled, in the darkness, I saw her pale, lovely little face as though in a visor, clamped in a hat that covered her head down to her ears and the nape of the neck. A solitary blonde curl stole from the cloche down her forehead. I knew that at this time she usually went to the tobacconist's shop to supervise the more complicated part of its bookkeeping. But I had hoped to persuade her to wait for the short time I needed with her.

In the dark, she did not immediately recognize me. In a questioning tone she uttered a name, neither mine nor Misceli's, which I couldn't make out. When she did recognize me, she extended her hand friendlily, without a trace of coldness and with a certain curiosity. I clasped her cold hand in both of mine and grew bold. She let her hand lie still, but drew her head back.

Never had that pole within her arched back so far—so far that I felt like releasing her hand and seizing her by the waist, if only to steady her.

And that far-away face, adorned with the single curl, studied me. Or was it actually studying me? Wasn't it really studying a problem which she had brought on herself and which demanded an immediate solution, then and there, on the stairs?

"It's impossible just at the moment," she said, after a long pause.

She was still looking at me. Then every shadow of hesitancy vanished.

She stood there, that lovely body of hers stiff in its precarious position, immobile, her little face pale and serious below the yellow ringlet; but slowly, just as if she were acting upon a serious resolution, she withdrew her hand.

"Yes!—it's impossible," she said again.

It was repeated to convince me that she was still considering the matter to see if there might be some way to satisfy me, but apart from this repetition there was no other evidence that she was really thinking about it. She had already made her final decision.

And then she said to me, "You might return on the first of the month, if you can…I'll see…I'll think about it."

It is only recently, only since I have put this account of my liaison with Felicita down on paper, that I have become objective enough to judge both of us fairly. I had come there to assert my rights to the few days outstanding on my subscription. She, on the other hand, was letting me know that by my renunciation I had lost my rights. I think if she had proposed that I there and then paid a fresh subscription I would have been less upset. I am sure I would not have run away. At the moment I was bent on love, and at my age, one is rather like a crocodile on dry land—it takes a long time to change direction. I would willingly have paid for the whole month, though I was only going to make love for one last time.

Instead, things being as they were, I fell into a fury. I could not find words; indeed, I could hardly breathe. I said: "Ouf!"

with intense indignation. I had the impression that I had said something articulate, and I even waited there for a moment or two as if I thought that my "ouf"—a cry meant to wound and give an outlet to my profound chagrin—called for a reply. But neither she nor I had anything more to say. I started down the stairs. A few steps down, I turned to look at her again. Perhaps on that pale face there would now be some sign contradicting such hard-hearted selfishness, such cold calculation. I could not see her face. She was completely absorbed in locking the flat, which she had to leave unoccupied for some hours.

Once again I said: "Ouf!" but not so loudly as to be heard by her. I said it to all the world, society, to our institutions, and to Mother Nature—to everything that had permitted me to find myself on that staircase in that situation.

It was my last love. Now that the whole affair has been fitted into the past, I no longer consider it so disgraceful; for Felicita— with that blonde hair of hers, that pallid face, the slender nose and inscrutable eyes, and the paucity of her words, only seldom betraying the iciness of her heart—Felicita was worth regretting. But after her there was no room for another mistress. She had educated me. Until then, whenever I was with a woman for more than ten minutes, I used to feel hope and desire surging in my heart. Of course, I wanted to conceal them both, but I wanted still more to let them grow, so as to feel an intenser sense of life and of belonging to life. And the only way to make them grow was to express them in words. There's no telling how many times I must have been laughed at. It was Felicita who educated me in my present role of old man. And I can still scarcely bring myself to realize that now, in the sphere of love, I am worth only as much as I pay.

My ugliness is ever before my eyes. This morning, on waking up, I studied the position I found my mouth in the moment I opened my eyes. My lower jaw was sagging on the side I had been lying on, and I felt my tongue out of place too, and stiff and swollen.

I thought of Felicita, whom I very often think of, with desire and hatred. And at that moment I murmured: "She's right."

"Who's right?" asked Augusta who was dressing.

And I promptly replied: "A certain Misceli, whom I ran into yesterday; he told me that he doesn't understand why one is born, lives and grows old—and he's right."

Thus I had really told her everything, without compromising myself in the least.

And until now no one has ever taken Felicita's place. Nevertheless, I still seek to deceive Mother Nature, who is keeping an eye on me to liquidate me as soon as it's apparent that I can no longer reproduce. With wise dosages, in Hahnemann's prescribed quantities, I take a little of the medicine every day. I watch women passing by; I follow them with my eyes, trying to discover in their legs something more than a mere motor apparatus, so that I may again feel the craving to stop them and fondle them. Even here, the doses are becoming more sparing than Hahnemann or I would choose. That is, I have to control my eyes lest they betray what they are looking for, and so, as you will understand, the medicine only rarely works. One can do without actual caresses, and still experience the feeling; but one can't feign total indifference without risking chilling one's own emotions.

And having written this, I can better understand my adventure with Signorina Dondi. I bowed to her so as to be able to make some kind of gesture to her, and feel her beauty more fully. It is the destiny of old men to make pretty bows.

One should not believe that such ephemeral relations, entered upon merely to rescue oneself from death, do not also leave their mark, or help to embellish or trouble one's life, just like my affairs with Carla and Felicita. Sometimes—very occasionally— they leave an indelible memory. I remember a girl sitting opposite me in a tram. She left me with a memory. We reached a certain intimacy, because I gave her a name: Amphora. She did not have a very striking face, but her eyes, luminous and rather round ones, stared at everything with great curiosity and something of a little girl's inquisitiveness. She might have been over twenty, but I would not have been surprised if, for fun, she had tugged the pigtails of the child sitting next to her. I can't say whether because she had an uncommon figure, or because her dress made her appear to have one, but from the waist up her slender body was like some graceful amphora on its base. I was greatly taken by that bosom of hers, and I said to myself, so as to deceive Nature, who had her eye on me: "It's clearly not time for me to die yet; for if this girl wanted me to, I would still be ready to procreate."

My face must have taken an odd look as I gazed at the amphora. But I won't admit that it was the look of a lecher, for I was thinking of death. Nevertheless, others interpreted it as ill-concealed lust. As I now noticed, the girl, who must have belonged to a well-to-do family, was accompanied by an old maidservant, who got off the tram with her. And it was this old woman who, as she passed me, looked at me and whispered: "Old lecher."

She had called me old. She was summoning death!

I said to her: "Old fool!"

But she went her way without replying.

MR. HIGGINBOTHAM'S CATASTROPHE

Nathaniel Hawthorne
(1804–1864)

By all accounts, Nathaniel Hawthorne was one of the most solitary and private authors who has ever lived. He was a virtual recluse in his twenties and early thirties, and even after his marriage and public success as an author he remained extremely shy and retiring. He wrote in his notebook once that he doubted whether he had ever had real conversations with half a dozen people. And yet, like many writers, he took refuge in a wonderful imaginative life, finding there the adventure and society he craved.

"Mr. Higginbotham's Catastrophe" certainly doesn't seem to be the product of an introverted mind. It has everything: mystery, romance, horror, comedy, suspense, social satire. Here, then, is a delightful little bauble from a writer more usually preoccupied with weightier issues.

 young fellow, a tobacco pedlar by trade, was on his way from Morristown, where he had dealt largely with the Deacon of the Shaker settlement, to the village of Parker's Falls, on Salmon River. He had a neat little cart, painted green, with a box of cigars depicted on each side panel, and an Indian chief, holding a pipe and a golden tobacco stalk, on the rear. The pedlar drove a smart little mare, and was a young man of excellent character, keen at a bargain, but none the worse liked by the Yankees; who, as I have heard them say, would rather be shaved with a sharp razor than a dull one. Especially was he beloved by

the pretty girls along the Connecticut, whose favour he used to court by presents of the best smoking tobacco in his stock; knowing well that the country lasses of New England are generally great performers on pipes. Moreover, as will be seen in the course of my story, the pedlar was inquisitive, and something of a tattler, always itching to hear the news and anxious to tell it again.

After an early breakfast at Morristown, the tobacco pedlar, whose name was Dominicus Pike, had travelled seven miles through a solitary piece of woods, without speaking a word to anybody but himself and his little grey mare. It being nearly seven o'clock, he was as eager to hold a morning gossip as a city shopkeeper to read the morning paper. An opportunity seemed at hand when, after lighting a cigar with a sun-glass, he looked up, and perceived a man coming over the brow of the hill, at the foot of which the pedlar had stopped his green cart. Dominicus watched him as he descended, and noticed that he carried a bundle over his shoulder on the end of a stick, and travelled with a weary, yet determined pace. He did not look as if he had started in the freshness of the morning, but had footed it all night, and meant to do the same all day.

"Good morning, mister," said Dominicus, when within speaking distance. "You go a pretty good jog. What's the latest news at Parker's Falls?"

The man pulled the broad brim of a grey hat over his eyes, and answered, rather suddenly, that he did not come from Parker's Falls, which, as being the limit of his own day's journey, the pedlar had naturally mentioned in his inquiry.

"Well then," rejoined Dominicus Pike, "let's have the latest news where you did come from. I'm not particular about Parker's Falls. Any place will answer."

Being thus importuned, the traveller—who was as ill looking a fellow as one would desire to meet in a solitary piece of woods—appeared to hesitate a little, as if he was either searching his memory for news, or weighing the expediency of telling it. At last, mounting on the step of the cart, he whispered in the ear of Dominicus, though he might have shouted aloud and no other mortal would have heard him.

"I do remember one little trifle of news," said he. "Old Mr. Higginbotham, of Kimballton, was murdered in his orchard, at eight o'clock last night, by an Irishman and a nigger. They strung him up to the branch of a St. Michael's pear-tree, where nobody would find him till the morning."

As soon as this horrible intelligence was communicated, the stranger betook himself to his journey again, with more speed than ever, not even turning his head when Dominicus invited him to smoke a Spanish cigar and relate all the particulars. The pedlar whistled to his mare and went up the hill, pondering on the doleful fate of Mr. Higginbotham whom he had known in the way of trade, having sold him many a bunch of long nines, and a great deal of pigtail, lady's twist, and fig tobacco. He was rather astonished at the rapidity with which the news had spread. Kimballton was nearly sixty miles distant in a straight line; the murder had been perpetrated only at eight o'clock the preceding night; yet Dominicus had heard of it at seven in the morning, when, in all probability, poor Mr. Higginbotham's own family had but just discovered his corpse, hanging on the St. Michael's pear-tree. The stranger on foot must have worn seven-league boots to travel at such a rate.

"Ill news flies fast, they say," thought Dominicus Pike; "but this beats railroads. The fellow ought to be hired to go express with the President's Message."

The difficulty was solved by supposing that the narrator had made a mistake of one day in the date of the occurrence; so that our friend did not hesitate to introduce the story at every tavern and country store along the road, expending a whole bunch of Spanish wrappers among at least twenty horrified audiences. He found himself invariably the first bearer of the intelligence, and was so pestered with questions that he could not avoid filling up the outline, till it became quite a respectable narrative. He met with one piece of corroborative evidence. Mr. Higginbotham was a trader; and a former clerk of his, to whom Dominicus related the facts, testified that the old gentleman was accustomed to return home through the orchard about nightfall, with the money and valuable papers of the store in his pocket. The clerk manifested but little grief at Mr. Higginbotham's catastrophe, hinting, what the pedlar had discovered in his own dealings with him, that he was a crusty old fellow, as close as a vice. His property would descend to a pretty niece who was now keeping school in Kimballton.

What with telling the news for the public good, and driving bargains for his own, Dominicus was so much delayed on the road that he chose to put up at a tavern, about five miles short of Parker's Falls. After supper, lighting one of his prime cigars, he seated himself in the bar-room, and went through the story of the murder, which had grown so fast that it took him half an hour to tell. There were as many as twenty people in the room, nineteen of whom received it all for gospel. But the twentieth was an elderly farmer, who had arrived on horseback a short time before, and was now seated in a corner smoking his pipe. When the story was concluded, he rose up very deliberately, brought his chair right in front of Dominicus, and stared him full in the face, puffing out the vilest tobacco smoke the pedlar had ever smelt.

"Will you make affidavit," demanded he, in the tone of a country justice taking an examination, "that old Squire Higginbotham of Kimballton was murdered in his orchard the night before last, and found hanging on his great pear-tree yesterday morning?"

"I tell the story as I heard it, mister," answered Dominicus, dropping his half-burnt cigar; "I don't say that I saw the thing done. So I can't take my oath that he was murdered exactly in that way."

"But I can take mine," said the farmer, "that if Squire Higginbotham was murdered night before last, I drank a glass of bitters with his ghost this morning. Being a neighbour of mine, he called me into his store, as I was riding by, and treated me, and then asked me to do a little business for him on the road. He didn't seem to know any more about his own murder than I did."

"Why, then, it can't be a fact!" exclaimed Dominicus Pike.

"I guess he'd have mentioned, if it was," said the old farmer; and he removed his chair back to the corner, leaving Dominicus quite down in the mouth.

Here was a sad resurrection of old Mr. Higginbotham! The pedlar had no heart to mingle in the conversation any more, but comforted himself with a glass of gin and water, and went to bed where, all night long, he dreamed of hanging on the St. Michael's pear-tree. To avoid the old farmer (whom he so detested that his suspension would have pleased him better than Mr. Higginbotham's), Dominicus rose in the grey of the morning, put the little mare into the green cart, and trotted swiftly away towards Parker's Falls. The fresh breeze, the dewy road, and the pleasant summer dawn, revived his spirits, and might have encouraged him to repeat the old story had there been anybody awake to hear it. But he met neither ox team, light wagon chaise, horseman, nor foot traveller, till, just as he crossed Salmon River, a man came trudging down to the bridge with a bundle over his shoulder, on the end of a stick.

"Good morning, mister," said the pedlar, reining in his mare. "If you come from Kimballton or that neighbourhood, maybe you can tell me the real fact about this affair of old Mr. Higginbotham. Was the old fellow actually murdered two or three nights ago, by an Irishman and a nigger?"

Dominicus had spoken in too great a hurry to observe, at first, that the stranger himself had a deep tinge of negro blood. On hearing this sudden question, the Ethiopian appeared to change his skin, its yellow hue becoming a ghastly white, while, shaking and stammering, he thus replied:

"No! no! There was no coloured man! It was an Irishman that hanged him last night, at eight o'clock. I came away at seven! His folks can't have looked for him in the orchard yet."

Scarcely had the yellow man spoken, when he interrupted himself, and though he seemed weary enough before, continued his journey at a pace which would have kept the pedlar's mare on a smart trot. Dominicus started after him in great perplexity. If the murder had not been committed till Tuesday night, who was the prophet that had foretold it, in all its circumstances, on Tuesday morning? If Mr. Higginbotham's corpse were not yet discovered by his own family, how came the mulatto, at above thirty miles' distance, to know that he was hanging in the orchard, especially as he had left Kimballton before the unfortunate man was hanged at all? These ambiguous circumstances, with the stranger's surprise and terror, made Dominicus think of raising a hue and cry after him, as an accomplice in the murder; since a murder, it seemed, had really been perpetrated.

"But let the poor devil go," thought the pedlar. "I don't want his black blood on my head; and hanging the nigger wouldn't unhang Mr. Higginbotham. Unhang the old gentleman! It's a sin, I know; but I should hate to have him come to life a second time, and give me the lie!"

With these meditations, Dominicus Pike drove into the street of Parker's Falls, which, as everybody knows, is as thriving a village as three cotton factories and a slitting mill can make it. The machinery was not in motion, and but a few of the shop doors unbarred, when he alighted in the stable yard of the tavern, and made it his first business to order the mare four quarts of oats. His second duty, of course, was to impart Mr. Higginbotham's catastrophe to the hostler. He deemed it advisable, however, not to be too positive as to the date of the direful fact, and also to be uncertain whether it were perpetrated by an Irishman and a mulatto, or by the son of Erin alone. Neither did he profess to relate it on his own authority, or that of any one person; but mentioned it as a report generally diffused.

The story ran through the town like fire among girdled trees, and became so much the universal talk that nobody could tell whence it had originated. Mr. Higginbotham was as well known at Parker's Falls as any citizen of the place, being part owner of the slitting mill, and a considerable stockholder in the cotton factories. The inhabitants felt their own prosperity interested in his fate. Such was the excitement, that the Parker's Falls *Gazette* anticipated its regular day of publication, and came out with half a form of blank paper and a column of double pica emphasized with capitals, and headed HORRID MURDER OF MR. HIGGINBOTHAM! Among other dreadful details, the printed account described the mark of the cord round the dead man's neck, and stated the number of thousand dollars of which he had been robbed; there was much pathos also about the affliction of his niece, who had gone from one fainting fit to another, ever since her uncle was found hanging on the St. Michael's pear-tree with his pockets inside out. The village poet likewise commemorated the young lady's grief in seventeen stanzas of a ballad. The selectmen held a meeting, and, in consideration of Mr. Higginbotham's claims on the town, determined to issue handbills, offering a reward of five hundred dollars for the apprehension of his murderers, and the recovery of the stolen property.

Meanwhile the whole population of Parker's Falls, consisting of shopkeepers, mistresses of boarding-houses, factory girls, millmen, and schoolboys, rushed into the street and kept up such a terrible loquacity as more than compensated for the silence of the cotton machines, which refrained from their usual din out of respect to the deceased. Had Mr. Higginbotham cared about posthumous renown, his untimely ghost would have exulted in this tumult. Our friend Dominicus, in his vanity of heart, forgot his intended precautions, and mounting on the town pump, announced himself as the bearer of the authentic intelligence which had caused so wonderful a sensation. He immediately became the great man of the moment, and had just begun a new edition of the narrative, with a voice like a field preacher, when the mail stage drove into the village street. It had travelled all night, and must have shifted horses at Kimballton at three in the morning.

"Now we shall hear all the particulars," shouted the crowd.

The coach rumbled up to the piazza of the tavern, followed by a thousand people; for if any man had been minding his own business till then, he now left it at sixes and sevens, to hear the news. The pedlar, foremost in the race, discovered two passengers both of whom had been startled from a comfortable nap to find themselves in the centre of a mob. Every man assailing them with separate questions, all propounded at once, the couple were struck speechless, though one was a lawyer and the other a young lady.

"Mr. Higginbotham! Mr. Higginbotham! Tell us the particulars about old Mr. Higginbotham!" bawled the mob. "What is the coroner's verdict? Are the murderers apprehended? Is Mr.

Higginbotham's niece come out of her fainting fits? Mr. Higginbotham! Mr. Higginbotham!!"

The coachman said not a word, except to swear awfully at the hostler for not bringing him a fresh team of horses. The lawyer inside had generally his wits about him even when asleep; the first thing he did, after learning the cause of the excitement, was to produce a large, red pocketbook. Meantime Dominicus Pike, being an extremely polite young man, and also suspecting that a female tongue would tell the story as glibly as a lawyer's, had handed the lady out of the coach. She was a fine, smart girl, now wide awake and bright as a button, and had such a sweet pretty mouth, that Dominicus would almost as lief have heard a love tale from it as a tale of murder.

"Gentlemen and ladies," said the lawyer to the shopkeepers, the millmen, and the factory girls, "I can assure you that some unaccountable mistake, or, more probably, a wilful falsehood, maliciously contrived to injure Mr. Higginbotham's credit, has excited this singular uproar. We passed through Kimballton at three o'clock this morning, and most certainly should have been informed of the murder had any been perpetrated. But I have proof nearly as strong as Mr. Higginbotham's own oral testimony, in the negative. Here is a note relating to a suit of his in the Connecticut courts, which was delivered me from that gentleman himself. I find it dated at ten o'clock last evening."

So saying, the lawyer exhibited the date and signature of the note, which irrefragably proved, either that this perverse Mr. Higginbotham was alive when he wrote it, or—as some deemed the more probable case, of two doubtful ones—that he was so absorbed in worldly business as to continue to transact it even after his death. But unexpected evidence was forthcoming. The young lady, after listening to the pedlar's explanation, merely seized a moment to smooth her gown and put her curls in order, and then appeared at the tavern door, making a modest signal to be heard.

"Good people," said she, "I am Mr. Higginbotham's niece."

A wondering murmur passed through the crowd on beholding her so rosy and bright; that same unhappy niece, whom they had supposed, on the authority of the Parker's Falls *Gazette*, to be lying at death's door in a fainting fit. But some shrewd fellows had doubted, all along, whether a young lady would be quite so desperate at the hanging of a rich old uncle.

"You see," continued Miss Higginbotham, with a smile, "that this strange story is quite unfounded as to myself; and I believe I may affirm it to be equally so in regard to my dear uncle Higginbotham. He has the kindness to give me a home in his house, though I contribute to my own support by teaching a school. I left Kimballton this morning to spend the vacation of commencement week with a friend, about five miles from Parker's Falls. My generous uncle, when he heard me on the stairs, called me to his bedside, and gave me two dollars and fifty cents to pay my stage fare, and another dollar for my extra expenses. He then laid his pocketbook under his pillow, shook hands with me, and advised me to take some biscuit in my bag, instead of breakfasting on the road. I feel confident, therefore, that I left my beloved relative alive, and trust that I shall find him so on my return."

The young lady courtesied at the close of her speech, which was so sensible and well worded, and delivered with such grace and propriety, that everybody thought her fit to be preceptress of the best academy in the State. But a stranger would have supposed that Mr. Higginbotham was an object of abhorrence at Parker's Falls, and that a thanksgiving had been proclaimed for his murder; so excessive was the wrath of the inhabitants on learning their mistake. The millmen resolved to bestow public honours on Dominicus Pike, only hesitating whether to tar and feather him, ride him on a rail, or refresh him with an ablution at the town pump, on the top of which he had declared himself the bearer of the news. The selectmen, by advice of the lawyer, spoke of prosecuting him for a misdemeanour, in circulating unfounded reports, to the great disturbance of the peace of the Commonwealth. Nothing saved Dominicus, either from mob law or a court of justice, but an eloquent appeal made by the young lady in his behalf. Addressing a few words of heartfelt gratitude to his benefactress, he mounted the green cart and rode out of town, under a discharge of artillery from the schoolboys, who found plenty of ammunition in the neighbouring clay pits and mud holes. As he turned his head to exchange a farewell glance with Mr. Higginbotham's niece, a ball, of the consistence of hasty pudding, hit him slap in the mouth, giving him a most grim aspect. His whole person was so bespattered with the like filthy missiles, that he had almost a mind to ride back, and supplicate for the threatened ablution at the town pump; for, though not meant in kindness, it would now have been a deed of charity.

However, the sun shone bright on poor Dominicus, and the mud, an emblem of all stains of undeserved opprobrium, was easily brushed off when dry. Being a funny rogue, his heart soon cheered up; nor could he refrain from a hearty laugh at the uproar which his story had excited. The handbills of the selectmen would cause the commitment of all the vagabonds in the State; the paragraph in the Parker's Falls *Gazette* would be reprinted from Maine to Florida, and perhaps form an item in the London newspapers; and many a miser would tremble for his money bags and life, on learning the catastrophe of Mr. Higginbotham. The pedlar meditated with much fervour on the charms of the young schoolmistress, and swore that Daniel Webster never spoke nor looked so like an angel as Miss Higginbotham, while defending him from the wrathful populace at Parker's Falls.

Dominicus was now on the Kimballton turnpike, having all along determined to visit that place, though business had drawn him out of the most direct road from Morristown. As he approached the scene of the supposed murder, he continued to revolve the circumstances in his mind, and was astonished at the aspect which the whole case assumed. Had nothing occurred to corroborate the story of the first traveller, it might now have been considered as a hoax; but the yellow man was evidently acquainted either with the report or the fact; and there was a mystery in his dismayed and guilty look on being abruptly questioned. When, to this singular combination of incidents, it was added that the rumour tallied exactly with Mr. Higginbotham's character and habits of life; and that he had an orchard, and a St. Michael's pear-tree, near which he always passed at nightfall: the circumstantial evidence appeared so strong that Dominicus doubted whether the autograph produced by the lawyer, or even the niece's direct testimony, ought to be equivalent. Making cautious inquiries along the road, the pedlar further learned that Mr. Higginbotham had in his service an Irishman of doubtful character, whom he had hired without a recommendation, on the score of economy.

"May I be hanged myself," exclaimed Dominicus Pike aloud, on reaching the top of a lonely hill, "if I'll believe old Higginbotham is unhanged till I see him with my own eyes, and hear it from his own mouth! And as he's a real shaver, I'll have the minister or some other responsible man for an indorser."

It was growing dusk when he reached the toll-house on Kimballton turnpike, about a quarter of a mile from the village of this name. His little mare was fast bringing him up with a man on horseback, who trotted through the gate a few rods in advance of him, nodded to the toll-gatherer, and kept on towards the village. Dominicus was acquainted with the tollman, and, while making change, the usual remarks on the weather passed between them.

"I suppose," said the pedlar, throwing back his whiplash, to bring it down like a feather on the mare's flank, "you have not seen anything of old Mr. Higginbotham within a day or two?"

"Yes," answered the toll-gatherer. "He passed the gate just before you drove up, and yonder he rides now, if you can see him through the dusk. He's been to Woodfield this afternoon, attending a sheriff's sale there. The old man generally shakes hands and has a little chat with me; but tonight, he nodded—as if to say, 'Charge my toll,' and jogged on; for wherever he goes, he must always be at home by eight o'clock."

"So they tell me," said Dominicus.

"I never saw a man look so yellow and thin as the squire does," continued the toll-gatherer. "Says I to myself, tonight, he's more like a ghost or an old mummy than good flesh and blood."

The pedlar strained his eyes through the twilight, and could just discern the horseman now far ahead on the village road. He seemed to recognize the rear of Mr. Higginbotham; but, through the evening shadows, and amid the dust from the horse's feet, the figure appeared dim and insubstantial; as if the shape of the mysterious old man were faintly moulded of darkness and grey light. Dominicus shivered.

"Mr. Higginbotham has come back from the other world, by way of the Kimballton turnpike," thought he.

He shook the reins and rode forward, keeping about the same distance in the rear of the grey old shadow, till the latter was concealed by a bend of the road. On reaching this point, the pedlar no longer saw the man on horseback, but found himself at the head of the village street, not far from a number of stores and two taverns, clustered round the meeting-house steeple. On his left were a stone wall and a gate, the boundary of a wood-lot, beyond which lay an orchard, farther still, a mowing field, and last of all, a house. These were the premises of Mr. Higginbotham, whose dwelling stood beside the old highway, but had been left in the background by the Kimballton turnpike. Dominicus knew the place; and the little mare stopped short by instinct; for he was not conscious of tightening the reins.

"For the soul of me, I cannot get by this gate!" said he, trembling. "I never shall be my own man again, till I see whether Mr. Higginbotham is hanging on the St. Michael's pear-tree!"

He leaped from the cart, gave the rein a turn round the gatepost, and ran along the green path of the wood-lot as if Old Nick were chasing behind. Just then the village clock tolled eight, and as each deep stroke fell, Dominicus gave a fresh bound and flew faster than before, till, dim in the solitary centre of the orchard, he saw the fated pear-tree. One great branch stretched from the old contorted trunk across the path, and threw the darkest shadow on that one spot. But something seemed to struggle beneath the branch!

The pedlar had never pretended to more courage than befits a man of peaceable occupation, nor could he account for his valour on this awful emergency. Certain it is, however, that he rushed forward, prostrated a sturdy Irishman with the butt end of his whip, and found—not indeed hanging on the St. Michael's pear-tree, but trembling beneath it, with a halter round his neck—the old, identical Mr. Higginbotham!

"Mr. Higginbotham," said Dominicus tremulously, "you're an honest man, and I'll take your word for it. Have you been hanged or not?"

If the riddle be not already guessed, a few words will explain the simple machinery by which this "coming event" was made to "cast its shadow before." Three men had plotted the robbery and murder of Mr. Higginbotham; two of them, successively, lost courage and fled, each delaying the crime one night by their disappearance; the third was in the act of perpetration, when a champion, blindly obeying the call of fate, like the heroes of old romance, appeared in the person of Dominicus Pike.

It only remains to say, that Mr. Higginbotham took the pedlar into high favour, sanctioned his addresses to the pretty schoolmistress, and settled his whole property on their children, allowing themselves the interest. In due time, the old gentleman capped the climax of his favours, by dying a Christian death, in bed, since which melancholy event Dominicus Pike has removed from Kimballton, and established a large tobacco manufactory in my native village.

Lochinvar

Sir Walter Scott
(1771–1832)

When I was a young lad in school, we used to read a lot of Sir Walter Scott—poems like "Lochinvar" and novels like Waverley *and* Ivanhoe. *Scott seems to be out of fashion these days, but I still think his poems have an appealing energy to them, and I love the way they conjure up that wild country of feuding clans and beautiful, rosy-cheeked maidens. And you can't help but read this poem with a Scottish "burr" in your voice. Just try…*

 young Lochinvar is come out
        of the west,
Through all the wide Border his
        steed was the best;
And save his good broadsword
        he weapons had none,
He rode all unarmed, and he
        rode all alone.
So faithful in love, and so dauntless in war,
There never was knight like the young Lochinvar.

He stayed not for brake, and he stopped not for stone,
He swam the Eske river where ford there was none;
But ere he alighted at Netherby gate,
The bride had consented, the gallant came late:
For a laggard in love, and a dastard in war,

Was to wed the fair Ellen of brave Lochinvar.

So boldly he entered the Netherby Hall,
Among bride's-men, and kinsmen, and brothers, and all:
Then spoke the bride's father, his hand on the sword,
(For the poor craven bridegroom said never a word,)
"O come ye in peace here, or come ye in war,
Or to dance at our bridal, young Lord Lochinvar?"

"I long wooed your daughter, my suit you denied;—
Love swells like the Solway, but ebbs like its tide—
And now am I come, with this lost love of mine,
To lead but one measure, drink one cup of wine.
There are maidens in Scotland more lovely by far,
That would gladly be bride to the young Lochinvar."

The bride kissed the goblet: the knight took it up,
He quaffed off the wine, and he threw down the cup.
She looked down to blush, and she looked up to sigh,
With a smile on her lips, and a tear in her eye.
He took her soft hand, ere her mother could bar,—
"Now tread we a measure!" said young Lochinvar.

So stately his form, and so lovely her face,
That never a hall such a galliard did grace;
While her mother did fret, and her father did fume,
And the bridegroom stood dangling his bonnet and
          plume;
And the bride-maidens whispered, "'Twere better by far,
To have matched our fair cousin with young Lochinvar."

One touch to her hand, and one word in her ear,
When they reached the hall-door, and the charger stood
          near;
So light to the croup the fair lady he swung,
So light to the saddle before her he sprung!
"She is won! we are gone, over bank, bush, and scaur;

They'll have fleet steeds that follow," quoth young
      Lochinvar.
There was mounting 'mong Græmes of the Netherby clan;
Forsters, Fenwicks, and Musgraves, they rode and they
      ran:
There was racing and chasing, on Cannobie Lee,
But the lost bride of Netherby ne'er did they see.
So daring in love, and so dauntless in war,
Have ye e'er heard of gallant like young Lochinvar?

THE GRIFFIN AND THE MINOR CANON

Frank Stockton
(1834–1902)

Frank Stockton was born smack in the middle of a very large family: he had six older siblings and six younger ones. He entertained his brothers and sisters by telling them fairy tales of his own devising, but he insisted that his supernatural creatures behave with some degree of rationality.

The Griffin in the following story is certainly a thoughtful creature, although most people have a hard time seeing through his forbidding exterior. And he says some very wise things. I am especially fond of his comment that "If some things were different, other things would be otherwise." Hmmm. I'll have to think about that...

ver the great door of an old, old church, which stood in a quiet town of a far-away land, there was carved in stone the figure of a large griffin. The old-time sculptor had done his work with great care, but the image he had made was not a pleasant one to look at. It had a large head, with enormous open mouth and savage teeth. From its back arose great wings, armed with sharp hooks and prongs. It had stout legs in front, with projecting claws, but there were no legs behind, the body running out into a long and powerful tail, finished off at the end with a barbed point. This tail was coiled up under him, the end sticking up just back of his wings.

The sculptor, or the people who had ordered this stone figure, had evidently been very much pleased with it, for little copies of it, also in stone, had been placed here and there along the sides of the church, not very far from the ground, so that people could easily look at them and ponder on their curious forms. There were a great many other sculptures on the outside of this church—saints, martyrs, grotesque heads of men, beasts, and birds, as well as those of other creatures which cannot be named, because nobody knows exactly what they were. But none were so curious and interesting as the great griffin over the door and the little griffins on the sides of the church.

A long, long distance from the town, in the midst of dreadful wilds scarcely known to man, there dwelt the Griffin whose image had been put up over the church door. In some way or other the old-time sculptor had seen him, and afterwards, to the best of his memory, had copied his figure in stone. The Griffin had never known this until, hundreds of years afterwards, he heard from a bird, from a wild animal, or in some manner which it is not easy to find out, that there was a likeness of him on the old church in the distant town.

Now, this Griffin had no idea whatever how he looked. He had never seen a mirror, and the streams where he lived were so turbulent and violent that a quiet piece of water, which would reflect the image of anything looking into it, could not be found. Being, as far as could be ascertained, the very last of his race, he had never seen another griffin. Therefore it was that, when he heard of this stone image of himself, he became very anxious to know what he looked like, and at last he determined to go to the old church and see for himself what manner of being he was. So he started off from the dreadful wilds, and flew on and on until he came to the countries inhabited by men, where his appearance in the air created great consternation. But he alighted nowhere, keeping up a steady flight until he reached the suburbs of the town which had his image on its church. Here, late in the afternoon, he alighted in a green meadow by the side of a brook, and stretched himself on the grass to rest. His great wings were tired, for he had not made such a long flight in a century or more.

The news of his coming spread quickly over the town, and the people, frightened nearly out of their wits by the arrival of so extraordinary a visitor, fled into their houses and shut themselves up. The Griffin called loudly for someone to come to him; but the more he called, the more afraid the people were to show themselves. At length he saw two labourers hurrying to their homes through the fields, and in a terrible voice he commanded them to stop. Not daring to disobey, the men stood, trembling.

"What is the matter with you all?" cried the Griffin. "Is there not a man in your town who is brave enough to speak to me?"

"I think," said one of the labourers, his voice shaking so that his words could hardly be understood, "that—perhaps—the Minor Canon—would come."

"Go, call him, then!" said the Griffin. "I want to see him."

The Minor Canon, who filled a subordinate position in the old church, had just finished the afternoon service, and was coming out of a side door, with three aged women who had formed the weekday congregation. He was a young man of a kind disposition, and very anxious to do good to the people of the town. Apart from his duties in the church, where he conducted services every weekday, he visited the sick and the poor; counselled and assisted persons who were in trouble, and taught a school composed entirely of the bad children in the town, with whom nobody else would have anything to do. Whenever the people wanted something difficult done for them, they always went to the Minor Canon. Thus it was that the labourer thought of the young priest when he found that someone must come and speak to the Griffin.

The Minor Canon had not heard of the strange event, which was known to the whole town except himself and the three old women, and when he was informed of it, and was told that the Griffin had asked to see him, he was greatly amazed and frightened.

"Me!" he exclaimed. "He has never heard of me! What should he want with *me*?"

"Oh, you must go instantly!" cried the two men. "He is very angry now because he has been kept waiting so long, and nobody knows what may happen if you don't hurry to him."

The poor Minor Canon would rather have had his hand cut off than to go out to meet an angry griffin; but he felt that it was his duty to go, for it would be a woeful thing if injury should come to the people of the town because he was not brave enough to obey the summons of the Griffin; so, pale and frightened, he started off.

"Well," said the Griffin as soon as the young man came near, "I am glad to see that there is someone who has the courage to come to me."

The Minor Canon did not feel very courageous, but he bowed his head.

"Is this the town," said the Griffin, "where there is a church with a likeness of myself over one of the doors?"

The Minor Canon looked at the frightful creature before him, and saw that it was, without doubt, exactly like the stone image on the church. "Yes," he said, "you are right."

"Well, then," said the Griffin, "will you take me to it? I wish very much to see it."

The Minor Canon instantly thought that if the Griffin entered the town without the people knowing what he came for, some of them would probably be frightened to death, and so he sought to gain time to prepare their minds.

"It is growing dark now," he said, very much afraid, as he spoke, that his words might enrage the Griffin, "and objects on the front of the church cannot be seen clearly. It will be better to wait until morning, if you wish to get a good view of the stone image of yourself."

"That will suit me very well," said the Griffin. "I see you are a man of good sense. I am tired, and I will take a nap here on this soft grass, while I cool my tail in the little stream that runs near me. The end of my tail gets red-hot when I am angry or excited, and it is quite warm now. So you may go; but be sure and come early tomorrow morning, and show me the way to the church."

The Minor Canon was glad enough to take his leave, and hurried into the town. In front of the church he found a great many people assembled to hear his report of his interview with the

Griffin. When they found that he had not come to spread ruin and devastation, but simply to see his stony likeness on the church, they showed neither relief nor gratification, but began to upbraid the Minor Canon for consenting to conduct the creature into the town.

"What could I do?" cried the young man. "If I should not bring him he would come himself, and perhaps end by setting fire to the town with his red-hot tail."

Still the people were not satisfied, and a great many plans were proposed to prevent the Griffin from coming into the town. Some elderly persons urged that the young men should go out and kill him. But the young men scoffed at such a ridiculous idea. Then someone said that it would be a good thing to destroy the stone image, so that the Griffin would have no excuse for entering the town. This proposal was received with such favour that many of the people ran for hammers, chisels, and crowbars with which to tear down and break up the stone griffin. But the Minor Canon resisted this plan with all the strength of his mind and body. He assured the people that this action would enrage the Griffin beyond measure, for it would be impossible to conceal from him that his image had been destroyed during the night.

But they were so determined to break up the stone griffin that the Minor Canon saw that there was nothing for him to do but to stay there and protect it. All night he walked up and down in front of the church door, keeping away the men who brought ladders by which they might mount to the great stone griffin and knock it to pieces with their hammers and crowbars. After many hours the people were obliged to give up their attempts, and went home to sleep. But the Minor Canon remained at his post till early morning, and then he hurried away to the field where he had left the Griffin.

The monster had just awakened, and rising to his forelegs and shaking himself, he said that he was ready to go into the town. The Minor Canon, therefore, walked back, the Griffin flying slowly through the air at a short distance above the head of his guide. Not a person was to be seen in the streets, and they proceeded directly to the front of the church, where the Minor

Canon pointed out the stone griffin.

The real Griffin settled down in the little square before the church and gazed earnestly at his sculptured likeness. For a long time he looked at it. First he put his head on one side, and then he put it on the other. Then he shut his right eye and gazed with his left, after which he shut his left eye and gazed with his right. Then he moved a little to one side and looked at the image, then he moved the other way. After a while he said to the Minor Canon, who had been standing by all this time:

"It is, it must be, an excellent likeness! That breadth between the eyes, that expansive forehead, those massive jaws! I feel that it must resemble me. If there is any fault to find with it, it is that the neck seems a little stiff. But that is nothing. It is an admirable likeness—admirable!"

The Griffin sat looking at his image all the morning and all the afternoon. The Minor Canon had been afraid to go away and leave him, and had hoped all through the day that he would soon be satisfied with his inspection and fly away home. But by evening the poor young man was utterly exhausted, and felt that he must eat and sleep. He frankly admitted this fact to the Griffin, and asked him if he would not like something to eat. He said this because he felt obliged in politeness to do so; but as soon as he had spoken the words, he was seized with dread lest the monster should demand half a dozen babies, or some tempting repast of that kind.

"Oh, no," said the Griffin, "I never eat between the equinoxes. At the vernal and at the autumnal equinox I take a good meal, and that lasts me for half a year. I am extremely regular in my habits, and do not think it healthful to eat at odd times. But if you need food, go and get it, and I will return to the soft grass where I slept last night, and take another nap."

The next day the Griffin came again to the little square before the old church, and remained there until evening steadfastly regarding the stone griffin over the door. The Minor Canon came once or twice to look at him, and the Griffin seemed very glad to see him. But the young clergyman could not stay as he had done before, for he had many duties to perform. Nobody went to the church, but the people came to the Minor Canon's house, and anxiously asked him how long the Griffin was going to stay.

"I do not know," he answered, "but I think he will soon be satisfied with looking at his stone likeness, and then he will go away."

But the Griffin did not go away. Morning after morning he went to the church, but after a time he did not stay there all day. He seemed to have taken a great fancy to the Minor Canon, and followed him about as he pursued his various avocations. He would wait for him at the side door of the church, for the Minor Canon held services every day, morning and evening, though nobody came now. "If anyone should come," he said to himself, "I must be found at my post." When the young man came out, the Griffin would accompany him in his visits to the sick and the poor, and would often look into the windows of the schoolhouse where the Minor Canon was teaching his unruly scholars. All the other schools were closed, but the parents of the Minor Canon's scholars forced them to go to school, because they were so bad they could not endure them all day at home—griffin or no griffin. But it must be said they generally behaved very well when that great monster sat up on his tail and looked in at the school-room window.

When it was perceived that the Griffin showed no sign of going away, all the people who were able to do so, left the town. The canons and the higher officers of the church had fled away during the first day of the Griffin's visit, leaving behind only the Minor Canon and some of the men who opened the doors and swept the church. All the citizens who could afford it shut up their houses and travelled to distant parts, and only the working-people and the poor were left behind. After some days these ventured to go about and attend to their business, for if they did not work they would starve. They were getting a little used to seeing the Griffin, and having been told that he did not eat between equinoxes, they did not feel so much afraid of him as before.

Day by day the Griffin became more and more attached to the Minor Canon. He kept near him a great part of the time, and often spent the night in front of the little house where the young clergyman lived alone. This strange companionship was often burdensome to the Minor Canon. But, on the other hand, he could not deny that he derived a great deal of benefit and instruction from it. The Griffin had lived for hundreds of years, and had seen much, and he told the Minor Canon many wonderful things.

"It is like reading an old book," said the young clergyman to himself. "But how many books I would have had to read before I would have found out what the Griffin has told me about the earth, the air, the water, about minerals, and metals, and growing things, and all the wonders of the world!"

Thus the summer went on, and drew toward its close. And now the people of the town began to be very much troubled again.

"It will not be long," they said, "before the autumnal equinox is here, and then that monster will want to eat. He will be dreadfully hungry, for he has taken so much exercise since his last meal. He will devour our children. Without doubt, he will eat them all. What is to be done?"

To this question no one could give an answer, but all agreed that the Griffin must not be allowed to remain until the approaching equinox. After talking over the matter a great deal, a crowd of the people went to the Minor Canon, at a time when the Griffin was not with him.

"It is all your fault," they said, "that that monster is among us. You brought him here, and you ought to see that he goes away. It is only on your account that he stays here at all, for, although he visits his image every day, he is with you the greater part of the time. If you were not here he would not stay. It is your duty to go away, and then he will follow you, and we shall be free from the dreadful danger which hangs over us."

"Go away!" cried the Minor Canon, greatly grieved at being spoken to in such a way. "Where shall I go? If I go to some other town, shall I not take this trouble there? Have I a right to do that?"

"No," said the people, "you must not go to any other town. There is no town far enough away. You must go to the dreadful wilds where the Griffin lives, and then he will follow you and stay there."

They did not say whether or not they expected the Minor Canon to stay there also, and he did not ask them anything about it. He bowed his head, and went into his house to think. The more he thought, the more clear it became to his mind that it was his duty to go away, and thus free the town from the presence of the Griffin.

That evening he packed a leather bag full of bread and meat, and early the next morning he set out on his journey to the dreadful wilds. It was a long, weary, and doleful journey, especially after he had gone beyond the habitations of men; but the Minor Canon kept on bravely and never faltered. The way was longer than he had expected, and his provisions soon grew so scanty that he was obliged to eat but a little every day; but he kept up his courage, and pressed on, and after many days of toilsome travel he reached the dreadful wilds.

When the Griffin found that the Minor Canon had left the town, he seemed sorry, but showed no disposition to go and look for him. After a few days had passed, he became much annoyed, and asked some of the people where the Minor Canon had gone. But although the citizens had been so anxious that the young clergyman should go to the dreadful wilds, thinking that the Griffin would immediately follow him, they were now afraid to mention the Minor Canon's destination, for the monster seemed angry already, and if he should suspect their trick, he would doubtless become very much enraged. So everyone said he did not know, and the Griffin wandered about disconsolate. One morning he looked into the Minor Canon's schoolhouse, which was always empty now, and thought that it was a shame that everything should suffer on account of the young man's absence.

"It does not matter so much about the church," he said, "for nobody went there. But it is a pity about the school. I think I will teach it myself until he returns."

It was the hour for opening the school, and the Griffin went inside and pulled the rope which rang the school bell. Some of the children who heard the bell ran in to see what was the matter, supposing it to be a joke of one of their companions. But when they saw the Griffin they stood astonished and scared.

"Go tell the other scholars," said the monster, "that school is about to open, and that if they are not all here in ten minutes I shall come after them."

In seven minutes every scholar was in place.

Never was seen such an orderly school. Not a boy or girl moved or uttered a whisper. The Griffin climbed into the master's seat, his wide wings spread on each side of him, because he could not lean back in his chair while they stuck out behind, and his great tail coiled around in front of the desk, the barbed end sticking up, ready to tap any boy or girl who might misbehave. The Griffin now addressed the scholars, telling them that he intended to teach them while their master was away. In speaking he endeavoured to imitate, as far as possible, the mild and gentle tones of the Minor Canon, but it must be admitted that in this he was not very successful. He had paid a good deal of attention to the studies of the school, and he determined not to attempt to teach them anything new, but to review them in what they had been studying. So he called up the various classes, and questioned them upon their previous lessons. The children racked their brains to remember what they had learned. They were so afraid of the Griffin's displeasure that they recited as they had never recited before. One of the boys, far down in his class, answered so well that the Griffin was astonished.

"I should think you would be at the head," said he. "I am sure you have never been in the habit of reciting so well. Why is this?"

"Because I did not choose to take the trouble," said the boy, trembling in his boots. He felt obliged to speak the truth, for all the children thought that the great eyes of the Griffin could see right through them, and that he would know when they told a falsehood.

"You ought to be ashamed of yourself," said the Griffin. "Go down to the very tail of the class, and if you are not at the head in two days, I shall know the reason why."

The next afternoon this boy was number one.

It was astonishing how much these children now learned of what they had been studying. It was as if they had been educated over again. The Griffin used no severity toward them, but there was a look about him which made them unwilling to go to bed until they were sure they knew their lessons for the next day.

The Griffin now thought that he ought to visit the sick and the poor, and he began to go about the town for this purpose. The effect upon the sick was miraculous. All except those who were very ill indeed, jumped from their beds when they heard he was coming, and declared themselves quite well. To those who could not get up he gave herbs and roots, which none of them had ever before thought of as medicines, but which the Griffin had seen used in various parts of the world, and most of them recovered. But, for all that, they afterwards said that no matter what happened to them, they hoped that they should never again have such a doctor coming to their bedsides, feeling their pulses and looking at their tongues.

As for the poor, they seemed to have utterly disappeared. All those who had depended upon charity for their daily bread were now at work in some way or other, many of them offering to do odd jobs for their neighbours just for the sake of their meals—a thing which before had been seldom heard of in the town. The Griffin could find no one who needed his assistance.

The summer now passed, and the autumnal equinox was rapidly approaching. The Griffin showed no signs of going away, but seemed to have settled himself permanently among them. In a short time the day for his semi-annual meal would arrive, and then what would happen? The monster would certainly be very hungry, and would devour all their children.

Now they greatly regretted and lamented that they had sent away the Minor Canon. He was the only one on whom they could have depended in this trouble, for he could talk freely with the Griffin, and so find out what could be done. But it would not do to be inactive. Some step must be taken immediately. A meeting of the citizens was called, and two old men were appointed to go and talk to the Griffin. They were instructed to offer to prepare a splendid dinner for him on equinox day—one which would entirely satisfy his hunger. They would offer him the fattest mutton, the most tender beef, fish and game of various sorts, and anything of the kind he might fancy. If none of these suited, they were to mention that there was an orphan asylum in the next town.

"Anything would be better," said the citizens, "than to have our dear children devoured."

The old men went to the Griffin, but their propositions were not received with favour.

"From what I have seen of the people of this town," said the monster, "I do not think I could relish anything which was prepared by them. They appear to be all cowards, and, therefore, mean and selfish. As for eating one of them, old or young, I could not think of it for a moment. In fact, there was only one creature in the whole place for whom I could have had any appetite, and that is the Minor Canon, who has gone away. He was brave, and good, and honest, and I think I should have relished him."

"Ah!" said one of the old men, very politely, "in that case I wish we had not sent him to the dreadful wilds!"

"What!" cried the Griffin. "What do you mean? Explain instantly what you are talking about!"

The old man, terribly frightened at what he had said, was obliged to tell how the Minor Canon had been sent away by the people, in the hope that the Griffin might be induced to follow him.

When the monster heard this he became furiously angry. He dashed away from the old men and, spreading his wings, flew backward and forward over the town. He was so much excited that his tail became red-hot, and glowed like a meteor against the evening sky. When at last he settled down in the little field where he usually rested, and thrust his tail into the brook, the steam arose like a cloud, and the water of the stream ran hot through the town. The citizens were greatly frightened, and bitterly blamed the old man for telling about the Minor Canon.

"It is plain," they said, "that the Griffin intended at last to go and look for him, and we should have been saved. Now who can tell what misery you have brought upon us?"

The Griffin did not remain long in the little field. As soon as his tail was cool he flew to the town hall and rang the bell. The citizens knew that they were expected to come there, and although they were afraid to go, they were still more afraid to stay away, and they crowded into the hall. The Griffin was on the platform at one end, flapping his wings and walking up and down, and the end of his tail was still so warm that it slightly scorched the boards as he dragged it after him.

When everybody who was able to come was there, the Griffin stood still and addressed the meeting.

"I have had a contemptible opinion of you," he said, "ever since I discovered what cowards you are, but I had no idea that you were so ungrateful, selfish, and cruel as I now find you to be. Here was your Minor Canon, who laboured day and night for your good, and thought of nothing else but how he might bene-fit you and make you happy; and as soon as you imagine your-selves threatened with a danger—for well I know you are dread-fully afraid of me—you send him off, caring not whether he returns or perishes, hoping thereby to save yourselves. Now, I had conceived a great liking for that young man, and had intend-ed, in a day or two, to go and look him up. But I have changed my mind about him. I shall go and find him, but I shall send him back here to live among you, and I intend that he shall enjoy the reward of his labour and his sacrifices. Go, some of you, to the officers of the church, who so cowardly ran away when I first came here, and tell them never to return to this town under penal-ty of death. And if, when your Minor Canon comes back to you, you do not bow yourselves before him, put him in the highest place among you, and serve and honour him all his life, beware of my terrible vengeance! There were only two good things in this town: the Minor Canon and the stone image of myself over your church door. One of these you have sent away, and the other I shall carry away myself."

With these words he dismissed the meeting; and it was time, for the end of his tail had become so hot that there was danger of its setting fire to the building.

The next morning the Griffin came to the church, and tearing the stone image of himself from its fastenings over the great door, he grasped it with his powerful forelegs and flew up into the air.

Then, after hovering over the town for a moment, he gave his tail an angry shake, and took up his flight to the dreadful wilds. When he reached this desolate region, he set the stone griffin upon a ledge of a rock which rose in front of the dismal cave he called his home. There the image occupied a position somewhat similar to that it had had over the church door; and the Griffin, panting with the exertion of carrying such an enormous load to so great a distance, lay down upon the ground, and regarded it with much satisfaction. When he felt somewhat rested he went to look for the Minor Canon. He found the young man, weak and half starved, lying under the shadow of a rock. After picking him up and carrying him to his cave, the Griffin flew away to a distant marsh, where he procured some roots and herbs which he well knew were strengthening and beneficial to man, though he had never tasted them himself. After eating these the Minor Canon was greatly revived, and sat up and listened while the Griffin told him what had happened in the town.

"Do you know," said the monster, when he had finished, "that I have had, and still have, a great liking for you?"

"I am very glad to hear it," said the Minor Canon, with his usual politeness.

"I am not at all sure that you would be," said the Griffin, "if you thoroughly understood the state of the case, but we will not consider that now. If some things were different, other things would be otherwise. I have been so enraged by discovering the manner in which you have been treated that I have determined that you shall at last enjoy the rewards and honours to which you are entitled. Lie down and have a good sleep, and then I will take you back to the town."

As he heard these words, a look of trouble came over the young man's face.

"You need not give yourself any anxiety," said the Griffin, "about my return to the town. I shall not remain there. Now that I have that admirable likeness of myself in front of my cave, where I can sit at my leisure and gaze upon its noble features and magnificent proportions, I have no wish to see that abode of cowardly and selfish people."

The Minor Canon, relieved from his fears, lay back, and dropped into a doze; and when he was sound asleep, the Griffin took him up and carried him back to the town. He arrived just before daybreak, and putting the young man gently on the grass in the little field where he himself used to rest, the monster, without having been seen by any of the people, flew back to his home.

When the Minor Canon made his appearance in the morning among the citizens, the enthusiasm and cordiality with which he was received were truly wonderful. He was taken to a house which had been occupied by one of the banished high officers of the place, and everyone was anxious to do all that could be done for his health and comfort. The people crowded into the church when he held services, so that the three old women who used to be his weekday congregation could not get to the best seats, which they had always been in the habit of taking; and the parents of the bad children determined to reform them at home, in order that he might be spared the trouble of keeping up his former school. The Minor Canon was appointed to the highest office of the old church, and before he died he became a bishop.

During the first years after his return from the dreadful wilds, the people of the town looked up to him as a man to whom they were bound to do honour and reverence. But they often, also, looked up to the sky to see if there were any signs of the Griffin coming back. However, in the course of time they learned to honour and reverence their former Minor Canon without the fear of being punished if they did not do so.

But they need never have been afraid of the Griffin. The autumnal equinox day came round, and the monster ate nothing. If he could not have the Minor Canon, he did not care for anything. So, lying down with his eyes fixed upon the great stone griffin, he gradually declined, and died. It was a good thing for some of the people of the town that they did not know this.

If you should ever visit the old town, you would still see the little griffins on the sides of the church, but the great stone griffin that was over the door is gone.

The Elixir of Father Gaucher

Alphonse Daudet
(1840–1897)

What a genius of the short story was Alphonse Daudet! In his remarkable collection Lettres de mon moulin (Letters from My Windmill), *he offers a group of stories truly breathtaking in their scope and understanding of human nature. Unlike his compatriot Maupassant, whose stories are often heavily ironic and very dark, Daudet always looks at his characters with the utmost compassion and humour—as in the following account of a charmingly flawed monk.*

rink this, neighbour, and tell me what you think of it."

And drop by drop, with the painstaking care of a lapidary counting pearls, the curé of Gravenson poured out for me two fingers of a golden-green, warm, sparkling, exquisite liqueur. My stomach was as if bathed in sunlight.

"This is Father Gaucher's elixir, the joy and health of our Provence," said the worthy man, with a triumphant air; "it is made at the convent of Prémontrés, two leagues from your mill. Isn't it better than all the chartreuses on earth? And if you knew how interesting the story of this elixir is! Listen."

Thereupon, as artlessly as possible, without the slightest tinge of irony, in that parsonage dining-room, so placid and calm, with its *Road to the Cross* in tiny pictures, and its pretty light curtains ironed like surplices, the abbé began a somewhat sceptical and irreverent anecdote, after the fashion of a tale of Erasmus or d'Assoucy.

"Twenty years ago, the Prémontrés, or the White Fathers, as we Provençals call them, had fallen into utter destitution. If you had seen their convent in those days, it would have made your heart ache.

"The high wall, the Pacôme Tower, were falling in pieces. All around the grass-grown cloisters, the pillars were cracked, the stone saints crumbling in their recesses. Not a stained-glass window whole, not a door that would close. In the courtyards, in the chapels, the wind from the Rhône blew as it blows in Camargue, extinguishing the candles, breaking the leaden sashes of the windows, spilling the water from the holy-water vessels. But the saddest of all was the convent belfry, silent as an empty dovecote; and the fathers, in default of money to buy a bell, were obliged to ring for matins with clappers of almond-wood!

"Poor White Fathers! I can see them now, in the procession on Corpus Christi, pacing sadly along in their patched hoods, pale and thin, fed on pumpkins and watermelons; and behind them monseigneur the abbé, marching with downcast head, ashamed to exhibit in the sunlight his tarnished crook and his worm-eaten mitre of white wool. The ladies of the fraternity wept with compassion in the ranks, and the stout banner-bearers whispered sneeringly to one another as they pointed to the poor monks:

"'The starlings grow thin when they fly in flocks.'

"The fact is, the unfortunate White Fathers had reached the point where they asked themselves if they would not do better to fly out into the world and to seek pasturage each for himself.

"Now, one day when this grave question was being discussed in the chapter, the prior was informed that Brother Gaucher desired to be heard in the council. I must say for your information that this Brother Gaucher was the drover of the convent; that is to say, he passed his days waddling from arch to arch through the cloister, driving before him two consumptive cows, which tried to find grass between the cracks of the flagstones. Supported until he was twelve years old by an old madwoman of the Baux country, called Aunt Bégon, then taken in by the monks, the wretched drover had never been able to learn anything except to drive his beasts and to repeat his paternoster; and even that he said in Provençal, for his brain was thick and his mind as dull as a leaden dagger. A fervent Christian, however, although somewhat visionary, comfortable in his haircloth shirt, and inflicting discipline upon himself, with sturdy conviction, and such arms!

"When they saw him come into the chapter-hall, simple and stupid of aspect, saluting the assemblage with a leg thrown back, prior, canons, steward, and everybody began to laugh. That was always the effect produced by that good-natured face with its grizzly, goatlike beard and its slightly erratic eyes, whenever it appeared anywhere; so that Brother Gaucher was not disturbed thereby.

"'Reverend fathers,' he said in a wheedling voice, playing with his chaplet of olive-stones, 'it is quite true that empty casks make the best music. Just imagine that, by dint of cudgelling my poor brain, which was already so hollow, I believe that I have thought out a way to help us out of our poverty.

"'This is how. You know Aunt Bégon, that worthy woman who took care of me when I was small—God rest her soul, the old hag! she used to sing some very vile songs after drinking. I must tell you then, reverend fathers, that Aunt Bégon, in her lifetime, knew as much about the mountain herbs as an old Corsican blackbird, and more. In fact, towards the end of her life, she compounded an incomparable elixir by mixing five or six kinds of simples that we picked together in the mountains. That was a good many years ago; but I believe that with the aid of St. Augustine and the permission of our worshipful abbé, I might, by careful search, discover the composition of that mysterious elixir. Then we should only have to bottle it and sell it at a rather high price, to enable the community to get rich as nicely as you please, like our brothers of La Trappe and La Grande—'

"He was not allowed to finish. The prior sprang to his feet and fell upon his neck. The canons seized his hands. The steward, even more deeply moved than all the rest, kissed respectfully the ragged edge of his cowl. Then they all returned to their chairs to deliberate; and the chapter decided on the spot that the cows should be entrusted to Brother Thrasybule, so that Brother Gaucher might devote himself exclusively to the compounding of his elixir.

"How did the excellent monk succeed in discovering Aunt Bégon's recipe? At the price of what efforts, or what vigils? History does not say. But this much is sure, that after six months the elixir of the White Fathers was very popular. Throughout the Comtat, in all the Arles country, there was not a farmhouse, not a granary, which had not in the depths of its buttery, amid the bottles of mulled wine and the jars of olives *à la picholine*, a little jug of brown earthenware, sealed with the arms of Provence, and with a monk in a trance on a silver label. Thanks to the popularity of its elixir, the convent of the Prémontrés grew rich very rapidly. The Pacôme Tower was rebuilt. The prior had a new mitre, the church some pretty stained windows; and in the fine openwork of the belfry, a whole legion of bells, large and small, burst forth one fine Easter morning, jingling and chiming with all their might.

"As for Brother Gaucher, that unfortunate lay brother, whose rustic manners amused the chapter so much, was never spoken of in the convent. Henceforth they only knew the Reverend Father Gaucher, a man of brains and of great learning, who lived completely apart from the trivial and multifarious occupations of the cloister, and was shut up all day in his distillery, while thirty monks hunted the mountain for him, seeking fragrant herbs. That distillery which no one, not even the prior, had the right to enter, was an old abandoned chapel, at the end of the canons' garden. The simplicity of the worthy fathers had transformed it into something mysterious and redoubtable; and if by chance some audacious and inquisitive young monk happened to get as far as the rosework of the doorway, he retreated very quickly, terrified by the aspect of Father Gaucher, with his sorcerer's beard, leaning over his furnaces, scales in hand; and all about him retorts of red sandstone, huge alembics, serpentine glasses, a whole strange outfit, flaming as if bewitched, in the red gleam of the stained-glass.

"At nightfall, when the last Angelus rang, the door of that abode of mystery would open softly, and the father would betake himself to the church for the evening service. You should have seen the welcome that he received when he passed through the monastery! The brethren drew up in two lines for him to pass. They said to one another:

"'Hush! he knows the secret!'

"The steward followed him and spoke to him with downcast eyes. Amid all this adulation, the father walked along, mopping his forehead, his broad-brimmed, three-cornered hat placed on the back of his head like a halo, glancing with an air of condescension at the great courtyards full of orange-trees, the blue roofs surmounted by new weathervanes; and, in the cloister, glaringly white between the gracefully carved pillars, the monks, newly dressed, marching two by two with placid faces.

"'They owe all this to me!' the father would say to himself; and every time that thought caused his bosom to swell with pride.

"The poor man was well punished for it, as you will see.

"Imagine that one evening, during the service, he arrived in the church in a state of extraordinary excitement: red-faced, breathless, his hood awry, and so perturbed that when he took his holy-water he wet his sleeves to the elbow. They thought at first that his excitement was due to being late; but when they saw him make profound reverences to the organ and the galleries instead of saluting the main altar, when they saw him rush through the church like a gust of wind, wander about the choir for five minutes looking for his stall, and, when once seated, bow to the right and left with a beatific smile, a murmur of amazement ran through the three naves. From breviary to breviary the monks whispered:

"'What can be the matter with our Father Gaucher? What can be the matter with our Father Gaucher?'

"Twice the prior, in his annoyance, struck his crook on the flagstones to enjoin silence. In the choir the psalms continued; but the responses lacked vigour.

"Suddenly, in the very middle of the *Ave verum*, lo and behold Father Gaucher fell backward in his stall and chanted in a voice of thunder:

"'*In Paris, there is a White Father—*
Patatin, patatan, tarabin, taraban.'

"General consternation. Everybody rose.

"'Carry him away! he is possessed!' they cried.

"The canons crossed themselves. Monseigneur's crook waved frantically. But Father Gaucher neither saw nor heard anything; and two sturdy monks were obliged to drag him away through the small door of the choir, struggling like one bewitched and continuing his *patatans* and his *tarabans* louder than ever.

"The next morning, at daybreak, the poor wretch was on his knees in the prior's oratory, confessing his sin with a flood of tears.

"'It was the elixir, monseigneur, it was the elixir that took me by surprise,' he said, beating his breast. And seeing him so heart-broken, so penitent, the good prior was deeply moved himself.

"'Come, come, Father Gaucher, calm yourself: all this will dry up like the dew in the sunshine. After all, the scandal was not so great as you think. To be sure there was a song which was a lit-tle—however, we must hope that the novices did not hear it. Now, tell me just how the thing happened to you. It was while you were trying the elixir, was it not? Your hand was a little too heavy. Yes, yes, I understand. It was like Brother Schwartz, the inventor of powder; you were the victim of your invention. And tell me, my dear friend, is it really necessary that you should try this terrible elixir upon yourself?'

"'Unluckily, yes, monseigneur. The test-tube, to be sure, gives me the strength and degree of heat of the alcohol; but for the fin-ishing touch, the velvety smoothness, I can trust nothing but my tongue.'

"'Ah! very good. But listen to what I ask. When you taste the elixir thus as a duty, does it taste good to you? Do you enjoy it?'

"'Alas! yes, monseigneur,' said the unhappy father, turning as red as a beet; 'for two evenings now I have found such a bouquet, such an aroma in it! It is certainly the devil who has played me this vile trick. So I have determined only to use the test-tube henceforth. If the liqueur is not as fine, if it is not as smooth as before, so much the worse!'

"'Do nothing of the sort,' interrupted the prior, earnestly. 'We must not take the risk of displeasing our customers. All that you have to do now that you are warned is to be on your guard. Tell me, how much do you need to drink, for your test? Fifteen or twenty drops, is it not? Let us say twenty drops. The devil will be very smart if he can catch you with twenty drops. Moreover, to avert all chance of accident, I excuse you from coming to church henceforth. You will repeat the evening service in the distillery. And now, go in peace, my father, and, above all things, count your drops carefully.'

"Alas! the poor father counted his drops to no purpose; the demon had him in his clutch, and he did not let him go.

"The distillery heard some strange services!

"In the daytime everything went well. The father was tranquil enough; he prepared his retorts, his alembics, carefully assorted his herbs—all Provençal herbs, fine and grey, and burned with perfume and sunlight. But at night, when the simples were steeped and the elixir was cooling in great basins of red copper, the poor man's martyrdom began.

"'Seventeen, eighteen, nineteen, twenty.'

"The drops fell from the tube into the silver goblet. Those twenty, the father swallowed at one draught, almost without enjoyment. It was only the twenty-first that aroused his longing. Oh! that twenty-first drop! To avoid temptation, he would go and kneel at the end of the laboratory and bury himself in his paternosters. But from the still warm liqueur there ascended a wreath of smoke heavily laden with aromatic odours, which came prowling about him, and drew him back towards the basins, whether he would or no. The liqueur was a beautiful golden-green. Leaning over it, with distended nostrils, the father stirred it gently with his tube, and it seemed to him that he saw, in the sparkling little spangles on the surface of the emerald lake, Aunt Bégon's eyes laughing and snapping as they looked at him.

"'Nonsense! Just one more drop.'

"And from drop to drop the poor wretch ended by filling his goblet to the brim. Then, at the end of his strength, he would sink down in an easy-chair; and his body relaxed, his eyes half closed, he would enjoy his sin by little sips, murmuring to himself with ecstatic remorse:

"'Ah! I am damning myself! I am damning myself!'

"The most terrible part of it was, that in the depth of diabolical elixir, he remembered, by some witchery or other, all Aunt Bégon's naughty songs: 'There were three little gossips, who talked of giving a feast'; or, 'Master André's shepherdess goes to the woods alone'; and always the famous one of the White Fathers: 'Patatin, patatan!'

"Imagine his confusion the next day when his old neighbours said to him with a sly expression:

"'Ha! ha! Father Gaucher, you had grasshoppers in your head when you went to bed last night.'

"Then there were tears, despair, fasting, haircloth, and penance. But nothing could prevail against the demon of the elixir; and every evening, at the same hour, the possession began anew.

"Meanwhile, orders rained upon the abbey like a blessing from Heaven. They came from Nîmes, from Aix, from Avignon, from Marseille. From day to day the convent assumed the aspect of a factory. There were packing brothers, labelling brothers, brothers to attend to the correspondence, draymen brothers; the service of God lost a few strokes of the bell now and then, to be sure, but the poor people of the neighbourhood lost nothing, I assure you.

"But one fine Sunday morning, while the steward was reading to the chapter his annual inventory, and the good canons were listening with sparkling eyes and smiling lips, behold Father Gaucher rushed into the midst of the conference, exclaiming:

"'It is all over! I can't stand it any longer! Give me back my cows.'

"'What is the matter, pray, Father Gaucher?' asked the prior, who had a shrewd idea what the matter might be.

"'The matter, monseigneur? The matter is that I am laying up for myself an eternity of hell-fire and blows with the pitchfork. The matter is that I am drinking, drinking like a miserable wretch.'

"'But I told you to count your drops.'

"'Count my drops! Oh, yes! I should have to count them by goblets now. Yes, my fathers, I have reached that point. Three flasks an evening. You must see that that cannot last. So let whomsoever you choose make the elixir. May God's fire consume me if I touch it again!'

"The chapter laughed no longer.

"'But you are ruining us, unhappy man!' cried the steward, waving his ledger.

"'Do you prefer that I should damn myself for ever?'

"Thereupon the prior rose.

"'My fathers,' he said, putting forth his beautiful white hand, upon which the pastoral ring glistened, 'there is a way to arrange everything. It is at night, is it not, my dear son, that the demon tempts you?'

"'Yes, monsieur prior, regularly every evening. So now, when night comes, a cold sweat takes me, saving your presence, like Capitou's donkey when he saw the saddle coming.'

"''Tis well! be comforted. Henceforth, every evening, at the service, we will repeat in your favour the prayer of St. Augustine, to which plenary indulgence is attached. With that, whatever happens, you are safe. It affords absolution during sin.'

"'Oh well! in that case, thanks, monsieur prior!'

"And, without asking anything more, Father Gaucher returned to his laboratory, as light-hearted as a lark.

"And in truth, from that day forward, every evening at the end of the complines, the officiating father never failed to say:

"'Let us pray for our poor Father Gaucher, who is sacrificing his soul in the interest of the community. *Oremus, Dominie*—'

"And while the prayer ran quivering over those white hoods, prostrate in the shadow of the nave, as a light breeze rushes over the snow, yonder at the other end of the convent, behind the

flaming stained-glass of the distillery, Father Gaucher could be
heard singing at the top of his lungs:

> *"'In Paris there is a White Father,*
> *Patatin, patatan, tarabin, taraban;*
> *In Paris there is a White Father*
> *Who dances with the nuns,*
> *Trin, trin, trin, in a garden,*
> *Who dances with the—'"*

Here the good curé stopped, in dismay.

"Merciful Heaven!" he exclaimed, "suppose my parishioners
should hear me!"

Taste

Roald Dahl
(1916–1990)

Roald Dahl is undoubtedly one of the modern masters of the short story, and I don't hesitate to include him here in the company of Maupassant, Hawthorne and Saki. I really don't have much to say about the story that follows, except to advise you to enjoy the suspense, which Dahl cranks up with each and every sentence. (A glass of good wine might help to put you in the mood for this particular story, but "Taste" can be enjoyed equally well on its own.)

 here were six of us to dinner that night at Mike Schofield's house in London: Mike and his wife and daughter, my wife and I, and a man called Richard Pratt.

Richard Pratt was a famous gourmet. He was president of a small society known as the Epicures, and each month he circulated privately to its members a pamphlet on food and wines. He organized dinners where sumptuous dishes and rare wines were served. He refused to smoke for fear of harming his palate, and when discussing wine, he had a curious, rather droll habit of referring to it as though it were a living being. "A prudent wine," he would say, "rather diffident and evasive, but quite prudent." Or, "A good-humoured wine, benevolent and cheerful—slightly obscene, perhaps, but none the less good-humoured."

I had been to dinner at Mike's twice before when Richard Pratt was there, and on each occasion Mike and his wife had gone out of their way to produce a special meal for the famous gourmet. And this one, clearly, was to be no exception. The moment we entered the dining-room, I could see that the table was laid for a feast. The tall candles, the yellow roses, the quantity of shining silver, the three wineglasses to each person, and above all the faint scent of roasting meat from the kitchen brought the first warm oozings of saliva to my mouth.

As we sat down, I remembered that on both Richard Pratt's previous visits Mike had played a little betting game with him over the claret, challenging him to name its breed and its vintage. Pratt had replied that that should not be too difficult provided it was one of the great years. Mike had then bet him a case of the wine in question that he could not do it. Pratt had accepted, and had won both times. Tonight I felt sure that the little game would be played over again, for Mike was quite willing to lose the bet in order to prove that his wine was good enough to be recognized, and Pratt, for his part, seemed to take a grave, restrained pleasure in displaying his knowledge.

The meal began with a plate of whitebait, fried very crisp in butter, and to go with it there was a Moselle. Mike got up and poured the wine himself, and when he sat down again, I could see that he was watching Richard Pratt. He had set the bottle in front of me so that I could read the label. It said, "Geierslay Ohligsberg, 1945." He leaned over and whispered to me that Geierslay was a tiny village in the Moselle, almost unknown outside Germany. He said that this wine we were drinking was something unusual, that the output of the vineyard was so small that it was almost impossible for a stranger to get any of it. He had visited Geierslay personally the previous summer in order to obtain the few dozen bottles that they had finally allowed him to have.

"I doubt whether anyone else in the country has any of it at the moment," he said. I saw him glance again at Richard Pratt. "Great thing about Moselle," he continued, raising his voice, "it's the perfect wine to serve before a claret. A lot of people serve a Rhine wine instead, but that's because they don't know any better. A Rhine wine will kill a delicate claret, you know that? It's barbaric to serve a Rhine before a claret. But a Moselle—ah!—a

Moselle is exactly right."

Mike Schofield was an amiable, middle-aged man. But he was a stockbroker. To be precise, he was a jobber in the stock market, and like a number of his kind, he seemed to be somewhat embarrassed, almost ashamed to find that he had made so much money with so slight a talent. In his heart he knew that he was not really much more than a bookmaker—an unctuous, infinitely respectable, secretly unscrupulous bookmaker—and he knew that his friends knew it, too. So he was seeking now to become a man of culture, to cultivate a literary and aesthetic taste, to collect paintings, music, books, and all the rest of it. His little sermon about Rhine wine and Moselle was a part of this thing, this culture that he sought.

"A charming little wine, don't you think?" he said. He was still watching Richard Pratt. I could see him give a rapid furtive glance down the table each time he dropped his head to take a mouthful of whitebait. I could almost *feel* him waiting for the moment when Pratt would take his first sip, and look up from his glass with a smile of pleasure, of astonishment, perhaps even of wonder, and then there would be a discussion and Mike would tell him about the village of Geierslay.

But Richard Pratt did not taste his wine. He was completely engrossed in conversation with Mike's eighteen-year-old daughter, Louise. He was half turned towards her, smiling at her, telling her, so far as I could gather, some story about a chef in a Paris restaurant. As he spoke, he leaned closer and closer to her, seeming in his eagerness almost to impinge upon her, and the poor girl leaned as far as she could away from him, nodding politely, rather desperately, and looking not at his face but at the topmost button of his dinner jacket.

We finished our fish, and the maid came round removing the plates. When she came to Pratt, she saw that he had not yet touched his food, so she hesitated, and Pratt noticed her. He waved her away, broke off his conversation, and quickly began to eat, popping the little crisp brown fish quickly into his mouth with rapid jabbing movements of his fork. Then, when he had finished, he reached for his glass, and in two short swallows he tipped the wine down his throat and turned immediately to resume his conversation with Louise Schofield.

Mike saw it all. I was conscious of him sitting there, very still, containing himself, looking at his guest. His round jovial face seemed to loosen slightly and to sag, but he contained himself and was still and said nothing.

Soon the maid came forward with the second course. This was a large roast of beef. She placed it on the table in front of Mike, who stood up and carved it, cutting the slices very thin, laying them gently on the plates for the maid to take around. When he had served everyone, including himself, he put down the carving knife and leaned forward with both hands on the edge of the table.

"Now," he said, speaking to all of us but looking at Richard Pratt. "Now for the claret. I must go and fetch the claret, if you'll excuse me."

"You go and fetch it, Mike?" I said. "Where is it?"

"In my study, with the cork out—breathing."

"Why the study?"

"Acquiring room temperature, of course. It's been there twenty-four hours."

"But why the study?"

"It's the best place in the house. Richard helped me choose it last time he was here."

At the sound of his name, Pratt looked round.

"That's right, isn't it?" Mike said.

"Yes," Pratt answered, nodding gravely. "That's right."

"On top of the green filing cabinet in my study," Mike said. "That's the place we chose. A good draught-free spot in a room with an even temperature. Excuse me now, will you, while I fetch it."

The thought of another wine to play with had restored his humour, and he hurried out of the door, to return a minute later more slowly, walking softly, holding in both hands a wine basket in which a dark bottle lay. The label was out of sight, facing downwards. "Now!" he cried as he came towards the table. "What about this one, Richard? You'll never name this one!"

Richard Pratt turned slowly and looked up at Mike, then his eyes travelled down to the bottle nesting in its small wicker basket, and he raised his eyebrows, a slight, supercilious arching of the brows, and with it a pushing outward of the wet lower lip, suddenly imperious and ugly.

"You'll never get it," Mike said. "Not in a hundred years."

"A claret?" Richard Pratt asked, condescending.

"Of course."

"I assume, then, that it's from one of the smaller vineyards?"

"Maybe it is, Richard. And then again, maybe it isn't."

"But it's a good year? One of the great years?"

"Yes, I guarantee that."

"Then it shouldn't be too difficult," Richard Pratt said, drawling his words, looking exceedingly bored. Except that, to me, there was something strange about his drawling and his boredom: between the eyes a shadow of something evil, and in his bearing an intentness that gave me a faint sense of uneasiness as I watched him.

"This one is really rather difficult," Mike said. "I won't force you to bet on this one."

"Indeed. And why not?" Again the slow arching of the brows, the cool, intent look.

"Because it's difficult."

"That's not very complimentary to me, you know."

"My dear man," Mike said, "I'll bet you with pleasure, if that's what you wish."

"It shouldn't be too hard to name it."

"You mean you want to bet?"

"I'm perfectly willing to bet," Richard Pratt said.

"All right then, we'll have the usual. A case of the wine itself."

"You don't think I'll be able to name it, do you."

"As a matter of fact, and with all due respect, I don't," Mike said. He was making some effort to remain polite, but Pratt was not bothering overmuch to conceal his contempt for the whole proceeding. And yet, curiously, his next question seemed to betray a certain interest.

"You like to increase the bet?"

"No, Richard. A case is plenty."

"Would you like to bet fifty cases?"

"That would be silly."

Mike stood very still behind his chair at the head of the table, carefully holding the bottle in its ridiculous wicker basket. There was a trace of whiteness around his nostrils now, and his mouth was shut very tight.

Pratt was lolling back in his chair, looking up at him, the eyebrows raised, the eyes half closed, a little smile touching the corners of his lips. And again I saw, or thought I saw, something distinctly disturbing about the man's face, that shadow of intentness between the eyes, and in the eyes themselves, right in their centres where it was black, a small slow spark of shrewdness, hiding.

"So you don't want to increase the bet?"

"As far as I'm concerned, old man, I don't give a damn," Mike said. "I'll bet you anything you like."

The three women and I sat quietly, watching the two men. Mike's wife was becoming annoyed; her mouth had gone sour and I felt that at any moment she was going to interrupt. Our roast beef lay before us on our plates, slowly steaming.

"So you'll bet me anything I like?"

"That's what I told you. I'll bet you anything you damn well please, if you want to make an issue out of it."

"Even ten thousand pounds?"

"Certainly I will, if that's the way you want it." Mike was more confident now. He knew quite well that he could call any sum Pratt cared to mention.

"So you say I can name the bet?" Pratt asked again.

"That's what I said."

There was a pause while Pratt looked slowly around the table, first at me, then at the three women, each in turn. He appeared to be reminding us that we were witnesses to the offer.

"Mike!" Mrs. Schofield said. "Mike, why don't we stop this nonsense and eat out food. It's getting cold."

"But it isn't nonsense," Pratt told her evenly. "We're making a little bet."

I noticed the maid standing in the background holding a dish of vegetables, wondering whether to come forward with them or not.

"All right, then," Pratt said. "I'll tell you what I want you to bet."

"Come on, then," Mike said, rather reckless. "I don't give a damn what it is—you're on."

Pratt nodded, and again the little smile moved the corners of his lips, and then, quite slowly, looking at Mike all the time, he said, "I want you to bet me the hand of your daughter in marriage."

Louise Schofield gave a jump. "Hey!" she cried. "No! That's not funny! Look here, Daddy, that's not funny at all."

"No, dear," her mother said. "They're only joking."

"I'm not joking," Richard Pratt said.

"It's ridiculous," Mike said. He was off balance again now.

"You said you'd bet anything I liked."

"I meant money."

"You didn't say money."

"That's what I meant."

"Then it's a pity you didn't say it. But anyway, if you wish to go back on your offer, that's quite all right with me."

"It's not a question of going back on my offer, old man. It's a no-bet anyway, because you can't match the stake. You yourself don't happen to have a daughter to put up against mine in case you lose. And if you had, I wouldn't want to marry her."

"I'm glad of that, dear," his wife said.

"I'll put up anything you like," Pratt announced. "My house, for example. How about my house?"

"Which one?" Mike asked, joking now.

"The country one."

"Why not the other one as well?"

"All right then, if you wish it. Both my houses."

At that point I saw Mike pause. He took a step forward and placed the bottle in its basket gently down on the table. He moved the salt-cellar to one side, then the pepper, and then he picked up his knife, studied the blade thoughtfully for a moment, and put it down again. His daughter, too, had seen him pause.

"Now, Daddy!" she cried. "Don't be *absurd!* It's *too* silly for words. I refuse to be betted on like this."

"Quite right, dear," her mother said. "Stop it at once, Mike, and sit down and eat your food."

Mike ignored her. He looked over at his daughter and he smiled, a slow, fatherly, protective smile. But in his eyes, suddenly, there glimmered a little triumph. "You know," he said, smiling as he spoke. "You know, Louise, we ought to think about this a bit."

"Now, stop it, Daddy! I refuse even to listen to you! Why, I've never heard anything so ridiculous in my life!"

"No, seriously, my dear. Just wait a moment and hear what I have to say."

"But I don't *want* to hear it."

"Louise! Please! It's like this. Richard, here, has offered us a serious bet. He is the one who wants to make it, not me. And if he loses, he will have to hand over a considerable amount of property. Now, wait a minute, my dear, don't interrupt. The point is this. *He cannot possibly win.*"

"He seems to think he can."

"Now listen to me, because I know what I'm talking about. The expert, when tasting a claret—so long as it is not one of the famous great wines like Lafite or Latour—can only get a certain way towards naming the vineyard. He can, of course, tell you the Bordeaux district from which the wine comes, whether it is from St. Emilion, Pomerol, Graves, or Médoc. But then each district has several communes, little counties, and each county has many, many small vineyards. It is impossible for a man to differentiate between them all by taste and smell alone. I don't mind telling you that this one I've got here is a wine from a small vineyard that is surrounded by many other small vineyards, and he'll never get it. It's impossible."

"You can't be sure of that," his daughter said.

"I'm telling you I can. Though I say it myself, I understand quite a bit about this wine business, you know. And anyway, heavens alive, girl, I'm your father and you don't think I'd let you in for—for something you didn't want, do you? I'm trying to make you some money."

"Mike!" his wife said sharply. "Stop it now, Mike, please!"

Again he ignored her. "If you will take this bet," he said to his daughter, "in ten minutes you will be the owner of two large houses."

"But I don't want two large houses, Daddy."

"Then sell them. Sell them back to him on the spot. I'll arrange all that for you. And then, just think of it, my dear, you'll be rich! You'll be independent for the rest of your life!"

"Oh, Daddy, I don't like it. I think it's silly."

"So do I," the mother said. She jerked her head briskly up and down as she spoke, like a hen. "You ought to be ashamed of yourself, Michael, ever suggesting such a thing! Your own daughter, too!"

Mike didn't even look at her. "Take it!" he said eagerly, staring hard at the girl. "Take it, quick! I'll guarantee you won't lose."

"But I don't like it, Daddy."

"Come on, girl. Take it!"

Mike was pushing her hard. He was leaning towards her, fixing her with two hard bright eyes, and it was not easy for the daughter to resist him.

"But what if I lose?"

"I keep telling you, you can't lose. I'll guarantee it."

"Oh, Daddy, must I?"

"I'm making you a fortune. So come on now. What do you say, Louise? All right?"

For the last time, she hesitated. Then she gave a helpless little shrug of the shoulders and said, "Oh, all right, then. Just so long as you swear there's no danger of losing."

"Good!" Mike cried. "That's fine! Then it's a bet!"

"Yes," Richard Pratt said, looking at the girl. "It's a bet."

Immediately, Mike picked up the wine, tipped the first thimbleful into his own glass, then skipped excitedly around the table filling up the others. Now everyone was watching Richard Pratt, watching his face as he reached slowly for his glass with his right hand and lifted it to his nose. The man was about fifty years old and he did not have a pleasant face. Somehow, it was all mouth— mouth and lips—the full, wet lips of the professional gourmet, the lower lip hanging downward in the centre, a pendulous, permanently open taster's lip, shaped open to receive the rim of a glass or a morsel of food. Like a keyhole, I thought, watching it; his mouth is like a large wet keyhole.

Slowly he lifted the glass to his nose. The point of the nose entered the glass and moved over the surface of the wine, delicately sniffing. He swirled the wine gently around in the glass to receive the bouquet. His concentration was intense. He had closed his eyes, and now the whole top half of his body, the head and neck and chest, seemed to become a kind of huge sensitive smelling-machine, receiving, filtering, analysing the message from the sniffing nose.

Mike, I noticed, was lounging in his chair, apparently unconcerned, but he was watching every move. Mrs. Schofield, the wife, sat prim and upright at the other end of the table, looking straight ahead, her face tight with disapproval. The daughter, Louise, had shifted her chair away a little, and sidewise, facing the gourmet, and she, like her father, was watching closely.

For at least a minute, the smelling process continued; then, without opening his eyes or moving his head, Pratt lowered the glass to his mouth and tipped in almost half the contents. He paused, his mouth full of wine, getting the first taste; then, he permitted some of it to trickle down his throat and I saw his Adam's apple move as it passed by. But most of it he retained in his mouth. And now, without swallowing again, he drew in through his lips a thin breath of air which mingled with the fumes of the wine in the mouth and passed on down into his lungs. He held the breath, blew it out through his nose, and finally began to roll the wine around under the tongue, and chewed it, actually chewed it with his teeth as though it were bread.

It was a solemn, impassive performance, and I must say he did it well.

"Um," he said, putting down the glass, running a pink tongue over his lips. "Um—yes. A very interesting little wine—gentle and gracious, almost feminine in the after-taste."

There was an excess of saliva in his mouth, and as he spoke he spat an occasional bright speck of it on to the table.

"Now we can start to eliminate," he said. "You will pardon me for doing this carefully, but there is much at stake. Normally I would perhaps take a bit of a chance, leaping forward quickly and landing right in the middle of the vineyard of my choice. But this time—I must move cautiously this time, must I not?" He looked up at Mike and smiled, a thick-lipped, wet-lipped smile. Mike did not smile back.

"First, then, which district in Bordeaux does this wine come from? That's not too difficult to guess. It is far too light in the body to be from either St. Emilion or Graves. It is obviously a Médoc. There's no doubt about *that*.

"Now—from which commune in Médoc does it come? That also, by elimination, should not be too difficult to decide. Margaux? No. It cannot be Margaux. It has not the violent bouquet of a Margaux. Pauillac? It cannot be Pauillac, either. It is too tender, too gentle and wistful for Pauillac. The wine of Pauillac has a character that is almost imperious in its taste. And also, to me, a Pauillac contains just a little pith, a curious dusty, pithy flavour that the grape acquired from the soil of the district. No, no. This—this is a very gentle wine, demure and bashful in the first taste, emerging shyly but quite graciously in the second. A little arch, perhaps, in the second taste, and a little naughty also, teasing the tongue with a trace, just a trace of tannin. Then, in the after-taste, delightful—consoling and feminine, with a certain blithely generous quality that one associates only with the wines of the commune of St. Julien. Unmistakably this is a St. Julien."

He leaned back in his chair, held his hands up level with his chest, and placed the fingertips carefully together. He was becoming ridiculously pompous, but I thought that some of it was deliberate, simply to mock his host. I found myself waiting rather tensely for him to go on. The girl Louise was lighting a cigarette. Pratt heard the match strike and he turned to her, flaring suddenly with real anger. "Please!" he said. "Please don't do that! It's a disgusting habit, to smoke at table!"

She looked up at him, still holding the burning match in one hand, the big slow eyes settling on his face, resting there a moment, moving away again, slow and contemptuous. She bent her head and blew out the match, but continued to hold the unlighted cigarette in her fingers.

"I'm sorry, my dear," Pratt said, "but I simply cannot have smoking at table."

She didn't look at him again.

"Now, let me see—where were we?" he said. "Ah, yes. This wine is from Bordeaux, from the commune of St. Julien, in the district of Médoc. So far, so good. But now we come to the more difficult part—the name of the vineyard itself. For in St. Julien there are many vineyards, and as our host so rightly remarked earlier on, there is often not much difference between the wine of one and the wine of another. But we shall see."

He paused again, closing his eyes. "I am trying to establish the 'growth,'" he said. "If I can do that, it will be half the battle. Now, let me see. This wine is obviously not from a first-growth vineyard—nor even a second. It is not a great wine. The quality, the—the—what do you call it?—the radiance, the power, is lacking. But a third growth—that it could be. And yet I doubt it. We know it is a good year—our host has said so—and this is probably flattering it a little bit. I must be careful. I must be very careful here."

He picked up his glass and took another small sip.

"Yes," he said, sucking his lips, "I was right. It is a fourth growth. Now I am sure of it. A fourth growth from a very good year—from a great year, in fact. And that's what made it taste for a moment like a third—or even a second-growth wine. Good! That's better! Now we are closing in! What are the fourth-growth vineyards in the commune of St. Julien?"

Again he paused, took up his glass, and held the rim against that sagging, pendulous lower lip of his. Then I saw the tongue shoot out, pink and narrow, the tip of it dipping into the wine, withdrawing swiftly again—a repulsive sight. When he lowered the glass, his eyes remained closed, the face concentrated, only the lips moving, sliding over each other like two pieces of wet, spongy rubber.

"There it is again!" he cried. "Tannin in the middle taste, and the quick astringent squeeze upon the tongue. Yes, yes, of course! Now I have it! The wine comes from one of those small vineyards around Beychevelle. I remember now. The Beychevelle district, and the river and the little harbour that has silted up so the wine ships can no longer use it. Beychevelle ... could it actually be a Beychevelle itself? No, I don't think so. Not quite. But it is somewhere very close. Château Talbot? Could it be Talbot? Yes, it could. Wait one moment."

He sipped the wine again, and out of the side of my eye I noticed Mike Schofield and how he was leaning farther and farther forward over the table, his mouth slightly open, his small eyes fixed upon Richard Pratt.

"No. I was wrong. It is not a Talbot. A Talbot comes forward to you just a little quicker than this one, the fruit is nearer the surface. If it is a '34, which I believe it is, then it couldn't be Talbot. Well, well. Let me think. It is not a Beychevelle and it is not a Talbot, and yet—yet it is so close to both of them, so close, that the vineyard must be almost in between. Now, which could that be?"

He hesitated, and we waited, watching his face. Everyone, even Mike's wife, was watching him now. I heard the maid put down the dish of vegetables on the sideboard behind me, gently, so as not to disturb the silence.

"Ah!" he cried. "I have it! Yes, I think I have it!"

For the last time, he sipped the wine. Then, still holding the glass up near his mouth, he turned to Mike and he smiled, a slow, silky smile, and he said, "You know what this is? This is the little Château Branaire-Ducru."

Mike sat tight, not moving.

"And the year, 1934."

We all looked at Mike, waiting for him to turn the bottle around in its basket and show the label.

"Is that your final answer?" Mike said.

"Yes, I think so."

"Well, is it or isn't it?"

"Yes, it is."

"What was the name again?"

"Château Branaire-Ducru. Pretty little vineyard. Lovely old château. Know it quite well. Can't think why I didn't recognize it at once."

"Come on, Daddy," the girl said. "Turn it round and let's have a peek. I want my two houses."

"Just a minute," Mike said. "Wait just a minute." He was sitting very quiet, bewildered-looking, and his face was becoming puffy and pale, as though all the force was draining slowly out of him.

"Michael!" his wife called sharply from the other end of the table. "What's the matter?"

"Keep out of this, Margaret, will you please."

Richard Pratt was looking at Mike, smiling with his mouth, his eyes small and bright. Mike was not looking at anyone.

"Daddy!" the daughter cried, agonized. "But, Daddy, you don't mean to say he's guessed it right!"

"Now, stop worrying, my dear," Mike said. "There's nothing to worry about."

I think it was more to get away from his family than anything else that Mike then turned to Richard Pratt and said, "I'll tell you what, Richard. I think you and I better slip off into the next room and have a little chat."

"I don't want a little chat," Pratt said. "All I want is to see the label on that bottle." He knew he was a winner now; he had the bearing, the quiet arrogance of a winner, and I could see that he was prepared to become thoroughly nasty if there was any trouble. "What are you waiting for?" he said to Mike. "Go on and turn it round."

Then this happened: the maid, the tiny, erect figure of the maid in her white-and-black uniform, was standing beside Richard Pratt, holding something out in her hand. "I believe these are yours, sir," she said.

Pratt glanced around, saw the pair of thin horn-rimmed spectacles that she held out to him, and for a moment he hesitated. "Are they? Perhaps they are, I don't know."

"Yes, sir, they're yours." The maid was an elderly woman— nearer seventy than sixty—a faithful family retainer of many years' standing. She put the spectacles down on the table beside him.

Without thanking her, Pratt took them up and slipped them into his top pocket, behind the white handkerchief.

But the maid didn't go away. She remained standing beside and slightly behind Richard Pratt, and there was something so unusual in her manner and in the way she stood there, small, motionless and erect, that I for one found myself watching her with a sudden apprehension. Her old grey face had a frosty, determined look, the lips were compressed, the little chin was out, and the hands were clasped together tight before her. The curious cap on her head and the flash of white down the front of her uniform made her seem like some tiny, ruffled, white-breasted bird.

"You left them in Mr. Schofield's study," she said. Her voice was unnaturally, deliberately polite. "On top of the green filing cabinet in his study, sir, when you happened to go in there by yourself before dinner."

It took a few moments for the full meaning of her words to penetrate, and in the silence that followed I became aware of Mike and how he was slowly drawing himself up in his chair, and the colour coming to his face, and the eyes opening wide, and the curl of the mouth, and the dangerous little patch of whiteness beginning to spread around the area of the nostrils.

"Now, Michael!" his wife said. "Keep calm now, Michael, dear! Keep calm!"

THE MASQUE OF
THE RED DEATH

Edgar Allan Poe
(1809–1849)

When I was going over the selections for this anthology, I noticed a marked similarity between this story and "Come Again in the Spring." Both of them have Death in their cast of characters, and he visits at inopportune moments. There, however, the similarity between the two stories ends.

It would be difficult to find a darker tale in all of literature than "The Masque of the Red Death." Despite this bleakness, however, I cannot help but admire the rich and evocative language with which Poe recounts his haunting, fable-like story. Above all, this is a visual story, glittering with rich deep reds, black velvet, flickering firelight and the endless, hectic swaying and swishing of the pleasure-obsessed revellers.

he "Red Death" had long devastated the country. No pestilence had ever been so fatal, or so hideous. Blood was its Avatar and its seal—the redness and the horror of blood. There were sharp pains, and sudden dizziness, and then profuse bleeding at the pores, with dissolution. The scarlet stains upon the body and especially upon the face of the victim, were the pest ban which shut him out from the aid and from the sympathy of his fellow-men. And the whole seizure, progress, and termination of the disease, were the incidents of half an hour.

But the Prince Prospero was happy and dauntless and sagacious. When his dominions were half depopulated, he summoned to his presence a thousand hale and light-hearted friends from among the knights and dames of his court, and with these retired to the deep seclusion of one of his castellated abbeys. This was an extensive and magnificent structure, the creation of the prince's own eccentric yet august taste. A strong and lofty wall girdled it in. This wall had gates of iron. The courtiers, having entered, brought furnaces and massy hammers and welded the bolts. They resolved to leave means neither of ingress nor egress to the sudden impulses of despair or of frenzy from within. The abbey was amply provisioned. With such precautions the courtiers might bid defiance to contagion. The external world could take care of itself. In the meantime it was folly to grieve, or to think. The prince had provided all the appliances of pleasure. There were buffoons, there were improvisatori, there were ballet-dancers, there were musicians, there was Beauty, there was wine. All these and security were within. Without was the "Red Death."

It was toward the close of the fifth or sixth month of his seclusion, and while the pestilence raged most furiously abroad, that the Prince Prospero entertained his thousand friends at a masked ball of the most unusual magnificence.

It was a voluptuous scene, that masquerade. But first let me tell of the rooms in which it was held. There were seven—an imperial suite. In many palaces, however, such suites form a long and straight vista, while the folding doors slide back nearly to the walls on either hand, so that the view of the whole extent is scarcely impeded. Here the case was very different; as might have been expected from the duke's love of the bizarre. The apartments were so irregularly disposed that the vision embraced but little more than one at a time. There was a sharp turn at every twenty or thirty yards, and at each turn a novel effect. To the right and left, in the middle of each wall, a tall and narrow Gothic window looked out upon a closed corridor which pursued the windings of the suite. These windows were of stained glass whose colour varied in accordance with the prevailing hue of the decorations of the chamber into which it opened. That at the eastern extremity was hung, for example, in blue—and vividly blue were its windows. The second chamber was purple in its ornaments and tapestries, and here the panes were purple. The third was green throughout, and so were the casements. The fourth was furnished and lighted with orange—the fifth with white—the sixth with violet. The seventh apartment was closely shrouded in black velvet tapestries that hung all over the ceiling and down the walls, falling in heavy folds upon a carpet of the same material and hue. But in this chamber only, the colour of the windows failed to correspond with the decorations. The panes here were scarlet—a deep blood colour. Now in no one of the seven apartments was there any lamp or candelabrum, amid the profusion of golden ornaments that lay scattered to and fro or depended from the roof. There was no light of any kind emanating from lamp or candle within the suite of chambers. But in the corridors that followed the suite, there stood, opposite to each window, a heavy tripod, bearing a brazier of fire, that projected its rays through the tinted glass and so glaringly illumined the room. And thus were produced a multitude of gaudy and fantastic appearances. But in the western or black chamber the effect of the firelight that streamed upon the dark hangings through the blood-tinted panes was ghastly in the extreme, and produced so wild a look upon the countenances of those who entered, that there were few of the company bold enough to set foot within its precincts at all.

It was in this apartment, also, that there stood against the western wall, a gigantic clock of ebony. Its pendulum swung to and fro with a dull, heavy, monotonous clang; and when the minute-hand made the circuit of the face, and the hour was to be stricken, there came from the brazen lungs of the clock a sound which was clear and loud and deep and exceedingly musical, but of so peculiar a note and emphasis that, at each lapse of an hour, the musicians of the orchestra were constrained to pause, momentarily, in their performance, to hearken to the sound; and thus the waltzers perforce ceased their evolutions; and there was a brief disconcert of the whole gay company; and, while the chimes of the clock yet rang, it was observed that the giddiest grew pale, and the more aged and sedate passed their hands over their brows as if in confused revery or meditation. But when the echoes had fully ceased, a light laughter at once pervaded the assembly; the musicians looked at each other and smiled as if at their own nervousness and folly, and made whispering vows, each to the other, that the next chiming of the clock should produce in them no similar emotion; and then, after the lapse of sixty minutes (which embrace three thousand six hundred seconds of the Time that flies), there came yet another chiming of the clock, and then were the same disconcert and tremulousness and meditation as before.

But, in spite of these things, it was a gay and magnificent revel. The tastes of the duke were peculiar. He had a fine eye for colours and effects. He disregarded the *decora* of mere fashion. His plans were bold and fiery, and his conceptions glowed with barbaric lustre. There are some who would have thought him mad. His followers felt that he was not. It was necessary to hear and see and touch him to be *sure* that he was not.

He had directed, in great part, the movable embellishments of the seven chambers, upon occasion of this great *féte*; and it was his own guiding taste which had given character to the masqueraders. Be sure they were grotesque. There were much glare and glitter and piquancy and phantasm—much of what has been since seen in "Hernani." There were arabesque figures with unsuited limbs and appointments. There were delirious fancies such as the madman fashions. There were much of the beautiful, much of the wanton, much of the bizarre, something of the terrible, and not a little of that which might have excited disgust. To and fro in the seven chambers there stalked, in fact, a multitude of dreams. And these—the dreams—writhed in and about, taking hue from the rooms, and causing the wild music of the orchestra to seem as the echo of their steps. And, anon, there strikes the ebony clock which stands in the hall of the velvet. And then, for a moment, all is still, and all is silent save the voice of the clock. The dreams are stiff-frozen as they stand. But the echoes of the chime die away—they have endured but an instant—and a light, half-subdued laughter floats after them as they depart. And now again the music swells, and the dreams live, and writhe to and fro more merrily than ever, taking hue from the many-tinted windows through which stream the rays from the tripods. But to the chamber which lies most westwardly of the seven there are now none of the maskers who venture; for the night is waning away; and there flows a ruddier light through the blood-coloured panes; and the blackness of the sable drapery appals; and to him whose foot falls upon the sable carpet, there comes from the near clock of ebony a muffled peal more solemnly emphatic than any which reaches their ears who indulge in the more remote gaieties of the other apartments.

But these other apartments were densely crowded, and in them beat feverishly the heart of life. And the revel went whirlingly on, until at length there commenced the sounding of midnight upon the clock. And then the music ceased, as I have told; and the evolutions of the waltzers were quieted; and there was an uneasy cessation of all things as before. But now there were twelve strokes to be sounded by the bell of the clock; and thus it happened, perhaps, that more of thought crept, with more of time, into the meditations of the thoughtful people among those who revelled. And thus too, it happened, perhaps, that before the last echoes of the last chime had utterly sunk into silence, there were many individuals in the crowd who had found leisure to become aware of the presence of a masked figure which had arrested the attention of no single individual before. And the rumour of this new presence having spread itself whisperingly around, there arose at length from the whole company a buzz, or murmur, expressive of disapprobation and surprise—then, finally, of terror, of horror, and of disgust.

In an assembly of phantasms such as I have painted, it may well be supposed that no ordinary appearance could have excited such sensation. In truth the masquerade licence of the night was nearly unlimited; but the figure in question had out-Heroded Herod, and gone beyond the bounds of even the prince's indefinite decorum. There are chords in the hearts of the most reckless which cannot be touched without emotion. Even with the utterly lost, to whom life and death are equally jests, there are matters of which no jest can be made. The whole company, indeed, seemed now deeply to feel that in the costume and bearing of the stranger neither wit nor propriety existed. The figure was tall and gaunt, and shrouded from head to foot in the habiliments of the grave. The mask which concealed the visage was made so nearly to resemble the countenance of a stiffened corpse that the closest scrutiny must have had difficulty in detecting the cheat. And yet all this might have been endured, if not approved, by the mad revellers around. But the mummer had gone so far as to assume the type of the Red Death. His vesture was dabbled in *blood*— and his broad brow, with all the features of the face, was besprinkled with the scarlet horror.

When the eyes of Prince Prospero fell upon this spectral image (which, with a slow and solemn movement, as if more fully to sustain its *rôle*, stalked to and fro among the waltzers) he was seen to be convulsed, in the first moment with a strong shudder either of terror or distaste; but, in the next, his brow reddened with rage.

"Who dares"—he demanded hoarsely of the courtiers who stood near him—"who dares insult us with this blasphemous mockery? Seize him and unmask him—that we may know whom we have to hang, at sunrise, from the battlements!"

It was in the eastern or blue chamber in which stood the Prince Prospero as he uttered these words. They rang throughout the seven rooms loudly and clearly, for the prince was a bold and robust man, and the music had become hushed at the waving of his hand.

It was in the blue room where stood the prince, with a group of pale courtiers by his side. At first, as he spoke, there was a slight rushing movement of this group in the direction of the intruder, who at the moment was also near at hand, and now, with deliberate and stately step, made closer approach to the speaker. But from a certain nameless awe with which the mad assumptions of the mummer had inspired the whole party, there were found none who put forth hand to seize him; so that, unimpeded, he passed within a yard of the prince's person; and, while the vast assembly, as if with one impulse, shrank from the centres of the rooms to the walls, he made his way uninterruptedly, but with the same solemn and measured step which had distinguished

him from the first, through the blue chamber to the purple—
through the purple to the green—through the green to the
orange—through this again to the white—and even thence to the
violet, ere a decided movement had been made to arrest him. It
was then, however, that the Prince Prospero, maddening with
rage and the shame of his own momentary cowardice, rushed
hurriedly through the six chambers, while none followed him on
account of a deadly terror that had seized upon all. He bore aloft
a drawn dagger, and had approached, in rapid impetuosity, to
within three or four feet of the retreating figure, when the latter,
having attained the extremity of the velvet apartment, turned
suddenly and confronted his pursuer. There was a sharp cry—and
the dagger dropped gleaming upon the sable carpet, upon which,
instantly afterward, fell prostrate in death the Prince Prospero.
Then, summoning the wild courage of despair, a throng of the
revellers at once threw themselves into the black apartment, and,
seizing the mummer, whose tall figure stood erect and motionless
within the shadow of the ebony clock, gasped in unutterable horror at finding the grave cerements and corpse-like mask, which
they handled with so violent a rudeness, untenanted by any tan-
gible form.

And now was acknowledged the presence of the Red Death.
He had come like a thief in the night. And one by one dropped
the revellers in the blood-bedewed halls of their revel, and died
each in the despairing posture of his fall. And the life of the ebony
clock went out with that of the last of the gay. And the flames of
the tripods expired. And Darkness and Decay and the Red Death
held illimitable dominion over all.

THE LADY WITH THE DOG

Anton Checkhov
(1860–1904)

We travel now to Russia at the close of the nineteenth century, and visit the society that remains vibrant for us through the stories and plays of Anton Chekhov. A bit funny, a bit sad, a bit ridiculous (as life itself often is), "The Lady with the Dog" was written with the compassion and the detachment that are typical of Chekhov's mature works. He once wrote in his notebook: "Man will become better only when you make him see what he is like." In this tale of two "birds of passage, caught and forced to live in different cages," Chekhov once again holds up a mirror for us to see ourselves, and as always he provides no easy answers.

I

t was said that a new person had appeared on the sea-front: a lady with a little dog. Dmitri Dmitritch Gurov, who had by then been a fortnight at Yalta, and so was fairly at home there, had begun to take an interest in new arrivals. Sitting in Verney's pavilion, he saw, walking on the sea-front, a fair-haired young lady of medium height, wearing a beret; a white Pomeranian dog was running behind her.

And afterwards he met her in the public gardens and in the square several times a day. She was walking alone, always wearing the same beret, and always with the same white dog; no one knew who she was, and everyone called her simply "the lady with the dog."

"If she is here alone without a husband or friends, it wouldn't be amiss to make her acquaintance," Gurov reflected.

He was under forty, but he had a daughter already twelve years old, and two sons at school. He had been married young, when he was a student in his second year, and by now his wife seemed half as old again as he. She was a tall, erect woman with dark eyebrows, staid and dignified, and, as she said of herself, intellectual. She read a great deal, used phonetic spelling, called her husband, not Dmitri, but Dimitri, and he secretly considered her unintelligent, narrow, inelegant, was afraid of her, and did not like to be at home. He had begun being unfaithful to her long ago—had been unfaithful to her often, and, probably on that account, almost always spoke ill of women, and when they were talked about in his presence, used to call them "the lower race."

It seemed to him that he had been so schooled by bitter experience that he might call them what he liked, and yet he could not get on for two days together without "the lower race." In the society of men he was bored and not himself, with them he was cold and uncommunicative; but when he was in the company of women he felt free, and knew what to say to them and how to behave; and he was at ease with them even when he was silent. In his appearance, in his character, in his whole nature, there was something attractive and elusive which allured women and disposed them in his favour; he knew that, and some force seemed to draw him, too, to them.

Experience often repeated, truly bitter experience, had taught him long ago that with decent people, especially Moscow people—always slow to move and irresolute—every intimacy, which at first so agreeably diversifies life and appears a light and charming adventure, inevitably grows into a regular problem of extreme intricacy, and in the long run the situation becomes unbearable. But at every fresh meeting with an interesting woman this experience seemed to slip out of his memory, and he was eager for life, and everything seemed simple and amusing.

One evening he was dining in the gardens, and the lady in the beret came up slowly to take the next table. Her expression, her gait, her dress, and the way she did her hair told him that she was a lady, that she was married, that she was in Yalta for the first time and alone, and that she was dull there... The stories told of the immorality in such places as Yalta are to a great extent untrue; he despised them, and knew that such stories were for the most part made up by persons who would themselves have been glad to sin if they had been able; but when the lady sat down at the next table three paces from him, he remembered these tales of easy conquests, of trips to the mountains, and the tempting thought of a swift, fleeting love affair, a romance with an unknown woman, whose name he did not know, suddenly took possession of him.

He beckoned coaxingly to the Pomeranian, and when the dog came up to him he shook his finger at it. The Pomeranian growled: Gurov shook his finger at it again.

The lady looked at him and at once dropped her eyes.

"He doesn't bite," she said, and blushed.

"May I give him a bone?" he asked; and when she nodded he asked courteously, "Have you been long in Yalta?"

"Five days."

"And I have already dragged out a fortnight here."

There was a brief silence.

"Time goes fast, and yet it is so dull here!" she said, not looking at him.

"That's only the fashion to say it is dull here. A provincial will live in Belyov or Zhidra and not be dull, and when he comes here it's 'Oh, the dullness! Oh, the dust!' One would think he came from Grenada."

She laughed. Then both continued eating in silence, like strangers, but after dinner they walked side by side; and there sprang up between them the light jesting conversation of people who are free and satisfied, to whom it does not matter where they go or what they talk about. They walked and talked of the strange light on the sea: the water was of a soft warm lilac hue, and there was a golden streak from the moon upon it. They talked of how sultry it was after a hot day. Gurov told her that he came from Moscow, that he had taken his degree in Arts, but had a post in a bank; that he had trained as an opera-singer, but had given it up, that he owned two houses in Moscow... And from her he learnt that she had grown up in Petersburg, but had lived in S—— since her marriage two years before, that she was staying another month in Yalta, and that her husband, who needed a holiday too, might perhaps come and fetch her. She was not sure whether her husband had a post in a Crown Department or under the Provincial Council—and was amused by her own ignorance. And Gurov learnt, too, that she was called Anna Sergeyevna.

Afterwards he thought about her in his room at the hotel— thought she would certainly meet him next day; it would be sure to happen. As he got into bed he thought how lately she had been a girl at school, doing lessons like his own daughter; he recalled the diffidence, the angularity, that was still manifest in her laugh and her manner of talking with a stranger. This must have been the first time in her life she had been alone in surroundings in which she was followed, looked at, and spoken to merely from a secret motive which she could hardly fail to guess. He recalled her slender, delicate neck, her lovely grey eyes.

"There's something pathetic about her, anyway," he thought, and fell asleep.

II

A week had passed since they had made acquaintance. It was a holiday. It was sultry indoors, while in the street the wind whirled the dust round and round, and blew people's hats off. It was a thirsty day, and Gurov often went into the pavilion, and pressed Anna Sergeyevna to have syrup and water or an ice. One did not know what to do with oneself.

In the evening when the wind had dropped a little, they went out on to the groyne to see the steamer come in. There were a great many people walking about the harbour; they had gathered to welcome someone, bringing bouquets. And two peculiarities of a well-dressed Yalta crowd were very conspicuous: the elderly ladies were dressed like young ones, and there were great numbers of generals.

Owing to the roughness of the sea, the steamer arrived late, after the sun had set, and it was a long time turning about before it reached the groyne. Anna Sergeyevna looked through her lorgnette at the steamer and the passengers as though looking for acquaintances, and when she turned to Gurov her eyes were shining. She talked a great deal and asked disconnected questions, forgetting next moment what she had asked; then she dropped her lorgnette in the crush.

The festive crowd began to disperse; it was too dark to see people's faces. The wind had completely dropped, but Gurov and Anna Sergeyevna still stood as though waiting to see someone else come from the steamer. Anna Sergeyevna was silent now, and sniffed the flowers without looking at Gurov.

"The weather is better this evening," he said. "Where shall we go now? Shall we drive somewhere?"

She made no answer.

Then he looked at her intently, and all at once put his arm round her and kissed her on the lips, and breathed in the moisture and the fragrance of the flowers; and he immediately looked round him, anxiously wondering whether anyone had seen them.

"Let us go to your hotel," he said softly. And both walked quickly.

The room was close and smelt of the scent she had bought at the Japanese shop. Gurov looked at her and thought: "What different people one meets in the world!" From the past he preserved memories of careless, good-natured women, who loved cheerfully and were grateful to him for the happiness he gave them, however brief it might be; and of women like his wife who loved without any genuine feeling, with superfluous phrases, affectedly, hysterically, with an expression that suggested that it was not love nor passion, but something more significant; and of two or three others, very beautiful, cold women, on whose faces he had caught a glimpse of a rapacious expression—an obstinate desire to snatch from life more than it could give, and these were capricious, unreflecting, domineering, unintelligent women not in their first youth, and when Gurov grew cold to them their beauty excited his hatred, and the lace on their linen seemed to him like scales.

But in this case there was still the diffidence, the angularity of inexperienced youth, an awkward feeling; and there was a sense of consternation as though someone had suddenly knocked at the door. The attitude of Anna Sergeyevna—"the lady with the dog"—to what had happened was somehow peculiar, very grave, as though it were her fall—so it seemed, and it was strange and inappropriate. Her face dropped and faded, and on both sides of it her long hair hung down mournfully; she mused in a dejected attitude like "the woman who was a sinner" in an old-fashioned picture.

"It's wrong," she said. "You will be the first to despise me now."

There was a water-melon on the table. Gurov cut himself a slice and began eating it without haste. There followed at least half an hour of silence.

Anna Sergeyevna was touching; there was about her the purity of a good, simple woman who had seen little of life. The solitary candle burning on the table threw a faint light on her face, yet it was clear that she was very unhappy.

"How could I despise you?" asked Gurov. "You don't know what you are saying."

"God forgive me," she said, and her eyes filled with tears. "It's awful."

"You seem to feel you need to be forgiven."

"Forgiven? No. I am a bad, low woman; I despise myself and don't attempt to justify myself. It's not my husband but myself I have deceived. And not only just now; I have been deceiving myself for a long time. My husband may be a good, honest man, but he is a flunkey! I don't know what he does there, what his work is, but I know he is a flunkey! I was twenty when I was married to him. I have been tormented by curiosity; I wanted something better. 'There must be a different sort of life,' I said to myself. I wanted to live! To live, to live!... I was fired by curi-

osity... you don't understand it, but, I swear to God, I could not
control myself; something happened to me: I could not be
restrained. I told my husband I was ill, and came here... And here
I have been walking about as though I were dazed, like a mad
creature...and now I have become a vulgar, contemptible woman
whom anyone may despise."

Gurov felt bored already, listening to her. He was irritated by
the naïve tone, by this remorse, so unexpected and inopportune;
but for the tears in her eyes, he might have thought she was jesting or playing a part.

"I don't understand," he said softly. "What is it you want?"
She hid her face on his breast and pressed close to him.

"Believe me, believe me, I beseech you..." she said. "I love a
pure, honest life, and sin is loathsome to me. I don't know what
I am doing. Simple people say: 'The Evil One has beguiled me.'
And I may say of myself now that the Evil One has beguiled me."

"Hush, hush!..." he muttered.

He looked at her fixed, scared eyes, kissed her, talked softly
and affectionately, and by degrees she was comforted, and her
gaiety returned; they both began laughing.

Afterwards when they went out there was not a soul on the
sea-front. The town with its cypresses had quite a deathlike air,
but the sea still broke noisily on the shore; a single barge was
rocking on the waves, and a lantern was blinking sleepily on it.

They found a cab and drove to Oreanda.

"I found out your surname in the hall just now: it was written on the board—Von Diderits," said Gurov. "Is your husband
a German?"

"No; I believe his grandfather was a German but he is an
Orthodox Russian himself."

At Oreanda they sat on a seat not far from the church, looked
down at the sea, and were silent. Yalta was hardly visible through
the morning mist; white clouds stood motionless on the moun-
tain-tops. The leaves did not stir on the trees, grasshoppers
chirruped, and the monotonous hollow sound of the sea, rising
up from below, spoke of the peace, of the eternal sleep awaiting
us. So it must have sounded when there was no Yalta, no

Oreanda here; so it sounds now, and it will sound as indifferently and monotonously when we are all no more. And in this constancy, in this complete indifference to the life and death of each of us, there lies hid, perhaps, a pledge of our eternal salvation, of the unceasing movement of life upon earth, of unceasing progress towards perfection. Sitting beside a young woman who in the dawn seemed so lovely, soothed and spellbound in these magical surroundings—the sea, mountains, clouds, the open sky—Gurov thought how in reality everything is beautiful in this world when one reflects: everything except what we think or do ourselves when we forget our human dignity and the higher aims of our existence.

A man walked up to them—probably a keeper—looked at them and walked away. And this detail seemed mysterious and beautiful, too. They saw a steamer come from Theodosia, with its lights out in the glow of dawn.

"There is dew on the grass," said Anna Sergeyevna, after a silence.

"Yes. It's time to go home."

They went back to the town.

Then they met every day at twelve o'clock on the sea-front, lunched and dined together, went for walks, admired the sea. She complained that she slept badly, that her heart throbbed violently; asked the same questions, troubled now by jealousy and now by the fear that he did not respect her sufficiently. And often in the square or gardens, when there was no one near them, he suddenly drew her to him and kissed her passionately. Complete idleness, these kisses in broad daylight while he looked round in dread of someone's seeing them, the heat, the smell of the sea, and the continual passing to and fro before him of idle, well-dressed, well-fed people, made a new man of him; he told Anna Sergeyevna how beautiful she was, how fascinating. He was impatiently passionate, he would not move a step away from her, while she was often pensive and continually urged him to confess that he did not respect her, did not love her in the least, and thought of her as nothing but a common woman. Rather late almost every evening they drove somewhere out of town, to

Oreanda or to the waterfall; and the expedition was always a success, the scenery invariably impressed them as grand and beautiful.

They were expecting her husband to come, but a letter came from him, saying that there was something wrong with his eyes, and he entreated his wife to come home as quickly as possible. Anna Sergeyevna made haste to go.

"It's a good thing I am going away," she said to Gurov. "It's the finger of destiny!"

She went by coach and he went with her. They were driving the whole day. When she had got into a compartment of the express, and when the second bell had rung, she said:

"Let me look at you once more... look at you once again. That's right."

She did not shed tears, but was so sad that she seemed ill, and her face was quivering.

"I shall remember you... think of you," she said. "God be with you; be happy. Don't remember evil against me. We are parting for ever—it must be so, for we ought never to have met. Well, God be with you."

The train moved off rapidly, its lights soon vanished from sight, and a minute later there was no sound of it, as though everything had conspired together to end as quickly as possible that sweet delirium, that madness. Left alone on the platform, and gazing into the dark distance, Gurov listened to the chirrup of the grasshoppers and the hum of the telegraph wires, feeling as though he had only just waked up. And he thought, musing, that there had been another episode or adventure in his life, and it, too, was at an end, and nothing was left of it but a memory... He was moved, sad, and conscious of a slight remorse. This young woman whom he would never meet again had not been happy with him; he was genuinely warm and affectionate with her, but yet in his manner, his tone, and his caresses there had been a shade of light irony, the coarse condescension of a happy man who was, besides, almost twice her age. All the time she had called him kind, exceptional, lofty; obviously he had seemed to her different from what he really was, so he had unintentionally deceived her...

Here at the station was already a scent of autumn; it was a cold evening.

"It's time for me to go north," thought Gurov as he left the platform. "High time!"

III

At home in Moscow everything was in its winter routine; the stoves were heated, and in the morning it was still dark when the children were having breakfast and getting ready for school, and the nurse would light the lamp for a short time. The frosts had begun already. When the first snow has fallen, on the first day of sledge-driving it is pleasant to see the white earth, the white roofs, to draw soft, delicious breath, and the season brings back the days of one's youth. The old limes and birches, white with hoar-frost, have a good-natured expression; they are nearer to one's heart than cypresses and palms, and near them one doesn't want to be thinking of the sea and the mountains.

Gurov was Moscow born; he arrived in Moscow on a fine frosty day, and when he put on his fur coat and warm gloves, and walked along Petrovka, and when on Saturday evening he heard the ringing of the bells, his recent trip and the places he had seen lost all charm for him. Little by little he became absorbed in Moscow life, greedily read three newspapers a day, and declared he did not read the Moscow papers on principle! He already felt a longing to go to restaurants, clubs, dinner parties, anniversary celebrations, and he felt flattered at entertaining distinguished lawyers and artists, and at playing cards with a professor at the doctor's club. He could already eat a whole plateful of salt fish and cabbage...

In another month, he fancied, the image of Anna Sergeyevna would be shrouded in a mist in his memory, and only from time to time would visit him in his dreams with a touching smile as others did. But more than a month passed, real winter had come, and everything was still clear in his memory as though he had parted with Anna Sergeyevna only the day before. And his mem-

ories glowed more and more vividly. When in the evening stillness
he heard from his study the voices of his children, preparing their
lessons, or when he listened to a song or the organ at the restaurant, or the storm howled in the chimney, suddenly everything
would rise up in his memory: what had happened on the groyne,
and the early morning with the mist on the mountains, and the
steamer coming from Theodosia, and the kisses. He would pace
a long time about his room, remembering it all and smiling; then
his memories passed into dreams, and in his fancy the past was
mingled with what was to come. Anna Sergeyevna did not visit
him in dreams, but followed him about everywhere like a shadow and haunted him. When he shut his eyes he saw her as though
she were living before him, and she seemed to him lovelier,
younger, tenderer than she was; and he imagined himself finer
than he had been in Yalta. In the evenings she peeped out at him
from the bookcase, from the fireplace, from the corner—he heard
her breathing, the caressing rustle of her dress. In the street he
watched the women, looking for someone like her.

He was tormented by an intense desire to confide his memories to someone. But in his home it was impossible to talk of his
love, and he had no one outside; he could not talk to his tenants
nor to anyone at the bank. And what had he to talk of? Had he
been in love, then? Had there been anything beautiful, poetical,
or edifying or simply interesting in his relations with Anna
Sergeyevna? And there was nothing for him but to talk vaguely
of love, of woman, and no one guessed what it meant; only his
wife twitched her black eyebrows, and said: "The part of a lady-
killer does not suit you at all, Dimitri."

One evening, coming out of the doctors' club with an official
with whom he had been playing cards, he could not resist saying:

"If only you knew what a fascinating woman I made the
acquaintance of in Yalta!"

The official got into his sledge and was driving away, but
turned suddenly and shouted:

"Dmitri Dmitritch!"

"What?"

"You were right this evening: the sturgeon was a bit too

strong!"

These words, so ordinary, for some reason moved Gurov to indignation, and struck him as degrading and unclean. What savage manners, what people! What senseless nights, what uninteresting, uneventful days! The rage for card-playing, the gluttony, the drunkenness, the continual talk always about the same thing. Useless pursuits and conversations always about the same things absorb the better part of one's time, the better part of one's strength, and in the end there is left a life grovelling and curtailed, worthless and trivial, and there is no escaping or getting away from it—just as though one were in a madhouse or a prison.

Gurov did not sleep all night, and was filled with indignation. And he had a headache all next day. And the next night he slept badly; he sat up in bed, thinking, or paced up and down his room. He was sick of his children, sick of the bank; he had no desire to go anywhere or to talk of anything.

In the holidays in December he prepared for a journey, and told his wife he was going to Petersburg to do something in the interests of a young friend—and he set off for S——. What for? He did not very well know himself. He wanted to see Anna Sergeyevna and to talk with her—to arrange a meeting, if possible.

He reached S—— in the morning, and took the best room at the hotel, in which the floor was covered with grey army cloth, and on the table was an inkstand, grey with dust and adorned with a figure on horseback, with its hat in its hand and its head broken off. The hotel porter gave him the necessary information; Von Diderits lived in a house of his own in Old Gontcharny Street—it was not far from the hotel: he was rich and lived in good style, and had his own horses; everyone in the town knew him. The porter pronounced the name "Dridirits."

Gurov went without haste to Old Gontcharny Street and found the house. Just opposite the house stretched a long grey fence adorned with nails.

"One would run away from a fence like that," thought Gurov, looking from the fence to the windows of the house and back again.

He considered: today was a holiday, and the husband would probably be at home. And in any case it would be tactless to go into the house and upset her. If he were to send her a note it might fall into her husband's hands, and then it might ruin everything. The best thing was to trust to chance. And he kept walking up and down the street by the fence, waiting for the chance. He saw a beggar go in at the gate and dogs fly at him; then an hour later he heard a piano, and the sounds were faint and indistinct. Probably it was Anna Sergeyevna playing. The front door suddenly opened, and an old woman came out, followed by the familiar white Pomeranian. Gurov was on the point of calling to the dog, but his heart began beating violently, and in his excitement he could not remember the dog's name.

He walked up and down, and loathed the grey fence more and more, and by now he thought irritably that Anna Sergeyevna had forgotten him, and was perhaps already amusing herself with someone else, and that that was very natural in a young woman who had nothing to look at from morning till night but that confounded fence. He went back to his hotel room and sat for a long while on the sofa, not knowing what to do, then he had dinner and a long nap.

"How stupid and worrying it is!" he thought when he woke and looked at the dark windows: it was already evening. "Here I've had a good sleep for some reason. What shall I do in the night?"

He sat on the bed, which was covered by a cheap grey blanket, such as one sees in hospitals, and he taunted himself in his vexation:

"So much for the lady with the dog...so much for the adventure... You're in a nice fix..."

That morning at the station a poster in large letters had caught his eye. "The Geisha" was to be performed for the first time. He thought of this and went to the theatre.

"It's quite possible she may go to the first performance," he thought.

The theatre was full. As in all provincial theatres, there was a fog above the chandelier, the gallery was noisy and restless; in the front row the local dandies were standing up before the beginning of the performance, with their hands behind them; in the Governor's box the Governor's daughter, wearing a boa, was sitting in the front seat, while the Governor himself lurked modestly behind the curtain with only his hands visible; the orchestra was a long time tuning up; the stage curtain swayed. All the time the audience were coming in and taking their seats Gurov looked at them eagerly.

Anna Sergeyevna, too, came in. She sat down in the third row, and when Gurov looked at her his heart contracted, and he understood clearly that for him there was in the whole world no creature so near, so precious, and so important to him; she, this little woman, in no way remarkable, lost in a provincial crowd, with a vulgar lorgnette in her hand, filled his whole life now, was his sorrow and his joy, the one happiness that he now desired for himself, and to the sounds of the inferior orchestra, of the wretched provincial violins, he thought how lovely she was. He thought and dreamed.

A young man with small side-whiskers, tall and stooping, came in with Anna Sergeyevna and sat down beside her; he bent his head at every step and seemed to be continually bowing. Most likely this was the husband whom at Yalta, in a rush of bitter feeling, she had called a flunkey. And there really was in his long figure, his side-whiskers, and the small bald patch on his head, something of the flunkey's obsequiousness; his smile was sugary, and in his buttonhole there was some badge of distinction like the number on a waiter.

During the first interval the husband went away to smoke; she remained alone in her stall. Gurov, who was sitting in the stalls, too, went up to her and said in a trembling voice, with a forced smile:

"Good evening."

She glanced at him and turned pale, then glanced again with horror, unable to believe her eyes, and tightly gripped the fan and the lorgnette in her hands, evidently struggling with herself not to faint. Both were silent. She was sitting, he was standing, frightened by her confusion and not venturing to sit down beside her.

The violins and the flute began tuning up. He felt suddenly frightened; it seemed as though all the people in the boxes were looking at them. She got up and went quickly to the door; he followed her, and both walked senselessly along passages, and up and down stairs, and figures in legal, scholastic, and civil service uniforms, all wearing badges, flitted before their eyes. They caught glimpses of ladies, of fur coats hanging on pegs; the draughts blew on them, bringing a smell of stale tobacco. And Gurov, whose heart was beating violently, thought:

"Oh, heavens! Why are these people here and this orchestra!..."

And at that instant he recalled how when he had seen Anna Sergeyevna off at the station he had thought that everything was over and they would never meet again. But how far they were still from the end!

On the narrow, gloomy staircase over which was written "To the Amphitheatre," she stopped.

"How you have frightened me!" she said, breathing hard, still pale and overwhelmed. "Oh, how you have frightened me! I am half dead. Why have you come? Why?"

"But do understand, Anna, do understand..." he said hastily in a low voice. "I entreat you to understand..."

She looked at him with dread, with entreaty, with love; she looked at him intently, to keep his features more distinctly in her memory.

"I am so unhappy," she went on, not heeding him. "I have thought of nothing but you all the time; I live only in the thought of you. And I wanted to forget, to forget you; but why, oh why, have you come?"

On the landing above them two schoolboys were smoking and looking down, but that was nothing to Gurov; he drew Anna Sergeyevna to him, and began kissing her face, her cheeks, and her hands.

"What are you doing, what are you doing!" she cried in horror, pushing him away. "We are mad. Go away today; go away at once ... I beseech you by all that is sacred, I implore you ... There are people coming this way!"

Someone was coming up the stairs.

"You must go away," Anna Sergeyevna went on in a whisper. "Do you hear, Dmitri Dmitritch? I will come and see you in Moscow. I have never been happy; I am miserable now, and I never, never shall be happy, never! Don't make me suffer still more! I swear I'll come to Moscow. But now let us part. My precious, good, dear one, we must part!"

She pressed his hand and began rapidly going downstairs, looking round at him, and from her eyes he could see that she really was unhappy. Gurov stood for a little while, listened, then, when all sound had died away, he found his coat and left the theatre.

IV

And Anna Sergeyevna began coming to see him in Moscow. Once in two or three months she left S——, telling her husband that she was going to consult a doctor about an internal complaint— and her husband believed her, and did not believe her. In Moscow she stayed at the Slaviansky Bazaar hotel, and at once sent a man in a red cap to Gurov. Gurov went to see her, and no one in Moscow knew of it.

Once he was going to see her in this way on a winter morning (the messenger had come the evening before when he was out). With him walked his daughter, whom he wanted to take to school: it was on the way. Snow was falling in big wet flakes.

"It's three degrees above freezing-point, and yet it is snowing," said Gurov to his daughter. "The thaw is only on the surface of the earth; there is quite a different temperature at a greater height in the atmosphere."

"And why are there no thunderstorms in the winter, father?"

He explained that, too. He talked, thinking all the while that he was going to see *her*, and no living soul knew of it, and probably never would know. He had two lives: one open, seen and known by all who cared to know, full of relative truth and of relative falsehood, exactly like the lives of his friends and acquaintances; and another life running its course in secret. And through some strange, perhaps accidental, conjunction of circumstances, everything that was essential, of interest and of value to him, everything in which he was sincere and did not deceive himself, everything that made the kernel of his life, was hidden from other people; and all that was false in him, the sheath in which he hid himself to conceal the truth—such, for instance, as his work in the bank, his discussions at the club, his "lower race," his presence with his wife at anniversary festivities—all that was open. And he judged of others by himself, not believing in what he saw, and always believing that every man had his real, most interesting life under the cover of secrecy and under the cover of night. All personal life rested on secrecy, and possibly it was partly on that account that civilized man was so nervously anxious that personal privacy should be respected.

After leaving his daughter at school, Gurov went on to the Slaviansky Bazaar. He took off his fur coat below, went upstairs, and softly knocked at the door. Anna Sergeyevna, wearing his favourite grey dress, exhausted by the journey and the suspense, had been expecting him since the evening before. She was pale; she looked at him, and did not smile, and he had hardly come in when she fell on his breast. Their kiss was slow and prolonged, as though they had not met for two years.

"Well, how are you getting on there?" he asked. "What news?"

"Wait; I'll tell you directly... I can't talk."

She could not speak; she was crying. She turned away from him, and pressed her handkerchief to her eyes.

"Let her have her cry out. I'll sit down and wait," he thought, and he sat down in an armchair.

Then he rang and asked for tea to be brought him, and while he drank his tea she remained standing at the window with her back to him. She was crying from emotion, from the miserable consciousness that their life was so hard for them; they could only meet in secret, hiding themselves from people, like thieves! Was not their life shattered?

"Come, do stop!" he said.

It was evident to him that this love of theirs would not soon be over, that he could not see the end of it. Anna Sergeyevna grew more and more attached to him. She adored him, and it was unthinkable to say to her that it was bound to have an end someday; besides, she would not have believed it!

He went up to her and took her by the shoulders to say something affectionate and cheering, and at that moment he saw himself in the looking-glass.

His hair was already beginning to turn grey. And it seemed strange to him that he had grown so much older, so much plainer during the last few years. The shoulders on which his hands rested were warm and quivering. He felt compassion for this life, still so warm and lovely, but probably already not far from beginning to fade and wither like his own. Why did she love him so much? He always seemed to women different from what he was, and they loved in him not himself, but the man created by their imagination, whom they had been eagerly seeking all their lives; and afterwards, when they noticed their mistake, they loved him all the same. And not one of them had been happy with him. Time passed, he had made their acquaintance, got on with them, parted, but he had never once loved; it was anything you like, but not love.

And only now when his head was grey he had fallen properly, really in love—for the first time in his life.

Anna Sergeyevna and he loved each other like people very close and akin, like husband and wife, like tender friends; it seemed to them that fate itself had meant them for one another, and they could not understand why he had a wife and she a husband; and it was as though they were a pair of birds of passage, caught and forced to live in different cages. They forgave each other for what they were ashamed of in their past, they forgave everything in the present, and felt that this love of theirs had changed them both.

In moments of depression in the past he had comforted himself with any arguments that came into his mind, but now he no longer cared for arguments; he felt profound compassion, he wanted to be sincere and tender...

"Don't cry, my darling," he said. "You've had your cry; that's enough… Let us talk now, let us think of some plan."

Then they spent a long while taking counsel together, talked of how to avoid the necessity for secrecy, for deception, for living in different towns and not seeing each other for long at a time. How could they be free from this intolerable bondage?

"How? How?" he asked, clutching his head. "How?"

And it seemed as though in a little while the solution would be found, and then a new and splendid life would begin; and it was clear to both of them that they had still a long, long way to go, and that the most complicated and difficult part of it was only just beginning.

THE
SCHARTZ–METTERKLUME
METHOD

Saki
(H.H. Munro, 1870–1916)

Saki's particular genius is to introduce elements of anarchy, cruelty and wildness—even violence—into that most genteel of worlds, upper-class Edwardian England. Certainly the Quabarls have no idea what they have unleashed into their household when they welcome the apparently civilized Lady Carlotta...

ady Carlotta stepped out on to the platform of the small wayside station and took a turn or two up and down its uninteresting length, to kill time till the train should be pleased to proceed on its way. Then, in the roadway beyond, she saw a horse struggling with a more than ample load, and a carter of the sort that seems to bear a sullen hatred against the animal that helps him to earn a living. Lady Carlotta promptly betook her to the roadway, and put rather a different complexion on the struggle. Certain of her acquaintances were wont to give her plentiful admonition as to the undesirability of interfering on behalf of a distressed animal, such interference being "none of her business." Only once had she put the doctrine of non-interference into practice, when one of its most eloquent exponents had been besieged for nearly three hours in a small and extremely uncomfortable may-tree by an angry boar-pig, while Lady Carlotta, on the other side of the fence, had proceeded with the water-colour sketch she was engaged on, and refused to interfere between the boar and his prisoner. It is to be feared that she lost the friendship of the ultimately rescued lady. On this occasion she merely lost the

train, which gave way to the first sign of impatience it had shown throughout the journey, and steamed off without her. She bore the desertion with philosophical indifference; her friends and relations were thoroughly well used to the fact of her luggage arriving without her. She wired a vague noncommittal message to her destination to say that she was coming on "by another train." Before she had time to think what her next move might be, she was confronted by an imposingly attired lady, who seemed to be taking a prolonged mental inventory of her clothes and looks.

"You must be Miss Hope, the governess I've come to meet," said the apparition, in a tone that admitted of very little argument.

"Very well, if I must I must," said Lady Carlotta to herself with dangerous meekness.

"I am Mrs. Quabarl," continued the lady; "and where, pray, is your luggage?"

"It's gone astray," said the alleged governess, falling in with the excellent rule of life that the absent are always to blame; the luggage had, in point of fact, behaved with perfect correctitude. "I've just telegraphed about it," she added, with a nearer approach to truth.

"How provoking," said Mrs. Quabarl; "these railway companies are so careless. However, my maid can lend you things for the night," and she led the way to her car.

During the drive to the Quabarl mansion Lady Carlotta was impressively introduced to the nature of the charge that had been thrust open her; she learned that Claude and Wilfrid were delicate, sensitive young people, that Irene had the artistic temperament highly developed, and that Viola was something or other else of a mould equally commonplace among children of that class and type in the twentieth century.

"I wish them not only to be *taught*," said Mrs. Quabarl, "but *interested* in what they learn. In their history lessons, for instance, you must try to make them feel that they are being introduced to the life-stories of men and women who really lived, not merely committing a mass of names and dates to memory. French, of course, I shall expect you to talk at mealtimes several days in the week."

"I shall talk French four days of the week and Russian in the remaining three."

"Russian? My dear Miss Hope, no one in the house speaks or understands Russian."

"That will not embarrass me in the least," said Lady Carlotta coldly.

Mrs. Quabarl, to use a colloquial expression, was knocked off her perch. She was one of those imperfectly self-assured individuals who are magnificent and autocratic as long as they are not seriously opposed. The least show of unexpected resistance goes a long way towards rendering them cowed and apologetic. When the new governess failed to express wondering admiration of the large, newly purchased and expensive car, and lightly alluded to the superior advantages of one or two makes which had just been put on the market, the discomfiture of her patroness became almost abject. Her feelings were those which might have animated a general of ancient warfaring days, on beholding his heaviest battle-elephant ignominiously driven off the field by slingers and javelin throwers.

At dinner that evening, although reinforced by her husband, who usually duplicated her opinions and lent her moral support generally, Mrs. Quabarl regained none of her lost ground. The governess not only helped herself well and truly to wine, but held forth with considerable show of critical knowledge on various vintage matters, concerning which the Quabarls were in no wise able to pose as authorities. Previous governesses had limited their conversation on the wine topic to a respectful and doubtless sincere expression of a preference for water. When this one went as far as to recommend a wine firm in whose hands you could not go very far wrong, Mrs. Quabarl thought it time to turn the conversation into more usual channels.

"We got very satisfactory references about you from Canon Teep," she observed; "a very estimable man, I should think."

"Drinks like a fish and beats his wife, otherwise a very lovable character," said the governess imperturbably.

"My *dear* Miss Hope! I trust you are exaggerating,"

exclaimed the Quabarls in unison.

"One must in justice admit that there is some provocation," continued the romancer. "Mrs. Teep is quite the most irritating bridge-player that I have ever sat down with; her leads and declarations would condone a certain amount of brutality in her partner, but to souse her with the contents of the only soda-water siphon in the house on a Sunday afternoon, when one couldn't get another, argues an indifference to the comfort of others which I cannot altogether overlook. You may think me hasty in my judgments, but it was practically on account of the siphon incident that I left."

"We will talk of this some other time," said Mrs. Quabarl hastily.

"I shall never allude to it again," said the governess with decision.

Mr. Quabarl made a welcome diversion by asking what studies the new instructress proposed to inaugurate on the morrow.

"History to begin with," she informed him.

"Ah, history," he observed sagely; "now in teaching them history you must take care to interest them in what they learn. You must make them feel that they are being introduced to the life-stories of men and women who really lived—"

"I've told her all that," interposed Mrs. Quabarl.

"I teach history on the Schartz–Metterklume method," said the governess loftily.

"Ah, yes," said her listeners, thinking it expedient to assume an acquaintance at least with the name.

"What are you children doing out here?" demanded Mrs. Quabarl the next morning, on finding Irene sitting rather glumly at the head of the stairs, while her sister was perched in an attitude of depressed discomfort on the window-seat behind her, with a wolfskin rug almost covering her.

"We are having a history lesson," came the unexpected reply. "I am supposed to be Rome, and Viola up there is the she-wolf; not a real wolf, but the figure of one that the Romans used to set store by—I forget why. Claude and Wilfrid have gone to fetch the shabby women."

"The shabby women?"

"Yes, they've got to carry them off. They didn't want to, but Miss Hope got one of father's fives-bats and said she'd give them a number nine spanking if they didn't, so they've gone to do it."

A loud, angry screaming from the direction of the lawn drew Mrs. Quabarl thither in hot haste, fearful lest the threatened castigation might even now be in process of infliction. The outcry, however, came principally from the two small daughters of the lodge-keeper, who were being hauled and pushed towards the house by the panting and dishevelled Claude and Wilfrid, whose task was rendered even more arduous by the incessant, if not very effectual, attacks of the captured maidens' small brother. The governess, fives-bat in hand, sat negligently on the stone balustrade, presiding over the scene with the cold impartiality of a Goddess of Battles. A furious and repeated chorus of "I'll tell muvver" rose from the lodge children, but the lodge-mother, who was hard of hearing, was for the moment immersed in the preoccupation of her washtub. After an apprehensive glance in the direction of the lodge (the good woman was gifted with the highly militant temper which is sometimes the privilege of deafness) Mrs. Quabarl flew indignantly to the rescue of the struggling captives.

"Wilfrid! Claude! Let those children go at once. Miss Hope, what on earth is the meaning of this scene?"

"Early Roman history; the Sabine women, don't you know? It's the Schartz-Metterklume method to make children understand history by acting it themselves; fixes it in their memory, you know. Of course, if, thanks to your interference, your boys go through life thinking that the Sabine women ultimately escaped, I really cannot be held responsible."

"You may be very clever and modern, Miss Hope," said Mrs. Quabarl firmly, "but I should like you to leave here by the next train. Your luggage will be sent after you as soon as it arrives."

"I'm not certain exactly where I shall be for the next few days," said the dismissed instructress of youth; "you might keep my luggage till I wire my address. There are only a couple of trunks and some golf-clubs and a leopard cub."

"A leopard cub!" gasped Mrs. Quabarl. Even in her departure, this extraordinary person seemed destined to leave a trail of embarrassment behind her.

"Well, it's rather left off being a cub; it's more than half-grown, you know. A fowl every day and a rabbit on Sundays is what it usually gets. Raw beef makes it too excitable. Don't trouble about getting the car for me, I'm rather inclined for a walk."

And Lady Carlotta strode out of the Quabarl horizon.

The advent of the genuine Miss Hope, who had made a mistake as to the day on which she was due to arrive, caused a turmoil which that good lady was quite unused to inspiring. Obviously, the Quabarl family had been woefully befooled, but a certain amount of relief came with the knowledge.

"How tiresome for you, dear Carlotta," said her hostess, when the overdue guest ultimately arrived; "how very tiresome losing your train and having to stop overnight in a strange place."

"Oh, dear, no," said Lady Carlotta; "not at all tiresome—for me."

A
LODGING FOR THE NIGHT

*A Story of Francis Villon
by Robert Louis Stevenson
(1850–1894)*

I sometimes discover that, without intending to, I have included stories in my collections which have striking similarities. For example, this story, like Jack London's "To Build a Fire," is about a man facing the elements of snow and cold. But Stevenson's story is set in fifteenth-century Paris while London's unfolds in the barren wastes of Alaska. So much for similarities!

I cherish Stevenson's writing, and this story is brimming with the author's love of adventure and his sympathy for life's rogues and vagabonds, those who live for the moment. Has there ever been anyone better at capturing a mood, creating an atmosphere, defining a locale? Incidentally, this was Stevenson's first piece of published fiction—an auspicious début if ever there was one.

t was late in November, 1456. The snow fell over Paris with rigorous, relentless persistence; sometimes the wind made a sally and scattered it in flying vortices; sometimes there was a lull, and flake after flake descended out of black night air, silent, circuitous, interminable. To poor people, looking up under moist eyebrows, it seemed a wonder where it all came from. Master Francis Villon had propounded an alternative that afternoon, at a tavern window: was it only Pagan Jupiter plucking geese upon Olympus? or were the holy angels moulting? He was only a poor Master of Arts, he went on; and as the

question somewhat touched upon divinity, he durst not venture to conclude. A silly old priest from Montargis, who was among the company, treated the young rascal to a bottle of wine in honour of the jest and the grimaces with which it was accompanied, and swore on his own white beard that he had been just such another irreverent dog when he was Villon's age.

The air was raw and pointed, but not far below freezing; and the flakes were large, damp, and adhesive. The whole city was sheeted up. An army might have marched from end to end and not a footfall given the alarm. If there were any belated birds in heaven, they saw the island like a large white patch, and the bridges like slim white spars, on the black ground of the river. High up overhead the snow settled among the tracery of the cathedral towers. Many a niche was drifted full; many a statue wore a long white bonnet on its grotesque or sainted head. The gargoyles had been transformed into great false noses, drooping towards the point. The crockets were like upright pillows swollen on one side. In the intervals of the wind, there was a dull sound of dripping about the precincts of the church.

The cemetery of St. John had taken its own share of the snow. All the graves were decently covered; tall white housetops stood around in grave array; worthy burghers were long ago in bed, benightcapped like their domiciles; there was no light in all the neighbourhood but a little peep from a lamp that hung swinging in the church choir, and tossed the shadows to and fro in time to its oscillations. The clock was hard on ten when the patrol went by with halberds and a lantern, beating their hands; and they saw nothing suspicious about the cemetery of St. John.

Yet there was a small house, backed up against the cemetery wall, which was still awake, and awake to evil purpose, in that snoring district. There was not much to betray it from without; only a stream of warm vapour from the chimney-top, a patch where the snow melted on the roof, and a few half-obliterated footprints at the door. But within, behind the shuttered windows, Master Francis Villon the poet, and some of the thievish crew with whom he consorted, were keeping the night alive and passing round the bottle.

A great pile of living embers diffused a strong and ruddy glow from the arched chimney. Before this straddled Dom Nicolas, the Picardy monk, with his skirts picked up and his fat legs bared to the comfortable warmth. His dilated shadow cut the room in half; and the firelight only escaped on either side of his broad person, and in a little pool between his outspread feet. His face had the beery, bruised appearance of the continual drinker's; it was covered with a network of congested veins, purple in ordinary circumstances, but now pale violet, for even with his back to the fire the cold pinched him on the other side. His cowl had half fallen back, and made a strange excrescence on either side of his bull neck. So he straddled, grumbling, and cut the room in half with the shadow of his portly frame.

On the right, Villon and Guy Tabary were huddled together over a scrap of parchment; Villon making a ballade which he was to call the "Ballade of Roast Fish," and Tabary spluttering admiration at his shoulder. The poet was a rag of a man, dark, little, and lean, with hollow cheeks and thin black locks. He carried his four-and-twenty years with feverish animation. Greed had made folds about his eyes, evil smiles had puckered his mouth. The wolf and pig struggled together in his face. It was an eloquent, sharp, ugly, earthly countenance. His hands were small and prehensile, with fingers knotted like a cord; and they were continually flickering in front of him in violent and expressive pantomime. As for Tabary, a broad, complacent, admiring imbecility breathed from his squash nose and slobbering lips: he had become a thief, just as he might have become the most decent of burgesses, by the imperious chance that rules the lives of human geese and human donkeys.

At the monk's other hand, Montigny and Thevenin Pensete played a game of chance. About the first there clung some flavour of good birth and training, as about a fallen angel; something long, lithe, and courtly in the person; something aquiline and darkling in the face. Thevenin, poor soul, was in great feather: he had done a good stroke of knavery that afternoon in the Faubourg St. Jacques, and all night he had been gaining from Montigny. A flat smile illuminated his face; his bald head shone rosily in a garland of red curls; his little protuberant stomach shook with silent chucklings as he swept in his gains.

"Doubles or quits?" said Thevenin.

Montigny nodded grimly.

"*Some may prefer to dine in state,*" wrote Villon, "*On bread and cheese on silver plate.* Or—or—help me out, Guido!"

Tabary giggled.

"*Or parsley on a golden dish,*" scribbled the poet.

The wind was freshening without; it drove the snow before it, and sometimes raised its voice in a victorious whoop, and made sepulchral grumblings in the chimney. The cold was growing sharper as the night went on. Villon, protruding his lips, imitated the gust with something between a whistle and a groan. It was an eerie, uncomfortable talent of the poet's much detested by the Picardy monk.

"Can't you hear it rattle in the gibbet?" said Villon. "They are all dancing the devil's jig on nothing, up there. You may dance, my gallants, you'll be none the warmer! Whew; what a gust! Down went somebody just now! A medlar the fewer on the three-legged medlar-tree!—I say, Dom Nicolas, it'll be cold tonight on the St. Denis Road?" he asked.

Dom Nicolas winked both his big eyes, and seemed to choke upon his Adam's apple. Montfaucon, the great grisly Paris gibbet, stood hard by the St. Denis Road, and the pleasantry touched him on the raw. As for Tabary, he laughed immoderately over the medlars; he had never heard anything more light-hearted; and he held his sides and crowed. Villon fetched him a fillip on the nose, which turned his mirth into an attack of coughing.

"Oh, stop that row," said Villon, "and think of rhymes to 'fish.'"

"Doubles or quits," said Montigny doggedly.

"With all my heart," quoth Thevenin.

"Is there any more in that bottle?" asked the monk.

"Open another," said Villon. "How do you ever hope to fill that big hogshead, your body, with little things like bottles? And how do you expect to get to heaven? How many angels, do you fancy, can be spared to carry up a single monk from Picardy? Or do you think yourself another Elias—and they'll send the coach for you?"

"*Hominibus impossible,*" replied the monk, as he filled his glass.

Tabary was in ecstasies.

Villon filliped his nose again.

"Laugh at my jokes, if you like," he said.

"It was very good," objected Tabary.

Villon made a face at him. "Think of rhymes to 'fish,'" he said. "What have you to do with Latin? You'll wish you knew none of it at the great assizes, when the devil calls for Guido Tabary, clericus—the devil with the humpback and the red-hot fingernails. Talking of the devil," he added in a whisper, "look at Montigny!"

All three peered covertly at the gamester. He did not seem to be enjoying his luck. His mouth was a little to a side; one nostril nearly shut, and the other much inflated. The black dog was on his back, as people say, in terrifying nursery metaphor; and he breathed hard under the gruesome burden.

"He looks as if he could knife him," whispered Tabary, with round eyes.

The monk shuddered, and turned his face and spread his open hands to the red embers. It was the cold that thus affected Dom Nicolas, and not any excess of moral sensibility.

"Come now," said Villon—"about this ballade. How does it run so far?" And, beating time with his hand, he read it aloud to Tabary.

They were interrupted at the fourth rhyme by a brief and fatal movement among the gamesters. The round was completed, and Thevenin was just opening his mouth to claim another victory, when Montigny leaped up, swift as an adder, and stabbed him to the heart. The blow took effect before he had time to utter a cry, before he had time to move. A tremor or two convulsed his frame; his hands opened and shut, his heels rattled on the floor; then his head rolled backward over one shoulder with the eyes wide open; and Thevenin Pensete's spirit had returned to Him who made it.

Everyone sprang to his feet; but the business was over in two twos. The four living fellows looked at each other in rather a ghastly fashion; the dead man contemplating a corner of the roof with a singular and ugly leer.

"My God!" said Tabary; and he began to pray in Latin.

Villon broke out into hysterical laughter. He came a step forward and ducked a ridiculous bow to Thevenin, and laughed still louder. Then he sat down suddenly, all of a heap, upon a stool, and continued laughing bitterly as though he would shake himself to pieces.

Montigny recovered his composure first.

"Let's see what he has about him," he remarked; and he picked the dead man's pockets with a practised hand and divided the money into four equal portions on the table. "There's for you," he said.

The monk received his share with a deep sigh, and a single stealthy glance at the dead Thevenin, who was beginning to sink into himself and topple sideways off the chair.

"We're all in for it," cried Villon, swallowing his mirth. "It's a hanging job for every man jack of us that's here—not to speak of those who aren't." He made a shocking gesture in the air with his raised right hand, and put out his tongue and threw his head on one side, so as to counterfeit the appearance of one who has been hanged. Then he pocketed his share of the spoil, and executed a shuffle with his feet as if to restore the circulation.

Tabary was the last to help himself; he made a dash at the money, and retired to the other end of the apartment.

Montigny stuck Thevenin upright in the chair, and drew out the dagger, which was followed by a jet of blood.

"You fellows had better be moving," he said, as he wiped the blade on his victim's doublet.

"I think we had," returned Villon with a gulp. "Damn his fat head!" he broke out. "It sticks in my throat like phlegm. What right has a man to have red hair when he is dead?" And he fell all of a heap again upon the stool, and fairly covered his face with his hands.

Montigny and Dom Nicolas laughed aloud, even Tabary

feebly chiming in.

"Cry baby," said the monk.

"I always said he was a woman," added Montigny with a sneer. "Sit up, can't you?" he went on, giving another shake to the murdered body. "Tread out that fire, Nick!"

But Nick was better employed; he was quietly taking Villon's purse, as the poet sat, limp and trembling, on the stool where he had been making a ballade not three minutes before. Montigny and Tabary dumbly demanded a share of the booty, which the monk silently promised as he passed the little bag into the bosom of his gown. In many ways an artistic nature unfits a man for practical existence.

No sooner had the theft been accomplished than Villon shook himself, jumped to his feet, and began helping to scatter and extinguish the embers. Meanwhile Montigny opened the door and cautiously peered into the street. The coast was clear; there was no meddlesome patrol in sight. Still it was judged wiser to slip out severally; and as Villon was himself in a hurry to escape from the neighbourhood of the dead Thevenin, and the rest were in a still greater hurry to get rid of him before he should discover the loss of his money, he was the first by general consent to issue forth into the street.

The wind had triumphed and swept all the clouds from heaven. Only a few vapours, as thin as moonlight, fleeted rapidly across the stars. It was bitter cold; and by a common optical effect, things seemed almost more definite than in the broadest daylight. The sleeping city was absolutely still: a company of white hoods, a field full of little Alps, below the twinkling stars. Villon cursed his fortune. Would it were still snowing! Now, wherever he went, he left an indelible trail behind him on the glittering streets; wherever he went he was still tethered to the house by the cemetery of St. John; wherever he went he must weave, with his own plodding feet, the rope that bound him to the crime and would bind him to the gallows. The leer of the dead man came back to him with a new significance. He snapped his fingers as if to pluck up his own spirits, and, choosing a street at random, stepped boldly forward in the snow.

Two things preoccupied him as he went: the aspect of the gallows at Montfaucon in this bright windy phase of the night's existence, for one; and for another, the look of the dead man with his
bald head and garland of red curls. Both struck cold upon his
heart, and he kept quickening his pace as if he could escape from
unpleasant thoughts by mere fleetness of foot. Sometimes he
looked back over his shoulder with a sudden nervous jerk; but he
was the only moving thing in the white streets, except when the
wind swooped round a corner and threw up the snow, which was
beginning to freeze, in spouts of glittering dust.

Suddenly he saw, a long way before him, a black clump and
a couple of lanterns. The clump was in motion, and the lanterns
swung as though carried by men walking. It was a patrol. And
though it was merely crossing his line of march, he judged it wiser
to get out of eyeshot as speedily as he could. He was not in the
humour to be challenged, and he was conscious of making a very
conspicuous mark upon the snow. Just on his left hand there
stood a great hotel, with some turrets and a large porch before
the door; it was half-ruinous, he remembered, and had long stood
empty; and so he made three steps of it and jumped into the shelter of the porch. It was pretty dark inside, after the glimmer of
the snowy streets, and he was groping forward with outspread
hands, when he stumbled over some substance which offered an
indescribable mixture of resistance, hard and soft, firm and loose.
His heart gave a leap, and he sprang two steps back and stared
dreadfully at the obstacle. Then he gave a little laugh of relief. It
was only a woman, and she dead. He knelt beside her to make
sure upon this latter point. She was freezing cold, and rigid like a
stick. A little ragged finery fluttered in the wind about her hair,
and her cheeks had been heavily rouged that same afternoon. Her
pockets were quite empty; but in her stocking, underneath the
garter, Villon found two of the small coins that went by the name
of whites. It was little enough; but it was always something; and
the poet was moved with a deep sense of pathos that she should
have died before she had spent her money. That seemed to him a
dark and pitiable mystery; and he looked from the coins in his
hand to the dead woman, and back again to the coins, shaking

his head over the riddle of man's life. Henry V of England, dying at Vincennes just after he had conquered France, and this poor jade cut off by a cold draught in a great man's doorway, before she had time to spend her couple of whites—it seemed a cruel way to carry on the world. Two whites would have taken such a little while to squander; and yet it would have been one more good taste in the mouth, one more smack of the lips, before the devil got the soul, and the body was left to birds and vermin. He would like to use all his tallow before the light was blown out and the lantern broken.

While these thoughts were passing through his mind, he was feeling, half mechanically, for his purse. Suddenly his heart stopped beating; a feeling of cold scales passed up the back of his legs, and a cold blow seemed to fall upon his scalp. He stood petrified for a moment; then he felt again with one feverish movement; and then his loss burst upon him, and he was covered at once with perspiration. To spendthrifts money is so living and actual—it is such a thin veil between them and their pleasures! There is only one limit to their fortune—that of time; and a spendthrift with only a few crowns is the Emperor of Rome until they are spent. For such a person to lose his money is to suffer the most shocking reverse, and fall from heaven to hell, from all to nothing, in a breath. And all the more if he has put his head in the halter for it; if he may be hanged tomorrow for that same purse, so dearly earned, so foolishly departed! Villon stood and cursed; he threw the two whites into the street, he shook his fist at heaven; he stamped, and was not horrified to find himself trampling the poor corpse. Then he began rapidly to retrace his steps towards the house beside the cemetery. He had forgotten all fear of the patrol, which was long gone by at any rate, and had no idea but that of his lost purse. It was in vain that he looked right and left upon the snow: nothing was to be seen. He had not dropped it in the streets. Had it fallen in the house? He would have liked dearly to go in and see; but the idea of the grisly occupant unmanned him. And he saw besides, as he drew near, that their efforts to put out the fire had been unsuccessful; on the contrary, it had broken into a blaze, and a changeful light played in the chinks of door and window, and revived his terror for the authorities and Paris gibbet.

He returned to the hotel with the porch, and groped about upon the snow for the money he had thrown away in his childish passion. But he could only find one white; the other had probably struck sideways and sunk deeply in. With a single white in his pocket, all his projects for a rousing night in some wild tavern vanished utterly away. And it was not only pleasure that fled laughing from his grasp; positive discomfort, positive pain, attacked him as he stood ruefully before the porch. His perspiration had dried upon him; and though the wind had now fallen, a binding frost was setting in stronger with every hour, and he felt benumbed and sick at heart. What was to be done? Late as was the hour, improbable as was success, he would try the house of his adopted father, the chaplain of St. Benoît.

He ran there all the way, and knocked timidly. There was no answer. He knocked again and again, taking heart with every stroke; and at last steps were heard approaching from within. A barred wicket fell open in the iron-studded door, and emitted a gush of yellow light.

"Hold up your face to the wicket," said the chaplain from within.

"It's only me," whimpered Villon.

"Oh, it's only you, is it?" returned the chaplain; and he cursed him with foul unpriestly oaths for disturbing him at such an hour, and bade him be off to hell, where he came from.

"My hands are blue to the wrist," pleaded Villon; "my feet are dead and full of twinges; my nose aches with the sharp air; the cold lies at my heart. I may be dead before morning. Only this once, father, and before God I will never ask again!"

"You should have come earlier," said the ecclesiastic coolly. "Young men require a lesson now and then." He shut the wicket and retired deliberately into the interior of the house.

Villon was beside himself; he beat upon the door with his hands and feet, and shouted hoarsely after the chaplain.

"Wormy old fox!" he cried. "If I had my hand under your twist, I would send you flying headlong into the bottomless pit."

A door shut in the interior, faintly audible to the poet down long passages. He passed his hand over his mouth with an oath. And then the humour of the situation struck him, and he laughed and looked lightly up to heaven, where the stars seemed to be winking over his discomfiture.

What was to be done? It looked very like a night in the frosty streets. The idea of the dead woman popped into his imagination, and gave him a hearty fright; what had happened to her in the early night might very well happen to him before morning. And he so young! and with such immense possibilities of disorderly amusement before him! He felt quite pathetic over the notion of his own fate, as if it had been someone else's, and made a little imaginative vignette of the scene in the morning when they should find his body.

He passed all his chances under review, turning the white between his thumb and forefinger. Unfortunately he was on bad terms with some old friends who would once have taken pity on him in such a plight. He had lampooned them in verses, he had beaten and cheated them; and yet now, when he was in so close a pinch, he thought there was at least one who might perhaps relent. It was a chance. It was worth trying at least, and he would go and see.

On the way, two little accidents happened to him which coloured his musings in a very different manner. For, first, he fell in the track of a patrol, and walked in it for some hundred yards, although it lay out of his direction. And this spirited him up; at least he had confused his trail; for he was still possessed with the idea of people tracking him all about Paris over the snow, and collaring him next morning before he was awake. The other matter affected him very differently. He passed a street corner, where, not so long before, a woman and her child had been devoured by wolves. This was just the kind of weather, he reflected, when wolves might take it into their heads to enter Paris again; and a lone man in these deserted streets would run the chance of something worse than a mere scare. He stopped and looked upon the place with an unpleasant interest—it was a centre where several lanes intersected each other; and he looked down them all one after another, and held his breath to listen, lest he should detect some galloping black things on the snow or hear the sound of howling between him and the river. He remembered his mother telling him the story and pointing out the spot, while he was yet a child. His mother! If he only knew where she lived, he might make sure at least of shelter. He determined he would inquire upon the morrow; nay, he would go and see her too, poor old girl! So thinking, he arrived at his destination—his last hope for the night.

The house was quite dark, like its neighbours; and yet after a few taps, he heard a movement overhead, a door opening, and a cautious voice asking who was there. The poet named himself in a loud whisper, and waited, not without some trepidation, the result. Nor had he to wait long. A window was suddenly opened, and a pailful of slops splashed down upon the doorstep. Villon had not been unprepared for something of the sort, and had put himself as much in shelter as the nature of the porch admitted; but for all that, he was deplorably drenched below the waist. His hose began to freeze almost at once. Death from cold and exposure stared him in the face; he remembered he was of phthisical tendency, and began coughing tentatively. But the gravity of the danger steadied his nerves. He stopped a few hundred yards from the door where he had been so rudely used, and reflected with his finger to his nose. He could only see one way of getting a lodging, and that was to take it. He had noticed a house not far away, which looked as if it might be easily broken into, and thither he betook himself promptly, entertaining himself on the way with the idea of a room still hot, with a table still loaded with the remains of supper, where he might pass the rest of the black hours, and whence he should issue, on the morrow, with an armful of valuable plate. He even considered on what viands and what wines he should prefer; and as he was calling the roll of his favourite dainties, roast fish presented itself to his mind with an odd mixture of amusement and horror.

"I shall never finish that ballade," he thought to himself; and then, with another shudder at the recollection, "Oh, damn his fat head!" he repeated fervently, and spat upon the snow.

The house in question looked dark at first sight; but as Villon made a preliminary inspection in search of the handiest point of attack, a little twinkle of light caught his eye from behind a curtained window.

"The devil!" he thought. "People awake! Some student or some saint, confound the crew! Can't they get drunk and lie in bed snoring like their neighbours? What's the good of curfew, and poor devils of bell-ringers jumping at a rope's end in bell-towers? What's the use of day, if people sit up all night? The gripes to them!" He grinned as he saw where his logic was leading him. "Every man to his business, after all," added he, "and if they're awake, by the Lord, I may come by a supper honestly for this once, and cheat the devil."

He went boldly to the door and knocked with an assured hand. On both previous occasions, he had knocked timidly and with some dread of attracting notice; but now when he had just discarded the thought of a burglarious entry, knocking at the door seemed a mighty simple and innocent proceeding. The sound of his blows echoed through the house with thin, phantasmal reverberations, as though it were quite empty; but these had scarcely died away before a measured tread drew near, a couple of bolts were withdrawn, and one wing was opened broadly, as though no guile or fear of guile were known to those within. A tall figure of a man, muscular and spare, but a little bent, confronted Villon. The head was massive in bulk, but finely sculptured; the nose blunt at the bottom, but refining upward to where it joined a pair of strong and honest eyebrows; the mouth and eyes surrounded with delicate markings, and the whole face based upon a thick white beard, boldly and squarely trimmed. Seen as it was by the light of a flickering hand-lamp, it looked perhaps nobler than it had a right to do; but it was a fine face, honourable rather than intelligent, strong, simple, and righteous.

"You knock late, sir," said the old man in resonant, courteous tones.

Villon cringed, and brought up many servile words of apology; at a crisis of this sort, the beggar was uppermost in him, and the man of genius hid his head with confusion.

"You are cold," repeated the old man, "and hungry? Well, step in." And he ordered him into the house with a noble enough gesture.

"Some great seigneur," thought Villon, as his host, setting down the lamp on the flagged pavement of the entry, shot the bolts once more into their places.

"You will pardon me if I go in front," he said, when this was done; and he preceded the poet upstairs into a large apartment, warmed with a pan of charcoal and lit by a great lamp hanging from the roof. It was very bare of furniture: only some gold plate on a sideboard; some folios; and a stand of armour between the windows. Some smart tapestry hung upon the walls, representing the crucifixion of our Lord in one piece, and in another a scene of shepherds and shepherdesses by a running stream. Over the chimney was a shield of arms.

"Will you seat yourself," said the old man, "and forgive me if I leave you? I am alone in my house tonight, and if you are to eat I must forage for you myself."

No sooner was his host gone than Villon leaped from the chair on which he had just seated himself, and began examining the room, with the stealth and passion of a cat. He weighed the gold flagons in his hand, opened all the folios, and investigated the arms upon the shield, and the stuff with which the seats were lined. He raised the window curtains, and saw that the windows were set with rich stained glass in figures, so far as he could see, of martial import. Then he stood in the middle of the room, drew a long breath, and retaining it with puffed cheeks, looked round and round him, turning on his heels, as if to impress every feature of the apartment on his memory.

"Seven pieces of plate," he said. "If there had been ten, I would have risked it. A fine house, and a fine old master, so help me all the saints!"

And just then, hearing the old man's tread returning along the corridor, he stole back to his chair, and began humbly toasting his wet legs before the charcoal pan.

His entertainer had a plate of meat in one hand and a jug of wine in the other. He set down the plate upon the table, motioning Villon to draw in his chair, and, going to the sideboard, brought back two goblets, which he filled.

"I drink to your better fortune," he said, gravely touching Villon's cup with his own.

"To our better acquaintance," said the poet, growing bold. A mere man of the people would have been awed by the courtesy of the old seigneur, but Villon was hardened in that matter; he had made mirth for great lords before now, and found them as black rascals as himself. And so he devoted himself to the viands with a ravenous gusto, while the old man, leaning backward, watched him with steady, curious eyes.

"You have blood on your shoulder, my man," he said.

Montigny must have laid his wet right hand upon him as he left the house. He cursed Montigny in his heart.

"It was none of my shedding," he stammered.

"I had not supposed so," returned his host quietly. "A brawl?"

"Well, something of that sort," Villon admitted with a quaver.

"Perhaps a fellow murdered?"

"Oh no, not murdered," said the poet, more and more confused. "It was all fair play—murdered by accident. I had no hand in it, God strike me dead!" he added fervently.

"One rogue the fewer, I dare say," observed the master of the house.

"You may dare to say that," agreed Villon, infinitely relieved. "As big a rogue as there is between here and Jerusalem. He turned up his toes like a lamb. But it was a nasty thing to look at. I dare say you've seen dead men in your time, my lord?" he added, glancing at the armour.

"Many," said the old man. "I have followed the wars, as you imagine."

Villon laid down his knife and fork, which he had just taken up again.

"Were any of them bald?" he asked.

"Oh yes, and with hair as white as mine."

"I don't think I should mind the white so much," said Villon. "His was red." And he had a return of his shuddering and tendency to laughter, which he drowned with a great draught of wine. "I'm a little put out when I think of it," he went on. "I knew him—damn him! And then the cold gives a man fancies—or the fancies give a man cold, I don't know which."

"Have you any money?" asked the old man.

"I have one white," returned the poet, laughing. "I got it out of a dead jade's stocking in a porch. She was as dead as Caesar, poor wench, and as cold as a church, with bits of ribbon sticking in her hair. This is a hard world in winter for wolves and wenches and poor rogues like me."

"I," said the old man, "am Enguerrand de la Feuillée, seigneur de Brisetout, bailly du Patatrac. Who and what may you be?"

Villon rose and made a suitable reverence. "I am called Francis Villon," he said, "a poor Master of Arts of this university. I know some Latin, and a deal of vice. I can make chansons, ballades, lais, virelais, and roundels, and I am very fond of wine. I was born in a garret, and I shall not improbably die upon the gallows. I may add, my lord, that from this night forward I am your lordship's very obsequious servant to command."

"No servant of mine," said the knight; "my guest for this evening, and no more."

"A very grateful guest," said Villon politely; and he drank in dumb show to his entertainer.

"You are shrewd," began the old man, tapping his forehead, "very shrewd; you have learning; you are a clerk; and yet you take a small piece of money off a dead woman in the street. Is it not a kind of theft?"

"It is a kind of theft much practised in the wars, my lord."

"The wars are the field of honour," returned the old man proudly. "There a man plays his life upon the cast; he fights in the name of his lord the king, his Lord God, and all their lordships and holy saints and angels."

"Put it," said Villon, "that I were really a thief, should I not play my life also, and against heavier odds?"

"For gain, but not for honour."

"Gain?" repeated Villon with a shrug. "Gain! The poor fellow wants supper, and takes it. So does the soldier in a campaign. Why, what are all these requisitions we hear so much about? If they are not gain to those who take them, they are loss enough to the others. The men-at-arms drink by a good fire, while the burgher bites his nails to buy them wine and wood. I have seen a good many ploughmen swinging on trees about the country, ay, I have seen thirty on one elm, and a very poor figure they made; and when I asked someone how all these came to be hanged, I was told it was because they could not scrape together enough crowns to satisfy the men-at-arms."

"These things are a necessity of war, which the low-born must endure with constancy. It is true that some captains drive over hard; there are spirits in every rank not easily moved by pity; and indeed many follow arms who are not better than brigands."

"You see," said the poet, "you cannot separate the soldier from the brigand; and what is a thief but an isolated brigand with circumspect manners? I steal a couple of mutton chops, without so much as disturbing people's sleep; the farmer grumbles a bit, but sups none the less wholesomely of what remains. You come up blowing gloriously on a trumpet, take away the whole sheep, and beat the farmer pitifully into the bargain. I have no trumpet; I am only Tom, Dick, or Harry; I am a rogue and a dog, and hanging's too good for me—with all my heart; but just you ask the farmer which of us he prefers, just find out which of us he lies awake to curse on cold nights."

"Look at us two," said his lordship. "I am old, strong, and honoured. If I were turned from my house tomorrow, hundreds would be proud to shelter me. Poor people would go out and pass the night in the streets with their children, if I merely hinted that I wished to be alone. And I find you up, wandering homeless, and picking farthings off dead women by the wayside! I fear no man and nothing; I have seen you tremble and lose countenance at a word. I wait God's summons contentedly in my own house, or, if it please the king to call me out again, upon the field of battle. You look for the gallows; a rough, swift death, without hope or honour. Is there no difference between these two?"

"As far as to the moon," Villon acquiesced. "But if I had been born lord of Brisetout, and you had been the poor scholar Francis, would the difference have been any the less? Should not I have been warming my knees at this charcoal pan, and would not you have been groping for farthings in the snow? Should not I have been the soldier, and you the thief?"

"A thief!" cried the old man. "I a thief! If you understood your words, you would repent them."

Villon turned out his hands with a gesture of inimitable impudence. "If your lordship had done me the honour to follow my argument!" he said.

"I do you too much honour in submitting to your presence," said the knight. "Learn to curb your tongue when you speak with old and honourable men, or someone hastier than I may reprove you in a sharper fashion." And he rose and paced the lower end of the apartment, struggling with anger and antipathy. Villon surreptitiously refilled his cup, and settled himself more comfortably in the chair, crossing his knees and leaning his head upon one hand and the elbow against the back of the chair. He was now replete and warm; and he was in no wise frightened for his host, having gauged him as justly as was possible between two such different characters. The night was far spent, and in a very comfortable fashion after all; and he felt morally certain of a safe departure on the morrow.

"Tell me one thing," said the old man, pausing in his walk. "Are you really a thief?"

"I claim the sacred rights of hospitality," returned the poet. "My lord, I am."

"You are very young," the knight continued.

"I should never have been so old," replied Villon, showing his fingers, "if I had not helped myself with these ten talents. They have been my nursing mothers and my nursing fathers."

"You may still repent and change."

"I repent daily," said the poet. "There are few people more given to repentance than poor Francis. As for change, let somebody change my circumstances. A man must continue to eat, if it were only that he may continue to repent."

"The change must begin in the heart," returned the old man solemnly.

"My dear lord," answered Villon, "do you really fancy that I steal for pleasure? I hate stealing, like any other piece of work or of danger. My teeth chatter when I see a gallows. But I must eat, I must drink, I must mix in society of some sort. What the devil! Man is not a solitary animal—*cui Deus foeminam tradit*. Make me king's pantler—make me abbot of St. Denis; make me bailly of the Patatrac; and then I shall be changed indeed. But as long as you leave me the poor scholar Francis Villon, without a farthing, why, of course, I remain the same."

"The grace of God is all-powerful."

"I should be a heretic to question it," said Francis. "It has made you lord of Brisetout and bailly of the Patatrac; it has given me nothing but the quick wits under my hat and these ten toes upon my hands. May I help myself to wine? I thank you respectfully. By God's grace, you have a very superior vintage."

The lord of Brisetout walked to and fro with his hands behind his back. Perhaps he was not yet quite settled in his mind about the parallel between thieves and soldiers; perhaps Villon had interested him by some cross-thread of sympathy; perhaps his wits were simply muddled by so much unfamiliar reasoning; but whatever the cause, he somehow yearned to convert the young man to a better way of thinking, and could not make up his mind to drive him forth again into the street.

"There is something more than I can understand in this," he said at length. "Your mouth is full of subtleties, and the devil has led you very far astray; but the devil is only a very weak spirit before God's truth, and all his subtleties vanish at a word of true honour, like darkness at morning. Listen to me once more. I learned long ago that a gentleman should live chivalrously and lovingly to God, and the king, and his lady; and though I have seen many strange things done, I have still striven to command my ways upon that rule. It is not only written in all noble histories, but in every man's heart, if he will take care to read. You speak of food and wine, and I know very well that hunger is a difficult trial to endure; but you do not speak of other wants; you say nothing of honour, of faith to God and other men, of courtesy, of love without reproach. It may be that I am not very wise—and yet I think I am—but you seem to me like one who has lost his way and made a great error in life. You are attending to the little wants, and you have totally forgotten the great and only real ones, like a man who should be doctoring a toothache on the Judgment Day. For such things as honour and love and faith are not only nobler than food and drink, but indeed I think that we desire them more, and suffer more sharply for their absence. I speak to you as I think you will most easily understand me. Are you not, while careful to fill your belly, disregarding another appetite in your heart, which spoils the pleasure of your life and keeps you continually wretched?"

Villon was sensibly nettled under all this sermonizing. "You think I have no sense of honour!" he cried. "I'm poor enough, God knows! It's hard to see rich people with their gloves, and you blowing in your hands. An empty belly is a bitter thing, although you speak so lightly of it. If you had had as many as I, perhaps you would change your tune. Any way I'm a thief—make the most of that—but I'm not a devil from hell, God strike me dead. I would have you to know I've an honour of my own, as good as yours, though I don't prate about it all day long, as if it was a God's miracle to have any. It seems quite natural to me; I keep it in its box till it's wanted. Why now, look you here, how long have I been in this room with you? Did you not tell me you were alone in the house? Look at your gold plate! You're strong, if you like, but you're old and unarmed, and I have my knife. What did I want but a jerk of the elbow and here would have been you with the cold steel in your bowels, and there would have been me, linking in the streets, with an armful of gold cups! Did you suppose I hadn't wit enough to see that? And I scorned the action. There are your damned goblets, as safe as in a church; there are you, with your heart ticking as good as new; and here am I, ready to go out again as poor as I came in, with my one white that you threw in my teeth! And you think I have no sense of honour—God strike me dead!"

The old man stretched out his right arm. "I will tell you what you are," he said. "You are a rogue, my man, an impudent and a black-hearted rogue and vagabond. I have passed an hour with you. Oh! believe me, I feel myself disgraced! And you have eaten and drunk at my table. But now I am sick of your presence; the day has come, and the night-bird should be off to his roost. Will you go before, or after?"

"Which you please," returned the poet, rising. "I believe you to be strictly honourable." He thoughtfully emptied his cup. "I wish I could add you were intelligent," he went on, knocking on his head with his knuckles. "Age, age! the brains stiff and rheumatic."

The old man preceded him from a point of self-respect; Villon followed, whistling, with his thumbs in his girdle.

"God pity you," said the lord of Brisetout at the door.

"Goodbye, papa," returned Villon with a yawn. "Many thanks for the cold mutton."

The door closed behind him. The dawn was breaking over the white roofs. A chill, uncomfortable morning ushered in the day. Villon stood and heartily stretched himself in the middle of the road.

"A very dull old gentleman," he thought. "I wonder what his goblets may be worth."

The Canterville Ghost

Oscar Wilde
(1854–1900)

I wanted to include this in my anthology of scary stories, but when I read it I realized it's not really a ghost story. That is to say, it starts off as a kind of ghost story, but then turns into something quite different—gentle, and romantic, and lovely, a story about childhood innocence, and goodness, and redemption. I'm happy to be able to include it here, as the last story in this collection—one of my all-time favourites by one of my very favourite authors.

I

hen Mr. Hiram B. Otis, the American Minister, bought Canterville Chase, everyone told him he was doing a very foolish thing, as there was no doubt at all that the place was haunted. Indeed, Lord Canterville himself, who was a man of the most punctilious honour, had felt it his duty to mention the fact to Mr. Otis, when they came to discuss terms.

"We have not cared to live in the place ourselves," said Lord Canterville, "since my grand-aunt, the Dowager Duchess of Bolton, was frightened into a fit, from which she never really recovered, by two skeleton hands being placed on her shoulders as she was dressing for dinner, and I feel bound to tell you, Mr. Otis, that the ghost has been seen by several living members of my family, as well as by the rector of the parish, the Rev.

Augustus Dampier, who is a fellow of King's College, Cambridge. After the unfortunate accident to the Duchess, none of our younger servants would stay with us, and Lady Canterville often got very little sleep at night, in consequence of the mysterious noises that came from the corridor and the library."

"My Lord," answered the Minister, "I will take the furniture and the ghost at a valuation. I come from a modern country, where we have everything that money can buy; and with all our spry young fellows painting the Old World red, and carrying off your best actresses and prima-donnas, I reckon that if there were such a thing as a ghost in Europe, we'd have it at home in a very short time in one of our public museums, or on the road as a show."

"I fear that the ghost exists," said Lord Canterville, smiling, "though it may have resisted the overtures of your enterprising impresarios. It has been well known for three centuries, since 1584 in fact, and always makes its appearance before the death of any member of our family."

"Well, so does the family doctor for that matter, Lord Canterville. But there is no such thing, sir, as a ghost, and I guess the laws of nature are not going to be suspended for the British aristocracy."

"You are certainly very natural in America," answered Lord Canterville, who did not quite understand Mr. Otis's last observation, "and if you don't mind a ghost in the house, it is all right. Only you must remember I warned you."

A few weeks after this, the purchase was completed, and at the close of the season the Minister and his family went down to Canterville Chase. Mrs. Otis, who, as Miss Lucretia R. Tappan, of West 53rd Street, had been a celebrated New York belle, was now a very handsome middle-aged woman, with fine eyes, and a superb profile. Many American ladies on leaving their native land adopt an appearance of chronic ill-health, under the impression that it is a form of European refinement, but Mrs. Otis had never fallen into this error. She had a magnificent constitution, and a really wonderful amount of animal spirits. Indeed, in many respects, she was quite English, and was an excellent example of the fact that we have really everything in common with America nowadays, except, of course, language. Her eldest son, christened Washington by his parents in a moment of patriotism, which he never ceased to regret, was a fair-haired, rather good-looking young man, who had qualified himself for American diplomacy by leading the German at the Newport Casino for three successive seasons, and even in London was well known as an excellent dancer. Gardenias and the peerage were his only weaknesses. Otherwise he was extremely sensible. Miss Virginia E. Otis was a little girl of fifteen, lithe and lovely as a fawn, and with a fine freedom in her large blue eyes. She was a wonderful amazon, and had once raced old Lord Bilton on her pony twice round the park, winning by a length and a half, just in front of Achilles' statue, to the huge delight of the young Duke of Cheshire, who proposed to her on the spot, and was sent back to Eton that very night by his guardians, in floods of tears. After Virginia came the twins, who were usually called "The Stars and Stripes" as they were always getting swished. They were delightful boys, and with the exception of the worthy Minister the only true republicans of the family.

As Canterville Chase is seven miles from Ascot, the nearest railway station, Mr. Otis had telegraphed for a waggonette to meet them, and they started on their drive in high spirits. It was a lovely July evening, and the air was delicate with the scent of the pinewoods. Now and then they heard a woodpigeon brooding over its own sweet voice, or saw, deep in the rustling fern, the burnished breast of the pheasant. Little squirrels peered at them from the beech-trees as they went by, and the rabbits scudded away through the brushwood and over the mossy knolls, with their white tails in the air. As they entered the avenue of Canterville Chase, however, the sky became suddenly overcast with clouds, a curious stillness seemed to hold the atmosphere, a great flight of rooks passed silently over their heads, and, before they reached the house, some big drops of rain had fallen.

Standing on the steps to receive them was an old woman, neatly dressed in black silk, with a white cap and apron. This was Mrs. Umney, the housekeeper, whom Mrs. Otis, at Lady

Canterville's earnest request, had consented to keep on in her former position. She made them each a low curtsey as they alighted, and said in a quaint, old-fashioned manner, "I bid you welcome to Canterville Chase." Following her, they passed through the fine Tudor hall into the library, a long, low room, panelled in black oak, at the end of which was a large stained-glass window. Here they found tea laid out for them, and, after taking off their wraps, they sat down and began to look round, while Mrs. Umney waited on them.

Suddenly Mrs. Otis caught sight of a dull red stain on the floor just by the fireplace and, quite unconscious of what it really signified, said to Mrs. Umney, "I am afraid something has been spilt there."

"Yes, madam," replied the old housekeeper in a low voice, "blood has been spilt on that spot."

"How horrid," cried Mrs. Otis; "I don't at all care for bloodstains in a sitting-room. It must be removed at once."

The old woman smiled, and answered in the same low, mysterious voice. "It is the blood of Lady Eleanore de Canterville, who was murdered on that very spot by her own husband, Sir Simon de Canterville, in 1575. Sir Simon survived her nine years, and disappeared suddenly under very mysterious circumstances. His body has never been discovered, but his guilty spirit still haunts the Chase. The bloodstain has been much admired by tourists and others, and cannot be removed."

"That is all nonsense," cried Washington Otis; "Pinkerton's Champion Stain Remover and Paragon Detergent will clean it up in no time," and before the terrified housekeeper could interfere he had fallen upon his knees, and was rapidly scouring the floor with a small stick of what looked like a black cosmetic. In a few moments no trace of the bloodstain could be seen.

"I knew Pinkerton would do it," he exclaimed triumphantly, as he looked round at his admiring family; but no sooner had he said these words than a terrible flash of lightning lit up the sombre room, a fearful peal of thunder made them all start to their feet, and Mrs. Umney fainted.

"What a monstrous climate!" said the American Minister

calmly, as he lit a long cheroot. "I guess the old country is so overpopulated that they have not enough decent weather for everybody. I have always been of opinion that emigration is the only thing for England."

"My dear Hiram," cried Mrs. Otis, "what can we do with a woman who faints?"

"Charge it to her like breakages," answered the Minister; "she won't faint after that"; and in a few moments Mrs. Umney certainly came to. There was no doubt, however, that she was extremely upset, and she sternly warned Mr. Otis to beware of some trouble coming to the house.

"I have seen things with my own eyes, sir," she said, "that would make any Christian's hair stand on end, and many and many a night I have not closed my eyes in sleep for the awful things that are done here." Mr. Otis, however, and his wife warmly assured the honest soul that they were not afraid of ghosts, and, after invoking the blessings of Providence on her new master and mistress, and making arrangements for an increase of salary, the old housekeeper tottered off to her own room.

II

The storm raged fiercely all that night, but nothing of particular note occurred. The next morning, however, when they came down to breakfast, they found the terrible stain of blood once again on the floor. "I don't think it can be the fault of the Paragon Detergent," said Washington, "for I have tried it with everything. It must be the ghost." He accordingly rubbed out the stain a second time, but the second morning it appeared again. The third morning also it was there, though the library had been locked up at night by Mr. Otis himself, and the key carried upstairs. The whole family were now quite interested; Mr. Otis began to suspect that he had been too dogmatic in his denial of the existence of ghosts, Mrs. Otis expressed her intention of joining the Psychical Society, and Washington prepared a long letter to

Messrs. Myers and Podmore on the subject of the Permanence of Sanguineous Stains when connected with crime. That night all doubts about the objective existence of phantasmata were removed for ever.

The day had been warm and sunny; and, in the cool of the evening, the whole family went out for a drive. They did not return home till nine o'clock, when they had a light supper. The conversation in no way turned upon ghosts, so there were not even those primary conditions of receptive expectation which so often precede the presentation of psychical phenomena. The subjects discussed, as I have since learned from Mr. Otis, were merely such as form the ordinary conversation of cultured Americans of the better class, such as the immense superiority of Miss Fanny Davenport over Sarah Bernhardt as an actress; the difficulty of obtaining green corn, buckwheat cakes, and hominy, even in the best English houses; the importance of Boston in the development of the world-soul; the advantages of the baggage check system in railway travelling; and the sweetness of the New York accent as compared to the London drawl. No mention at all was made of the supernatural, nor was Sir Simon de Canterville alluded to in any way. At eleven o'clock the family retired, and by half past all the lights were out. Some time after, Mr. Otis was awakened by a curious noise in the corridor, outside his room. It sounded like the clank of metal, and seemed to be coming nearer every moment. He got up at once, struck a match, and looked at the time. It was exactly one o'clock. He was quite calm, and felt his pulse, which was not at all feverish. The strange noise still continued, and with it he heard distinctly the sound of footsteps. He put on his slippers, took a small oblong phial out of his dressing-case, and opened the door. Right in front of him he saw, in the wan moonlight, an old man of terrible aspect. His eyes were as red as burning coals; long grey hair fell over his shoulders in matted coils; his garments, which were of antique cut, were soiled and ragged, and from his wrists and ankles hung heavy manacles and rusty gyves.

"My dear sir," said Mr. Otis, "I really must insist on your oiling those chains, and have brought you for that purpose a small bottle of the Tammany Rising Sun Lubricator. It is said to be completely efficacious upon one application, and there are several testimonials to that effect on the wrapper from some of our most eminent native divines. I shall leave it here for you by the bedroom candles, and will be happy to supply you with more should you require it." With these words the United States Minister laid the bottle down on a marble table, and, closing his door, retired to rest.

For a moment the Canterville ghost stood quite motionless in natural indignation; then, dashing the bottle violently upon the polished floor, he fled down the corridor, uttering hollow groans, and emitting a ghastly green light. Just, however, as he reached the top of the great oak staircase, a door was flung open, two little white-robed figures appeared, and a large pillow whizzed past his head! There was evidently no time to be lost, so, hastily adopting the Fourth Dimension of Space as a means of escape, he vanished through the wainscoting, and the house became quite quiet.

On reaching a small secret chamber in the left wing, he leaned up against a moonbeam to recover his breath, and began to try and realize his position. Never, in a brilliant and uninterrupted career of three hundred years, had he been so grossly insulted. He thought of the Dowager Duchess, whom he had frightened into a fit as she stood before the glass in her lace and diamonds; of the four housemaids, who had gone off into hysterics when he merely grinned at them through the curtains of one of the spare bedrooms; of the rector of the parish, whose candle he had blown out as he was coming late one night from the library, and who had been under the care of Sir William Gull ever since, a perfect martyr to nervous disorders; and of old Madame de Tremouillac, who, having wakened up one morning early and seen a skeleton seated in an armchair by the fire reading her diary, had been confined to her bed for six weeks with an attack of brain fever, and, on her recovery, had become reconciled to the Church, and had broken off her connection with that notorious sceptic Monsieur de Voltaire. He remembered the terrible night when the wicked Lord Canterville was found choking in his dressing-room, with the knave of diamonds halfway down his throat, and confessed, just before he died, that he had cheated Charles James Fox out of £50,000 at Crockford's by means of that very card, and swore that the ghost had made him swallow it. All his great achievements came back to him again, from the butler who had shot himself in the pantry because he had seen a green hand tapping at the window-pane, to the beautiful Lady Stutfield, who was always obliged to wear a black velvet band round her throat to hide the mark of five fingers burnt upon her white skin, and who drowned herself at last in the carp-pond at the end of the King's Walk. With the enthusiastic egotism of the true artist he went over his most celebrated performances, and smiled bitterly to himself as he recalled to mind his last appearance as "Red Ruben, or the Strangled Babe," his début as "Gaunt Gibeon, the Bloodsucker of Bexley Moor," and the furore he had excited one lovely June evening by merely playing ninepins with his own bones upon the lawn-tennis ground. And after all this, some wretched modern Americans were to come and offer him the Rising Sun Lubricator, and throw pillows at his head! It was quite unbearable. Besides, no ghosts in history had ever been treated in this manner. Accordingly, he determined to have vengeance, and remained till daylight in an attitude of deep thought.

III

The next morning when the Otis family met at breakfast, they discussed the ghost at some length. The United States Minister was naturally a little annoyed to find that his present had not been accepted. "I have no wish," he said, "to do the ghost any personal injury, and I must say that, considering the length of time he has been in the house, I don't think it is at all polite to throw pillows at him"—a very just remark, at which, I am sorry to say, the twins burst into shouts of laughter. "Upon the other hand," he continued, "if he really declines to use the Rising Sun Lubricator, we shall have to take his chains from him. It would be quite impossible to sleep, with such a noise